The Killer Brand

ANOTHER SAGEBRUSH LARGE PRINT WESTERN BY
WILLIAM COLT MACDONALD

The Black Sombrero

The Killer Brand

WILLIAM COLT MACDONALD

Library of Congress Cataloging-in-Publication Data

MacDonald, William Colt, 1891-1968.
The killer brand / William Colt MacDonald.
p. cm.
ISBN 1-57490-497-3 (alk. paper)
1. Fathers—Death—Fiction. 2. Revenge—Fiction. 3. Large type books. I. Title.

PS3525.A2122K55 2003
813'.52—dc21 2003010605

Cataloging in Publication Data is available from the British Library and the National Library of Australia.

Sagebrush Large Print Westerns are published in the United States and Canada by Thomas T. Beeler, Publisher, PO Box 659, Hampton Falls, New Hampshire 03844-0659. ISBN 1-57490-497-3

Published in the United Kingdom, Eire, and the Republic of South Africa by Isis Publishing Ltd, 7 Centremead, Osney Mead, Oxford OX2 0ES England. ISBN 0-7531-6920-7

Published in Australia and New Zealand by Bolinda Publishing Pty Ltd, 17 Mohr Street, Tullamarine, Victoria, Australia, 3043 ISBN 1-74030-927-8

Manufactured by Sheridan Books in Chelsea, Michigan.

The Killer Brand

HOLDUP

THE CLOUDS OF ALKALI DUST which had been boiling up from the rear of the stagecoach the past three hours gradually diminished as the vehicle got into the foothills of the Triscador Range. The speed of the coach likewise slackened as it followed the gradually rising trail wending between low hills. Finally it came to a complete halt. Within the coach the lone passenger removed his derby hat and, thrusting his head through the open door window, inquired in a voice that definitely pigeonholed him as being of Eastern extraction the reason for the stop.

Trent Ziebold twisted around on his driver's seat and glanced down at his passenger's upthrust, inquiring face, then spat a long stream of tobacco juice. "Got to breathe muh hawsses a mite, mister. That"—gesturing with his whip to a point a short distance ahead—"is the Sepulvida grade. Ain't no stage hawss on earth figurin' to make that climb 'thout he gits hisself prepared for it fust. Anybody but a Billy-be-damned N'Yawker would've knowed that much 'thout askin'."

"No doubt you're correct," the passenger returned civilly enough. "Mind if I alight and stretch my legs? This long ride has—"

"They're yore laigs," the driver cackled, and spat another brown deluge into the dust beside the coach. "Stretch 'em nigh back to them alkali flats if you like." He twisted about on his seat and nudged in the ribs the stage guard seated at his side. "Them shawt-hawn Easterners!" he grunted derisively, as though speaking of some strange species from other worlds. "I jest can't make 'em out, Shotgun."

Shotgun Kerry frowned. "I dunno as you should be so short with that jasper, Trent. Put yourself in his place. Supposin' you was in N'Yawk. I'm bettin' you'd move plumb circumspect on a strange range like that—and ask plenty questions before you moved."

Trent Ziebold considered for a moment and finally admitted his pardner could be correct.

Kerry asked, "What's he out here for?"

"Whisky drummer. Name of Wagman."

"There, you see! Whisky! Cripes, Trent, this Wagman's doin' his part in bringin' civilization to the West. We need men like him. Just suppose everybody was like you, actin' so short and snubby with Eastern folks, scarin' 'em off from comin' out here. First thing you know, we wouldn't have no whisky."

Ziebold paled at the thought. "Reckon I'd best mind my tongue from now on," he mumbled.

Meanwhile the passenger had descended from the coach, slapping vigorously at the alkali dust on his clothing, and slammed the stage door. He stood gazing curiously at the surrounding country while the dust swam hazily in the air about him. To the rear of the coach, beyond the rock-studded tops of rolling hills, lay a desolate stretch of alkali flats shimmering brightly in the early afternoon sunlight. All around the coach grew clumps of wiry grass springing from the yellow-gray sandy soil; there was a good deal of stunted mesquite, prickly pear, and greasewood. Ahead rose a series of precipitous sandstone bluffs, between which ascended a narrow, wheel-rutted ribbon over which the stage must travel before reaching the crest of Sepulvida Pass. From that point the stage would have a long gradual descent until it reached the town of Toyah Wells, mining and cattle center of Cross Timbers County. Overhead the sky was an inverted bowl of turquoise, with not a bird or cloud within sight.

Finally Trent Ziebold gathered the reins in his hands and glanced over one shoulder at his passenger. " 'Bout ready to roll, mister. Hop in."

The passenger, Wagman, had been eying with some trepidation the trail ahead: for a short distance it seemed to run almost perpendicularly up the side of a bluff until it curved out of sight around one shoulder of badly eroded sandstone. The way was cluttered with chunks of loose rock; the roadbed itself seemed none too firm, and at the top it sloped away to a brush-filled canyon a hundred feet below.

Wagman hesitated, then raised one quivering finger. "Do you mean to say you—you drive straight up—there?" he demanded unbelievingly.

"Ain't no other way to reach the crest of the pass," Ziebold replied in bored tones.

"It looks dangerous," Wagman protested. "Suppose a wheel slipped off the edge . . . "

Ziebold yawned. "Ain't never happened—'ceptin' five or six times, in the last ten years."

"And you lived through it?" Wagman asked incredulously.

"Didn't nobody live through it," Ziebold stated flatly. "I wa'n't drivin' this route then. But git in if yo're goin'."

Wagman still hesitated. The guard took pity on him. "Tell you what, Mr. Wagman, it's just that first stretch that's so steep. After you get around that shoulder of rock the way levels some. From here you could walk to the crest in less'n a half-hour. Why'n't you stretch yore laigs some more?" Wagman started to ask a question, but Shotgun Kerry forestalled him: "No need of you frettin'. We won't be much ahead, and Trent always stops at the top of the pass to rest the hawsses some more 'fore startin' down. We'll be waitin' when you get there."

Wagman considered, glanced again at the road ahead, then nodded. "I—I believe I will walk, thank you." He smiled sheepishly. "It will do me good. This bracing air—not enough exercise, as it is—a short walk will—" He broke off, hesitating for further words.

Trent Ziebold nodded shortly. He and the guard settled back in the driver's seat. Ziebold gathered the reins more tightly, kicked off the brake, and snaked his long whip with a sharp cracking sound above the heads of his leaders. The four horses threw themselves into the traces, and the sturdy Concord coach lurched into motion, the spinning wheels throwing up clouds of dust at the rear. Again the long whip cracked sharply as Trent Ziebold urged his horses into a swiftly running start for the sharp incline ahead.

For some minutes sight of the coach was lost to Wagman as dust rose before the whisky drummer's eyes. When the atmosphere had cleared somewhat he saw that the swaying coach was already halfway up the steep roadway. Then gradually it slowed as the horses dug frantic hoofs into the earth. From some distance the sharp cracking of the whip reached Wagman's ears. The coach continued to ascend, approaching nearer and nearer the point where the road narrowed at the perilous turn around the shoulder of rock. The rear wheels skidded but slightly as Ziebold piloted his horses skillfully around the curve, then the coach disappeared from Wagman's view. Wagman shuddered, exhaled a long pent-up breath of relief, then commenced with long, deliberate steps the steep ascent of the trail. His pace, like the coach's, slowed before long, but he continued doggedly on his way, still believing in his heart he had chosen the safer way.

The coach, after having negotiated the turn around the shoulder, went on steadily, the way now being less steep. Ziebold turned to his guard. "That's one more time we made it, Shotgun."

Kerry shifted his double-barreled weapon to a more comfortable position across his knees. "We made it," he agreed in a placid voice, "but I'd like to bet you we go over one of these days."

Ziebold shook his head. "I ain't never yet bet on no sure thing," he replied with a chuckle.

The road had widened considerably by this time. On either side rose a thick wall of brush, mesquite, scrub oak, and cactus. On the left, beyond the brush, sheer rock walls rose toward the sky; on the right the brush sloped off to the canyon below. The coach, drawn by its four sweat-streaked horses, swayed easily on its thorough braces. Now and then one wheel lurched over a chunk of broken rock, or the vehicle was deftly guided around a chuckhole lying in its path. The afternoon sun beat down with a steady heat. Before long Ziebold drew the horses to a walk.

"Nearly to the top," he said, "and then the long slide down after we've rested and waited for that N'Yawker to catch up." He gazed out across the open stretch of range that lay far below. Already he could see the flat roofs of Toyah Wells quivering in the heat waves rising from the floor of the semi-desert country miles below. And then, quite abruptly, it happened.

The right lead horse stumbled; the left reared and emitted a sharp frightened snort. Even as they crashed into the dust, Trent Ziebold heard from either side, sounding almost simultaneously, two heavy gun explosions. Immediately the wheel horses commenced plunging frantically to the accompaniment of shrill neighings. The coach stopped abruptly. By the time Ziebold managed to quiet the wheelers he became conscious at once of various happenings: his left leader was dead; from the other came only a slight quivering of one leg; blood was seeping into the dirt near the horses' heads. At Ziebold's right, Shotgun Kerry sat quietly, both arms raised high in the air, the shotgun resting across his knees. On either side of the coach stood two masked men, four in all, holding leveled .45s on driver and guard.

Ziebold swore with some bitterness. "Damn you scuts! There wa'n't no need to kill my hawsses. I'd have pulled up to rest fifty yards farther on—"

"Shut your trap!" snapped one of the masked men.

Ziebold spat a contemptuous brown stream but remained silent.

On the other side of the coach a masked man had approached the vehicle and opened the door. "No passengers," he called to the others as he again backed to the side of the road.

A third bandit spoke. "You, Shotgun, toss that scatter-gun down here."

Shotgun Kerry said calmly, "Do you mind goin' to hell, mister?"

"Hey!" Ziebold blurted out. "I know that voice! Shotgun! That's the feller—"

A .45 roared again. Trent Ziebold groaned and slumped on his seat. Shotgun Kerry cursed and lowered his arms toward the weapon across his knees. Before his fingers could touch barrels or stock, the booming report of a six-shooter once more shattered the mountain silence. Kerry stiffened, half rose from his seat, then slowly toppled forward to land on one shoulder in the dust beside the coach, where he lay without movement. The ears of the wheel horses went back, their limbs quivered, but they remained quiet.

A stillness settled over the men on either side of the stagecoach, then one of them burst out angrily, "Dammit! There wasn't any need of that—"

"T'hell there wa'n't," a second man snapped. "Shotgun was reachin' for his scatter-gun. He might've got one of us—"

"Even so," the first persisted, "you promised there'd be no killin'. Least of all Trent Ziebold. He never harmed a soul—"

"He would've," the third bandit snarled. "He recognized my voice. Once he hit Toyah Wells, where would I be? It was him or me. If you don't like it, you don't got to stay. Get your horse and ride. Splittin' the money three ways 'stead of four suits me—"

"Yeah, I imagine it would. All right. What's done is done. I'm into this. I'll see it through." He swore long and bitterly under his breath as he stepped toward the stricken stage guard and knelt at his side. After a moment he arose, saying in a dull voice, "Finished Shotgun instanter, I reckon." He stepped to the side of the coach and climbed up while the other three watched. A minute later he swore again, adding something that had to do with murdering bustards. "If it's any satisfaction to you scuts, Trent Ziebold will never recognize any more voices."

No one replied. The bandit on the driver's seat reached to the railed roof of the coach, seized the strongbox it had been carrying, and tossed it to the earth. Then he followed it to the ground. His arrival was punctuated by the roar of a six-shooter as one of the bandits shot off the padlock of the box. The cover was flung back. Within lay a string-tied bundle of mail and three heavy canvas sacks that gave forth clinking sounds when they were lifted from the open box.

"Look," one of the masked men proposed, "why don't we split this money right now, then the four of us scatter in different directions?"

"Nothing doing," refused the one who had protested the killing. "We go through with the scheme as planned—"

"Maybe"—belligerently—"us others don't agree with you—"

"We go through with things as planned," came the harsh reply. "If you don't like it that-a-way, Scar, maybe you'd best fill your hand and we can settle the matter right pronto."

There was a tense moment of silence before the man called Scar shrugged his shoulders. "Oh, hell, no sense you gettin' proddy—"

"Correct. I ain't lookin' for trouble neither. There's already been too much killin' today. Let's get cleared up here and slope."

NO CLUES

MEANWHILE, THE WHISKY DRUMMER, WAGMAN, had already reached the curve in the road where it rounded the shoulder of eroded rock, and was walking wearily in pursuit of the coach. His feet were sore; he knew blisters had formed on his heels. His face streamed with perspiration. He had removed his coat and was carrying it over one arm; his black derby hat was clutched in the moist fingers of his other hand. The armpits of his shirt under his open vest were stained wetly. Now and then the tall brush at his right offered broad spots of shade for which he was grateful. And then, just as Wagman sighted the rear end of the coach, he heard two gunshots spaced closely together. He noticed now the coach wasn't moving, though he could see the heads and shoulders of Ziebold and Kerry still on the driver's seat.

Wagman froze in his tracks. A minute later he heard a third shot, quickly followed by a fourth. Now Kerry was no longer in sight on the driver's seat, and Ziebold's form seemed to have assumed a slumped position. Masked men, Wagman now noticed, had appeared from the brush on either side of the coach. The whisky drummer waited no longer but quickly directed his shaking legs in the direction of a sheltering mesquite at one side of the road, where he could observe without being seen. After a time a fifth shot reached his ears. How long he stayed hidden at that point, Wagman never knew, but it was some time after the bandits had left the scene of the holdup.

The time elapsed after the departure of the masked men and the arrival of the whisky drummer at the side of the stagecoach couldn't have been too long, however, as the sounds of moving horses through the trees and brush of the canyon bottom far below were still evident to Wagman's ears. Though he couldn't see the riders because of the thick growth of treetops and brush, he could hear their voices quite distinctly above the crackling of brush limbs and the occasional clatter of a horse's hoof against rock. Some sort of argument seemed in progress concerning the direction the bandits would take; one voice kept insisting that they would be through with the original plans. Finally both voices and crackling of brush faded away, and the whisky drummer forced his horrified gaze back toward the stagecoach.

His trembling limbs carried him completely around the vehicle. Cold beads of perspiration stood out on his forehead. A dead man lay on the earth, his shotgun near the body, his sightless eyes turned toward the blue sky. An ugly dark patch stained the front of the guard's shirt. Not far from the body was the open strong-box, empty except for some letters and other mail. More letters were scattered about the box. Wagman drew a deep sigh and steeled his nerves for the climb to the driver's seat. Once atop the coach, he realized instantly that Trent Ziebold was also dead. The driver was still on his seat, though slumped sidewise. Blood dripped steadily from the seat to the footboard below.

With heart beating like a trip hammer, the whisky drummer returned to the earth and studied the situation. Two horses lay dead amid a tangle of harness. The remaining pair stood quietly when Wagman approached. He studied the horses and harness, not at all sure he could unhitch one of them without trouble. Besides, he had never ridden a horse. The beast might throw him off. Arriving at a decision after a glance at the open range and distant roof tops of Toyah Wells miles below, he started off on foot, leaving the grisly scene at his rear as fast as possible . . .

It was after dark before Wagman reached Toyah Wells. It would have been still later had not a passing puncher from the A-Bar-3 crossed the trail and, hearing the whisky drummer's story, taken him up behind his saddle and headed pell-mell for town. Once in town, the puncher had taken Wagman to the sheriff's office, where the drummer's story was quickly related to

Sheriff Bob Tinsley, a middle-aged, bulky-shouldered man with wide sun-bleached mustaches. The sheriff asked a few swift questions. No, Wagman stated, he hadn't recognized any of the men; they had had bandannas drawn across their faces. He had heard them leaving through the canyon brush but couldn't decide what direction they had taken. Wagman forced a thin sheepish smile; after all, he was a stranger to this Western country. It was difficult for a man to orient himself as to directions.

By this time quite a crowd had collected about the sheriff's office and was listening, openmouthed, to the whisky drummer's story. The sheriff put another question. Wagman replied that, so far as he could determine, the bandits had been arguing as to the direction they would take. After a time Wagman recollected having heard one of the bandits called "Scar." The name ran through the crowd. Somebody said something about "Scar Hopkins." The crowd scattered toward the town's saloons. A short time later, though nobody in particular noticed it, a rider drove his pony hard and fast out of Toyah Wells.

By this time the sheriff was on his way to the Toyah Wells Bar, and Wagman was directing his weary steps toward the town's sole hotel. Halfway to the bar, Sheriff Tinsley spied in the light thrown from another saloon a tall dark man approaching with long even strides. On his vest Tinsley caught the glint of his deputy's badge. "Thought you was in bed sick, Gene," Tinsley said.

"Feelin' some better now," replied Deputy Sheriff Gene Talbert. "Just something I et, I reckon. Figured I'd get out for a breath of air. Then I heard about this holdup and I knowed this was no time for me to be ailin' when you needed my help—"

"Good." Briefly Sheriff Tinsley outlined what he knew of the tragedy on Sepulvida Pass; then: "Is Scar Hopkins around town?"

"Probably. I ain't seen him though."

"If you see him, grab him for questioning. Spread the word around for folks to keep an eye open for him. I'm roundin' up a posse. Saddle my hawss and your own Hold up! You able to ride?"

"I can ride when it's this serious."

The sheriff nodded and strode on toward the Toyah Wells Bar. Within at the long counter he spied a gathering of men talking excitedly of the stage robbery. The sheriff spoke with some directness. "You hombres already know of the holdup, I reckon. The guard, Shotgun Kerry, and Trent Ziebold were killed. That stage was carrying the Angela Mine pay roll. The strongbox was busted open and the money taken. I'm raisin' a posse." The sheriff paused, his eyes running swiftly over the assembled men at the bar, until they rested on a wide-shouldered man with hawk features and iron-gray hair, clad in denims, flannel shirt, cow boots, and wide-brimmed sombrero. A pair of cartridge belts crisscrossed the man's waist, each supporting the weight of a holstered .45 six-shooter. "You, Cyrus, I'll want you."

Cyrus Gallatin, otherwise known as Cougar, studied the sheriff's grim features a moment and nodded shortly. "You got me, Bob." He left the bar to get his horse.

The sheriff named other men; Rugger Hess, Bert Redmond, Johnny Barton, Tanner Reese, Jigs O'Keefe, and Joe Prince. A few minutes later the sheriff and his men were met on the street by the deputy with two horses. The posse mounted, then the sheriff gave the word to move, and the riders swept out of town in a cloud of dust.

The night passed. Shortly after dawn one of the posse, Rugger Hess by name, brought the stage into town drawn by two horses. The dead horses had been tumbled into the canyon below Sepulvida Pass for the coyotes to clean their bones. The stage stopped before the undertaker's, where the bodies of Ziebold and Kerry were removed from the vehicle. Only one saloon was open at the time, and it was here that Hess next stopped. A few early morning drinkers were at the bar, and to these Hess stated that the posse hadn't been able to uncover any sort of clue as to the direction the bandits had taken.

By noontime the posse, minus the sheriff, had come straggling back to town. They announced they had done a lot of riding but had learned nothing new. The sheriff had remained behind to study the terrain further but hadn't seen any reason for retaining the posse any longer. The posse broke up, its members going their separate ways in search of food, drink, or beds. Their features were grim, harshly lined; in the hearts of most welled a bitter resentment and a desire for the sudden death of the masked bandits who had murdered Trent Ziebold and Shotgun Kerry, when and if the killers could be apprehended.

COUGAR GALLATIN

TOYAH WELLS LAY SOMNOLENT under the heat of early afternoon sun. It wasn't much of a town, Toyah Wells wasn't—just a single unpaved dusty thoroughfare with a long line of high, false-fronted frame buildings on either side. Ranged along the plank sidewalks were hitch racks at which drowsy cow ponies stood on three legs and switched lazy tails at the myriad flies droning through the dust motes. Occasionally a vagrant gust of wind swirled down from the high Triscador peaks, lifting the dust of the street into miniature cyclones which quickly subsided after wafting gritty particles of sand throughout the nearby buildings.

Now and then a man strode along the sidewalk, keeping in the shade as much as possible. Other men, with hats drawn over their faces, snored comfortably in tilted-back chairs on various porches. Still other individuals sought the cool dimness of saloons, drinking and playing cards. Doubtless it was more comfortable in the residences on the low hills surrounding the town, but even there the leaves of the cottonwood trees drooped in the torrid heat, stirred only occasionally by an oppressive breeze. The only real activity displayed on Toyah Wells's dusty street was that stirred up by a hen and three small chickens scratching futilely in the dirt in search of something to eat. And then quite abruptly things commenced to happen.

Loud voices rose suddenly in the Toyah Wells Bar, and the next instant Cougar Gallatin came backing out, a smoking gun in either hand. Within, sprawled on the floor before the bar, two men writhed in pain. On the plank sidewalk Gallatin paused only long enough beyond the violently swinging saloon doors to send another shot roaring through a window. Shattered glass splintered from the frames as answering explosions were heard from within. But by this time Cougar Gallatin had whirled toward the hitch rack and was heading toward his pony.

A man yelled from inside the bar: "Stop Gallatin! It

was him held up the stage!"

Activity stirred along the street. Others took up the cry. "Stop Gallatin! Get the dirty murderin' son! It was Cougar done it!"

Doors were flung open. Tilted chairs came down with a bang on all four legs. A bullet kicked up dust some considerable distance from Gallatin's lean, wide-shouldered form. He cast a defiant glance of his stern, hawklike features toward the direction from which the bullet had come, and continued moving with quick lithe steps toward his pony at the tie rail.

"Get the killer!" sounded across the street.

Cougar Gallatin directed a shot toward the voice. A leaden slug thudded into a wooden upright. A door was slammed shut. A frightened cow pony neighed shrilly, reared, and whirled, taking with it a section of broken tie rail to which its reins had been tied. Two men with drawn guns were mowed down by the pony's maddened rush, the beast's shoulder striking one of them, sending the man spilling into the road; one end of the broken tie rail caught the other across the head as it flailed through the air and sent him hurtling toward the sidewalk, where he lay without movement. The pony reared again, started at a run along the street, tripped on the dangling tie rail, and went down in a cloud of dust and sharply scattered gravel. It also stayed down when a broken leg made rising impossible.

Gallatin had nearly reached his horse now. He thrust one gun into his holster and prepared to mount. A rifle cracked from some distance down the street. Gallatin staggered back from his horse, spun halfway around, then his legs let him down suddenly. A second bullet plowed sand at his side. Gallatin started to rise, then in a stooping, crawling position made his way to the partial shelter offered by a nearby watering trough, leaden slugs kicking up dirt all around him as he moved.

"I downed him!" came the triumphant yell as a man carrying a Winchester emerged from his hiding place between buildings.

A grim laugh was torn from Gallatin's lips. His hat had fallen off, and the sun shone brightly on his thick thatch of iron-gray hair and his chiseled features. Sure, he'd been downed. But that was no sign he was finished, Not yet. He reloaded his six-shooters swiftly, with steady fingers, and awaited the next attack. "There'll be more'n one go out with me before I pass on," he muttered through tight lips.

The man with the rifle was nearer now. Gallatin braced himself on one hand and peered across the top of the watering trough. A streak of white fire spurted from his right fist. The man with the rifle sat down with abrupt violence. "Damn you, Cougar—" he commenced, and then rolled on his face and was silent.

For a few minutes the noise subsided. Gallatin plugged out an empty shell and shoved in a fresh cartridge. He crouched behind the watering trough, waiting, feeling the congealing stickiness within one pant leg. The sun broiled down mercilessly on his gray head. Wind stirred gently the dust of the road. High overhead, three black shadows wheeled and floated on motionless wings. There was an odor of fresh blood in the air.

From across the street, at Gallatin's back, a six-shooter roared, shattering the hot silence. Gallatin winced, realizing now his left leg was broken. He grunted, then snapped a quick return fire, shooting from beneath one arm, not knowing if he hit anyone or not. Gun butts clenched in his powerful fists, he awaited the next move.

Now other men gained courage. Flying missiles of death buzzed and whined around the half-prone figure at the watering trough. More figures emerged into view on the street. From their hands came sudden puffs of black powder smoke penetrated by white spears of flame. Bullets were coming from all directions. At intervals the watering trough seemed to be fringed with sharp jets of fire. Here and there a man dropped, or fled hurriedly for shelter between buildings.

Old Cougar Gallatin was dying hard.

He grunted contemptuously: "The coyotes are workin' around to encircle me. Betcha I take a couple of more to hell with me when—" He paused, grimacing horribly as something like molten steel seared his ribs, then drew a long hard breath. "Sure 'pears like my time has come," he grated through set teeth. "I just wish I could see the boy first, though. Anyway, he'll know that I went out with my guns smokin'."

A shower of splinters from one edge of the trough struck his face. A bullet ricocheted and whined viciously off into space. A sudden blinding rage filled Gallatin. "Dammit! I'm sick of this sort of palaverin'! Let's get this business finished . . . "

He struggled upright on his one good leg, bracing himself against the watering trough. "Come into the open, you measly low-down bustards!" he yelled his challenge. "I'm waitin' on you!"

His voice carried the length of the street. Four men, guns in hands, stepped somewhat hesitantly into full view. Cougar Gallatin held his fire. The four came on, striding without haste. Gallatin knew it was the end this time. A harsh laugh parted his pallid lips. The four came nearer.

Gallatin raised his voice. "Thank Gawd some of you has still got your nerve left!"

Hammers clicked back under his gnarled thumbs. The four raised their guns. There ensued a moment's silence, as though Toyah Wells waited breathlessly for the final curtain to descend on the tragedy. Abruptly the spell was broken and hell broke loose.

Leaden messengers of death crossed and crisscrossed over the short stretch of sandy road that intervened between Cougar Gallatin and his four opponents. Two of the four dropped instantly. The other two continued their advance, one with dragging steps, the other unhit as yet.

Again Gallatin unleashed his fire. The third man dropped. Gallatin swayed back, lost his balance, and fell heavily. The fourth man still came on, but now he was stumbling drunkenly and was unable to control his fire.

Overhead the three black shadows had drawn nearer, their wide-winged forms making dark patterns against the blue sky as they wheeled and soared like vagrant bits of paper caught in a breeze.

Gallatin twisted his body around, forcing himself to a sitting position. One arm hung limply at his side. His face was a contorted mask of crimson. A wet blot seeped slowly across his woolen shirt. He raised the gun in his one good arm and eyed the shambling steps of the fourth man, who was still doggedly approaching. Hank Bevens, a good man. More than once Cougar Gallatin and Bevens had bought each other drinks at the Toyah Wells Bar. Gallatin raised his voice. "Here's looking at you, Hank. One more down the long dark hatch and this business is finished." He called again, "Here's looking at you, Hank."

Hank Bevens straightened with an effort. Everything

was swimming crazily before his vision now. He swayed on his heels, looked back at the crumpled forms of his three companions sprawled in the road, then with an effort faced Cougar Gallatin once more.

In that moment Cougar Gallatin could have finished Bevens, but that wasn't according to Gallatin's code. Killer that he was, had been, no man could say that Gallatin didn't give the other man an even chance. And after all, Galatin mused, Bevens was a square sort of cuss. He'd always liked Hank Bevens.

Gallatin frowned through the crimson trickling down from a scalp wound, frowned impatiently. "For cripes sake, come alive, Hank! I can't be waiting much longer."

Bevens halted, focused his bleary gaze, forced a thin smile. "Be right with you, Cougar—and thanks for waitin'. I'm plumb sorry to do this—"

His gun came up, roared once. Then Gallatin unleashed everything in his cylinder, toppling sidewise as he fired the final shot. Bevens spun twice around from the impact of the heavy lead bullets, then pitched forward on his face. Gallatin didn't strive to rise and look at Bevens. That wasn't necessary. Cougar Gallatin *knew*.

And now a dark-haired man wearing a deputy's badge came running from between buildings, flourishing a sawed-off shotgun. Other men appeared on the street. With Cougar Gallatin down, courage had taken an appreciable rise.

From the eastern end of town there came a sudden drumming of horse's hoofs. An angry yell left the lips of the rider as he came tearing along the rutted street. The deputy with the sawed-off shotgun uttered a startled exclamation and turned back toward the buildings from which he had come. Other men paused in their tracks.

The rider was closer now and was recognized as Sheriff Bob Tinsley. Straight toward the watering trough the sheriff rode, slipped from the saddle, and bent to the prone form of Cougar Gallatin. A crowd started to gather, but the sheriff warned it to stay back. He ordered one man to bring some whisky and water. Then Tinsley bent again to the prone Gallatin and slipped one arm under the stricken man's shoulders.

"It looks like they ganged up on you, Cyrus," Tinsley said. "I didn't know what was going on until I hit the edge of town, then some blame fool yelled out that they had the stage robber cornered and mentioned your name. Of all the idiots—"

"It's true, Bob."

"Don't say that, Cyrus." The sheriff's voice was almost a wail.

Gallatin smiled faintly at the use of his given name, smiled through the blood and pain. Bob Tinsley was the only one who ever remembered to call him Cyrus instead of Cougar. Also, Tinsley was one of the few who remembered when the Gallatin brand had really meant something in that section of the cow country.

A man approached with a flask of whisky and a glass of water. Tinsley held some of both to Gallatin's ashen lips. "I'll get you moved to a bed, Cyrus," the sheriff was saying. "We'll get the sawbones and—"

"It's no use, Bob," Gallatin insisted. "I'm finished and I know it. Yes, and I'm guilty of that stage holdup too—guilty as hell." Tinsley started another protest, but Gallatin interrupted: "I know what I'm talking about, Bob. Now don't you talk. You just listen. I ain't got much time left, and there's things I want said to my boy."

For several minutes he talked in a faint, halting voice. Now and then Tinsley gave him water or whisky. Gallatin's eyes were commencing to have a glassy look, and his words could scarcely be heard. Quite suddenly, in mid-sentence, he ceased speaking.

It was several moments before the sheriff realized the old gun fighter was dead. High overhead, three black. shadows wheeled and floated on motionless wings. There was an odor of fresh blood in the air.

THE COUGAR'S WHELP

FIVE MILES OUT OF TOYAH WELLS, to the west, lay the eastern boundary of the Rafter-G Ranch—if ranch it could still be called. Time was when the Rafter-G had been known as one of the most prosperous outfits in the Toyah Wells section, but that had been years ago. Now there were no cattle at all left to carry the big G design with its inverted widespread V above. Rust had put the tall windmill out of commission. The buildings were sadly in need of paint or whitewash. Corral bars were down; that didn't mean a great deal, anyway: there weren't any horses to be penned within the enclosure. Only the huge live-oak trees surrounding what had once been the pleasant ranch house continued to flourish. Within the ranch house the furniture was covered with dust; there were no longer any Indian rugs or animal skins on the floor. Broken chairs and tables had gone without repair. In the barn a few bits of broken harness still hung from pegs. Nearby a buckboard sagged on three wheels. Mess shanty and bunkhouse were in a similar state of ruination. The Rafter-G, as one man put it, had gone completely to pot, along about the time the big G had commenced to stand for "gun fighter" rather than Gallatin, though the two names had become synonymous, as a matter of fact.

It was here they brought the stiffened form of Cougar Gallatin shortly before sundown. Gallatin's son, Whitlock—known as Whit—had seen them coming and was waiting on the gallery of the dilapidated ranch house. He wasn't more than twenty-one or -two, Whit Gallatin wasn't. Tall, wide-shouldered, slim-hipped, with his father's gray eyes, aquiline nose, and fighting jaw. Straight and dark-haired, he stood beside an upright of the gallery, his gaze fixed steadily on the wagon carrying its silent form under a pair of blankets. If he guessed it was his father who lay there, there was nothing in his features to show it. The half dozen riders accompanying the wagon eyed him warily and breathed a little easier when they saw he was unarmed. Whit Gallatin was known to be almost as fast as his father when it came to drawing and shooting, though as yet there were no killings placed against the son's name.

The cavalcade drew to a halt a few yards away from the gallery. Young Gallatin stood there, very erect, in overalls, spurred riding boots, woolen shirt, and battered sombrero, waiting for someone to speak. His face was an inscrutable mask as he eyed Sheriff Bob Tinsley, who sat his horse somewhat in advance of the others. The sheriff removed his hat, mopped at the perspiration on his forehead, seeming reluctant to start talking.

Finally Whit Gallatin said levelly, "Is that Dad you've brought?" knowing in his heart the reply would be in the affirmative. For years now he'd been expecting something like this, bracing himself for it. He was looking only at the sheriff, disregarding the stern glances the other riders were directing his way.

Tinsley swallowed hard and nodded. "I'm mighty regretful, Whit. There was—well—there was some shootin' in town, and—and—"

Whit nodded shortly, stepped down from the gallery and around to the end of the wagon.

The sheriff commenced, "Wait—I'll give you a hand."

If young Gallatin heard the words he gave no sign. Effortlessly, it seemed, he gathered the still form in his arms, returned to the gallery, and carried his burden through the open door of the ranch house. An instant later he reappeared in the doorway. "You can all clear out now," he said in toneless accents.

"Whit," the sheriff protested, "don't you want to hear—"

"You can all clear out," Gallatin repeated.

"T'hell we will," one of the riders snapped. "We're aiming to talk to you, Gallatin. It could be the Cougar's whelp is guilty too."

"You heard me," Whit said in the same flat voice. "Get out!"

The eyes of the two men clashed. The man on the horse backed his horse a little, one hand straying toward his holster.

Tinsley, glancing over his shoulder, caught the movement. "Don't do it, Royce!" the sheriff ordered sharply. A couple of the others started a protest. Tinsley swore. "I shouldn't have let you bustards come with the wagon in the first place. If Whit don't want you here, that goes for me too. I'm backing him up. You can all clear out." He turned back to Gallatin. "I want to *habla* with you a mite, boy, if you don't mind, before I leave."

"I'm aiming to be alone for a while, Bob," Gallatin replied shortly. "Won't it wait? I figure to ride into town later."

The sheriff shook his head. "Cyrus wanted me to talk to you right off, soon's I could."

Gallatin nodded ungracious consent. His eyes were hard and cold, his lips a straight colorless line.

Tinsley spoke to the others. This time there were no protests. Wagon and horses wheeled around and departed. The sheriff dismounted, led his horse to the end of the gallery where Gallatin's mount was tethered, then joined him near the doorway. Gallatin didn't invite him inside.

His cold eyes were steady on the sheriff. He said, "Let's be quick about it, Bob."

"I knew you'd got home," the sheriff commenced awkwardly. "Jake Arden mentioned you'd crossed his trail on his way to town this afternoon. It's—it's a hell of a home-coming."

"You had some message for me from Dad," Whit reminded.

"Yeah—yeah, I have." The sheriff again removed his hat and mopped at his brow before replacing the Stetson. "Cyrus—Cyrus wanted to be buried up on that hill yonderly, beside your mom."

"I'll take care of it." Still no break in the level flat tones.

"I'm mighty regretful about the whole business," Tinsley commenced again. "You see, I wa'n't in Toyah Wells when it happened. Got back just before Cyrus died. He went out fightin'."

Whit nodded, only half hearing, his eyes fixed on some far-off horizon. Words wouldn't come for a few moments. There was a gnawing pain in his breast that choked off any words he might form.

Tinsley was having a hard time explaining the

righteousness of the men who had killed Cougar Gallatin. "You see," he stumbled on, "it was your dad that—that—well, Cyrus was one of four men who stuck up the stage on Sepulvida Pass yesterday. They killed the driver, Trent Ziebold, and—"

"It wasn't Dad who killed that driver, nor Shotgun Kerry neither," Gallatin said.

"—and got away with the Angela Mine pay roll."

"It wasn't my dad who killed those men," Gallatin persisted dully.

The certainty in the tones impressed Tinsley. "You knew Cyrus was in that holdup?"

Whit nodded. "I found out about it—later."

Tinsley's eyes narrowed. "You weren't one of the bandits?"

Gallatin forced a thin, contemptuous smile. "What do you think, Bob Tinsley?"

The sheriff frowned. "I don't just reckon so, son. But them fellers that rode here with me ain't so sure of it. They want to talk to you."

"I won't be leaving here without giving 'em a chance." The words were clipped, brittle.

Tinsley hesitated, uncertain what to say next. "If you know anythin' that will lead to the apprehension—"

"I'm not talking now."

"I thought a heap of Cyrus Gallatin," Tinsley continued after a minute. "Your dad was right good to me, Whit, when I come down here from Montana twenty years back. At that time I couldn't believe the things folks told about him—how he'd been such a hell-roarin' gun fighter up until he'd met your mom and how that settled him to more peaceful ways. Time after time I've been glad to have Cyrus at my back when this country was being civilized. He's lent a hand in stoppin' the Comanches and runnin' out crooks and—and, oh, hell, the fools nowdays never will realize what's owin' to Cyrus Gallatin. I watched him build up the Rafter-G—and then I saw it fall apart—"

"I know." Whit's words were coming hard, though he was finding it good to talk to someone who understood. "I know," he repeated. "You stuck up for Dad even after he commenced to get a hard name. But Dad wasn't really bad. That stage stick-up was the first thing of that kind he ever did—" A lump rose in Gallatin's throat.

"Look here, son," Tinsley said kindly, "you're holdin' in too much. Mostly, cryin' is for women, but I bet if you'd just let down a mite you'd feel a heap relieved."

Young Gallatin's gaze rested on the sheriff a moment, then moved along the gallery toward the sheriff's horse standing at one end, as though about to suggest the sheriff mount and ride. Then his eyes hardened as they came back to rest on Tinsley once more, and he held a firm check on his emotions. "They called Dad a killer, but no man can say he didn't always give the other Teller an even break." A harsh laugh left his lips. "Maybe he was a killer. He had three notches carved on one gun butt, two on the other."

Tinsley said, "Cyrus took three more with him when he went out today. There's another may not live. Not to mention several carryin' wounds of various degrees." He said again. "He sure went out fightin'."

Whit Gallatin nodded briefly. "Tell me about it."

"Soon's I heard of the holdup I gathered my posse. Your dad was the first man I picked to go 'long. We all lined out to where the holdup had took place and found 'sign' where the four stick-up men had left the road and headed down into the canyon below. That canyon bottom is so choked with brush and trees that by the time we got down there and my riders had barged around for a spell, I couldn't figure which tracks was made by—by the bandits, and which by my posse. One of my posse, feller name of Rugger Hess, sent his hawss plunging back and forth until I'll bet he spoiled more sign than the rest of us found. I finally sent him back with the stage and the bodies."

The sheriff paused to draw out an ancient brier pipe and stuff it with tobacco. "I stood it as long as I could, then sent the whole posse back to town in charge of my deputy, Gene Talbert, while I stayed on alone to see could I pick up some clues. I rode to the east a spell but finally decided the holdup men wouldn't have gone that way, 'cause crossin' the alkali flats would leave a trail too easy to follow. They might have headed down toward Mexico, or they could have gone north, though there's some rugged country to travel up that way. Or they might have headed due west with the loot. I finally decided to come back to Toyah Wells and question folks hereabouts, to see if anyone had spotted any strangers ridin' through."

"That was your best bet." Whit Gallatin nodded.

"It was, but I didn't know that at the time, of course." Tinsley drew a match from his pocket, lighted it on one thumbnail, and applied flame to the bowl of his pipe. Evil-smelling blue smoke floated through the air along the gallery. The sheriff went on after a few meditative puffs: "When I was nearly to town I heard shots, so I spurred on in. On the outskirts some feller yelled at me that they had one of the bandits cornered and that he was Cougar Gallatin. You can imagine how I felt—'specially when I got to Cyrus too late to do anythin'."

A few more puffs from the pipe, then: "Now the next

part of the story, Whit, I got from one of my posse. I'd left my deputy in charge of the posse, figurin' to hold the riders together should they be needed in a hurry. Bert Redmond tells me that a short time before I got back to Toyah Wells my deputy, Gene Talbert, called him outside the Toyah Wells Bar, then told him to go back inside and accuse your dad of the holdup. Redmond thought Gene was aimin' to play some sort of joke, so he falls in with the idea. What made it all the funnier to Redmond was that I had picked Cyrus as one of my posse. So Redmond gets set to have a good laugh—"

"It could have been his last," Gallatin said without emotion.

"Lucky it wasn't," Tinsley said. "Anyway, he went back in the saloon and says, 'Cougar Gallatin, you're under arrest for the robbery of the Angela Mine pay roll.' The words was scarce out of Redmond's mouth when he saw the joke had misfired. He says Cyrus's guns come out like a pair of bats wingin' their way outten hell, and Cyrus starts backin' for the doorway. Redmond was too surprised to even think of drawin' his weapon, but a couple of others of the posse did. They figured your dad's actions was a plain confession of guilt. Well, that started the gunplay. Cyrus fought his way outten the saloon and took shelter behind a waterin' trough. And then"—the sheriff swallowed hard before he concluded—"well, there's no use repeatin' what happened after that."

Gallatin nodded. "How come Gene Talbert put Redmond up to accusin' my dad? Where'd he get his information?"

"Gene won't say. Says he got a tip on the identity of the bandits but promised to keep his source a secret for the time bein'. He hints that you were one of the bandits, Whit."

"I wouldn't advise him to do his hinting in my hearing." Young Gallatin's eyes had narrowed to thin slits.

"Now don't you go to flyin' off the handle, Whit," Tinsley said anxiously. "You might as well face the fact that a heap of folks suspect you—"

"Why, dammit"—Gallatin's face flamed—"I can prove I was over on the Cross-X range, lending a hand on beef roundup. Even if we can't run cows of our own any more, I can at least—and as you damn well know—take jobs where I can find 'em, and keep the taxes paid on the Rafter-G holdings—"

"Now don't get proddy, son. *I* ain't accusin' you of nothin'. I know you haven't been home half a dozen times in the past three years. You've always been workin' someplace and I admire you for your efforts to hold things together. But look at the facts. When did you leave the Cross-X country?"

"Soon's roundup was finished—three days ago."

"Three days ago," Tinsley said slowly. "Whit, by ridin' hard you could have got here in time for that holdup. And I don't know as you'd have had to kill any hawss flesh, at that. I—"

"You accusin' me?" Gallatin flared.

"I already told you I ain't, son. I'm just askin' that you look at the facts and realize how folks could be suspicious."

Gallatin said bitterly, "Oh hell!" He added more quietly a moment later: "You haven't any clues as to the other three stick-up men?"

"Not much. There's just one thing: that whisky drummer who brought news of the holdup said he heard the name of 'Scar' mentioned."

"This is the first I've heard of any whisky drummer."

"That's so. I been too riled up inside to think straight, I reckon. Here's the details." The sheriff lighted another match, held it to his pipe, and repeated the story Wagman had brought in. When he had concluded, Gallatin said:

"Scar? Do you know anybody named Scar, Bob?"

Tinsley said, "It could be Scar Hopkins. Hopkins disappeared from town shortly after the holdup was reported. No, I can't tell you much about him. He'd only been in Toyah Wells a short time. Never paid him much attention. Claimed he was lookin' for a job, but I never heard of him makin' any effort to get one. Somebody said he'd been workin' on some range up in Canada before he come here. Leastwise he'd dropped hints to that effect. He never caused any trouble here, so, like I say, I never paid him much attention."

"What sort of feller was he?"

"Stringy-built, dark-complected, what I could see of his face. He had black hair and wore a heavy beard. I'd judge him around thirty."

"I wonder, could that beard have covered up a scar?" Gallatin speculated.

"Maybe it did," the sheriff replied. "I never noticed any scar anyplace else. Why'd you bring that up?"

Gallatin shrugged. "Could be that a scar on a man's face could lead to identifying him. Maybe this Scar Hopkins lit out of Canada in a hurry, with the Mounties on his trail. You haven't any idea why he left Toyah Wells so sudden?"

"None. Unless hearing his name mentioned in connection with the stage holdup threw a scare into him and he figured he'd better slope fast." The sheriff hesitated. “Look, Whit, you wouldn’t have any ideas as to who your dad’s associates might have been, would you?”

“Scar Hopkins might have been one of them.”

“I figured that way too, of course. But who’s the other two?”

“If I know, I’m not stating,” Gallatin said flatly.

“By Gawd, you do know somethin’.”

“Nothing I’d put into words right now.”

“But won’t you even give me a hint as to what you think?” Tinsley pleaded.

“What I think,” Whit Gallatin said savagely, “is that three skunks framed my dad into something. They needed his guns if anything went wrong with the plans. Once they got the money cached, the three planned to get Dad killed so the money would only have to be split three ways. They knew Dad liked excitement, and with a couple of drinks under his belt he could be persuaded into anything that might make him forget, if only for a little time, my mother’s death.” Gallatin’s voice was like a cold wind from glacial waste country. “I’ll be squaring Dad’s killing.”

“Now you look here, son,” Tinsley said anxiously. “Certain members of my posse had a hand in your dad’s death. That posse was legal sworn in. It only done its duty. Good Gawd, boy! Ain’t it better that Cyrus Gallatin went that way, than to have him spendin’ the rest of his natural days inside a penitentiary?”

“Maybe so,” Whit admitted reluctantly, “but just the same, there’s certain things have to be squared—three double-crossin’ bustards are going to pay for Dad’s life—and might be there’ll be more than three. There’s things I want to know about this affair.”

“You’d best think twice before you do anythin’

foolish, son." Tinsley's voice sounded miserable. "Your dad feared you might feel this way. You see, he had killer blood in him. That's something he told me before he died, and he feared you'd turn killer just like him. It's something you've maybe inherited. Cyrus didn't want you to be like him, but he knows that killer streak is there, and he feared you'd get into a heap of trouble if you stay in these parts. I heard a parson talk one time on men that killed. He said they was branded with the mark of Cain and there wa'n't no hope for 'em."

Gallatin commenced a protest, but the sheriff interrupted: "Shootin' in self-defense is one thing, but sometimes when a man does that too often he gets so he's a mite too eager to throw lead, 'specially when he's fast with his irons like Cyrus Gallatin was. Before he died Cyrus told me he'd got so he fair loved a gun fight. I don't understand a thing like that, neither, unless it was that killer streak dominatin' his better instincts. Cyrus was always a right hombre until—"

"Dad sort of went haywire after Mother died," Whit said soberly. "That was when he started drinking and gambling away our herds. Now there's only the land left. Dad was all broken up when she died."

"I understand that, Whit. Cyrus loved you a heap too. He told me he only went into that holdup to get the money for an education for you. He'd planned to send you to some good college. He wanted you to be somebody and not have to go through life wearin' that killer brand. It's a handicap, boy. That's why Cyrus wanted you to go away from here. You can't lick all Toyah Wells just to square your dad's death."

"Where's his guns?" Whit broke in abruptly.

"He asked me to give 'em to you. They're on my saddle. Cyrus wanted that you'd never use 'em except in self-defense."

"Did he say anything else?"

"There wa'n't time for him to say much, 'ceptin' he didn't want you to be a killer like him. Oh yes, he did sort of wonder how Redmond come to accuse him of the holdup—couldn't figure out how Redmond had learned about it."

"What did Dad say when you told him your deputy had put Redmond up to it?" Gallatin's tones were grim.

Tinsley shook his head. "I didn't get to tell him that. Cyrus passed off too sudden." The sheriff looked into the hard dry eyes and felt something akin to a shudder course along his spine. There was grief in Whit Gallatin's eyes, but something else was there, too, something Tinsley didn't like to see: something greater, stronger than grief. The overwhelming desire to avenge his father's death dominated all else in Whit Gallatin's stony gaze.

"I'll be taking his guns now," Whit said in a voice that sounded like the harsh rustling of dry leaves.

Tinsley knew there was no use saying more. He walked to his horse, swung up to the saddle, and guided the animal to the edge of the gallery where Gallatin stood. From his saddle horn the sheriff took a pair of wide cartridge belts, each carrying its weight of loads and Colt's holstered six-shooters. He handed down the weapons, saying, "Now don't you go to doin' anything foolish, son."

"There's something to be squared," Whit repeated tonelessly, as though voicing a sort of sacred ritual.

The lump in the sheriff's throat made it difficult for the words to get through: "Now you looky here, Whit, you and me has been good friends, but I don't aim to stand for no promiscuous shooting. I've got to enforce the law. Don't make it hard for me. Why don't you leave here, go someplace where folks don't know the name of Gallatin?"

"And where would that be?" Whit asked tersely.

"I just don't know," the sheriff said slowly after some consideration. "Your dad's name is known pretty widely out here in the West. Course you might head East, but I don't know how—"

"I'll be going away," Gallatin interrupted, "but"—again that repetition—"there's something to be squared first."

Tinsley sighed and changed the subject: "Holdup man or not, Whit, I thought a heap of Cyrus. I'd consider it an honor to stay and help with the buryin'."

"Thanks, no, Bob." The words were hard, brittle-sounding. "He's mine. I'll take care of him."

"But, Whit—"

"Can't you understand?" Gallatin's voice was fiercely possessive. "He's mine! I want to do it alone."

The sheriff nodded and wheeled his horse. "All right, son. Have it your way. Adios!"

But Whit didn't hear him. He had already passed within the house to join his dead.

FRESH NOTCHES

THE SUN HAD ALREADY SETTLED behind the western hills, but Whit Gallatin sat without movement in the room where the blanket-draped figure of his father lay stretched on an ancient sofa. Shadows deepened within the house, but Whit still sat staring blindly off into space, his mind reverting to boyhood days when his mother still lived. Cougar Gallatin had been a model husband those days, the years of a turbulent youth put far behind him by the hand of that gentle woman who had restrained the tainted instinct that cropped up, generation after generation, in those bearing the name of Gallatin.

And now Whit was remembering old tales he had heard of that proud family which three hundred years before had boasted of a coat of arms and a king's royal favor, and of how each generation had produced at least one member of the family who had killed a man. But always in fair fight or self-defense. Whit experienced a momentary satisfaction in that. There had been that Hugo Gallatin who had done his killing with a dueling pistol under the New Orleans oaks. And Proctor Gallatin who had been on General Washington's staff and who had employed a flintlock weapon. There was that Gallatin who had ridden with Bonnie Prince Charlie—what was his name, Nigel?—who had favored the claymore. And that English Gallatin who had known no equal with long thin rapiers. Doubtless, Whit reflected, there had been a Gallatin drawing the longbow at the Battle of Crécy. He remembered his mother's stories of those ancient days and wondered now if that same killer strain had dominated certain cave men of prehistoric days when they used brutally clubs and huge chunks of rock in overthrowing an enemy.

Until today Whit Gallatin had never felt the slightest desire to take life, but now, slowly, inexorably, there was seeping into his veins the same relentless urge that for so long had controlled Cougar Gallatin's life. Whit, for the first time, was commencing to feel there might be a sort of grim satisfaction in pitting himself against some other man—men?—who was trying to "wipe him out," and beating him to the shot. After all, he considered, it was something primitive that had come, down to him from his ancestors, something not quite compatible with man-made laws, something that could overrule all else when the blood ran hot with anger and hate and a desire for revenge.

Never before had Whit Gallatin felt that overpowering urge to lift his gun against another man. Such shooting as he had done had been at targets composed of tin cans, or trees, or playing cards. Until now he had been satisfied to work and dream of the time when his father would once more settle down and the Gallatin Rafter-G stock could again be placed on the beef markets of the country. But now all these dreams were abruptly swept aside in the overwhelming desire to avenge his father's death—nay, murder. For to Whit Gallatin, it was murder, nothing less.

It was dark by the time he rose and lighted a lantern, then made his way out to the rickety old barn. Here he found a rusty saw, a hammer, some nails. There were some old packing crates and other heavy lumber. By the flickering light of the lantern he fashioned a coffin which he carried to an oak-covered hill back of the ranch house. There was already one low mound of earth there, a mound with a slab of granite rising from one end and loose chunks of rock piled over it. Beside this mound Whit Gallatin dug the grave. Later he brought out the body of his father and placed it within the blanket-lined coffin.

The moon was edging above the western horizon by the time he scraped the last particle of gravelly earth back into the grave. That done, he piled loose rock over this second mound to keep the coyotes from disturbing Cyrus Gallatin's last resting place. Later—if he lived—

he would return and erect another headstone of some sort. But for the present there was other work to be done—a task to be completed first.

Carrying the lantern, Whit Gallatin re-entered the house. Some time was spent in removing various papers from an old tin box, glancing through them and then placing them inside his shirt. He wrote a note, leaving certain of Cougar Gallatin's possessions—horse, rifle, and a few other objects so necessary to men of the cow country—to friends of his father. The note he left in plain view on the table, knowing that someone would come to the house to investigate before many hours had passed.

His own .45 six-shooter and belt he left hanging on the back of a chair. He glanced over the twin .45s Cougar Gallatin had left him, cut fresh notches in the butts with his barlow knife, then strapped on the pair of cartridge belts. They fitted snugly about his hips, allowing the holsters to hang low for a quick draw. The bottoms of the holsters were tied with leather thongs to his thighs. He hesitated then only long enough to get a thin roll of bills from a coat pocket. His gaze went swiftly around the house in one long last look, then he donned his Stetson and blew out the light in the lantern. The next instant the door had closed softly at his back. The moon was higher now when he stepped from the house gallery. Gathering the reins of his waiting pony, he stepped up to the saddle and headed for town.

Sheriff Bob Tinsley caught sight of Gene Talbert as the deputy crossed Toyah Wells's dusty street. "Hey, Gene," Tinsley called, "just a minute."

The two came together in a square of yellow light shining from a nearby poolroom. "Oh, hello, Bob,"

Talbert said. "I didn't see you comin'." He stood tugging at his black mustache, waiting for the sheriff to speak.

"Where you been all evenin'?" Tinsley wanted to know.

"Layin' down for a spell. Me bein' sick when that holdup happened, and then losin' sleep ridin' with the posse, and the fight with Cougar Gallatin, and all, sort of laid me out. I been catchin' up on some shut-eye. I get a queer feelin' every time I think of it bein' old Cougar who pulled that holdup, and him bein' one of our posse. He was likely laughin' up his sleeve at us. D'you know, I was sorry to see him go like that. I always liked Cougar. It's a damn funny business when you come to think on it."

"Damn funny," Tinsley agreed. He looked at his deputy as though awaiting some further explanation of the matter. "I'm still wondering," he hinted finally "just who tipped you off that Cyrus was one of the bandits."

"I'll bet you are." Talbert nodded. "You know, that Cougar certainly put up one whale of a scrap. We all knew he was one tough old root, but I don't think any man in town figured him as that tough."

"I could have told you. Most folks in town haven't known Cyrus Gallatin like I have, and I ain't convinced that killin' him was best for all concerned."

"What do you mean?" Talbert asked sharply.

"You didn't act smart, Gene. A real smart deputy with the information you said you had would have taken Gallatin prisoner and got him to tell who his three pards were."

Talbert emitted a scornful laugh. "You claim to have known old Cougar? Do you think he would have ratted on his pals, Bob? Now you know better than that. Wild hawsses couldn't have dragged such information outten him if he didn't feel like talkin'."

"Yeah"—Tinsley nodded glumly—"I reckon you're correct. Cyrus wa'n't no squealer . . . Just who was it gave you that tip on Cyrus, Gene?"

Talbert chuckled. "I'm goin' to have to keep you guessin' on that score for a spell, Bob. The information was given me in confidence. Until the other three bandits are rounded up, I'd rather not tell you anything." He paused. "Maybe there'll just be two more to round up, with Scar Hopkins disappearin' the way he did."

"You feel pretty certain Scar was one of 'em?"

"I don't think there's any doubt of it. He just lost his nerve and lit outten the country, the way I see it. That just leaves two to divide the loot."

"You got any ideas as to the identity of the two?"

Talbert said, "I feel right sure about one of 'em, anyway."

"You do? Who is he?"

Talbert's dark brow knitted. "We-ell, I don't rightly like to say yet. Not until I get a mite more proof."

"Can't you give me a hint? I'm willin' to hold my peace for a spell if it will lead to the arrest of the other bandits, but if you'd just give a hint I might be able to help work out this business," Tinsley persisted.

"Hell, Bob," Talbert said reluctantly, "I don't like to accuse anybody until I'm sure, but if you insist, I'd say we wouldn't go far wrong by nabbing Whit Gallatin. Him and his old man were probably leaders in the job—" He broke off to halt Tinsley's violent protests. "Now, no need you gettin' mad, Bob. You asked for my opinion and I gave it. And I'm not the only man in town that feels this way—not by a long shot. On the other hand, while I'm not actually sure, I'd like to go slow. If Whit is innocent, I'd sure feel like hell accusin' him, with old Cougar hardly cold yet. At the same time, I've got a strong hunch if we was to ride up to Gallatin's place right now we might find him countin' over his share of the payroll money."

"Oh hell," Tinsley growled angrily. "You're way off'n the trail, Gene, and so help me Gawd, if you make a move without my permission, I'll—"

"Take it easy, Bob. I ain't said I was goin' to do anythin' without proof, have I?" He laughed good-humoredly. "No use you and me scrappin' about somethin' that ain't yet come to pass. I'm headin' for a drink. Want to join me?"

Tinsley shook his head. "I'm going to perambulate around a mite first. Maybe I'll see you in the Toyah Wells Bar later."

The two men parted, Deputy Talbert heading in the direction of the saloon, which was half the length of a city block farther down the street. Tinsley headed in the opposite direction.

The sheriff had progressed only a short distance when, in the lights shining from windows, he caught sight of Whit Gallatin striding along the sidewalk. Gallatin was staring straight ahead, eyes cold and hard and dry. As he walked he swung his arms. At each step his fingertips brushed the gun butt at either hip. His face might have been hewn from cold granite.

Tinsley waited for Whit to come up. The other man recognized him, nodded, and would have kept on going. Tinsley said, "Where you headin', son?"

"Toyah Wells Bar." Whit gave the information in crisp, brittle tones. He didn't slacken pace either.

The sheriff fell in at his side. "I'll drift along with you. Just get in?"

"Hit town a couple of minutes back."

"Looking for anybody in particular, son?"

Whit stared straight ahead. Finally: "Would you be if someone had murdered your father?"

"Now look here, Whit, you can't term that murder. My posse was doin' its duty. You'd best not do anythin' foolish. Was I you, I'd take things easy. Maybe you don't realize it, but right now you're suspected of bein' an accomplice in that holdup. It wouldn't take much to have the whole town on your back, let alone the members of my posse—"

"I'm not surprised."

In the light from a window Tinsley saw the scorn in Gallatin's chiseled features. The sheriff was nonplused. He wanted to stop further trouble, but there wasn't anything he could arrest Gallatin for—yet. Neither did he feel justified in taking Whit up on suspicion. But there was trouble brewing, plenty of trouble. How to stop it? Tinsley said at last. "Whit, I think you'd better hand your guns over to me for a while until things cool down a mite."

Gallatin laughed harshly. "Just *think* about it, Bob. Don't go any farther. You tell me a lot of folks suspect me of playing a part in the holdup. Some of them are mighty likely to have itching trigger fingers. My dad was framed into something by three scuts, but at least he was armed. Are you planning to leave me defenseless?"

"No, I reckon not," Tinsley said dully. He added after they had walked a little farther, "I'm warnin' you, though, Whit, that I aim to place you under arrest if you start rolling lead without a damn good excuse."

"I've got an excuse, Bob, a mighty good one."

Anger welled in the sheriff, an anger induced by his sense of helplessness. "All right," he snapped, "but just remember that I warned you, Whit. I won't put up with no cold-blooded killin'. You mind what I tell you."

They continued to stride along, neither speaking now, Gallatin's eyes resting sharply on every passer-by who approached. In front of the Toyah Wells Bar, Gallatin halted. "I'm going in here, Bob," he stated. "I'll see you later."

"I'll go in with you," Tinsley said, injecting in his tones a certain geniality. "It's a coon's age since you and me drunk together. I'm buying."

"I'm not drinking right now," Gallatin said coldly. Abruptly he swung about and entered the building, Tinsley close at his heels.

The Toyah Wells Bar was the largest of the town's five saloons. A long scarred oaken bar ran along the right wall as one entered. Ranged along the opposite wall were card tables and chairs. There were probably fifteen men in the place. A few sat at tables, dealing cards or studying hands, but most of them were ranged at the long bar with drinks before them. Three oil lamps with smoky chimneys hung from the raftered ceiling. The room was thick with cigar and cigarette smoke; bottles and glasses made clinking sounds; poker chips rattled on the tables.

Deputy Gene Talbert stood at the entrance end of the bar, talking to the man named Rugger Hess. Hess was a barrel-torsoed individual with muddy blue eyes and colorless hair. A six-shooter hung in a scarred holster at one hip, and he carried the reputation of being a tough customer to mix with, though to date he'd never stirred up any particular trouble in Toyah Wells.

Men's voices gradually subsided as Whit Gallatin crossed the floor and took up a position midway of the bar. Someone coughed nervously as Whit's hard gaze flicked from man to man. Of the posse that had finished

Cougar Gallatin that day, only two members were present: Deputy Gene Talbert and Rugger Hess.

Sensing the tension, a slick-haired bartender moved up to the point at which Whit Gallatin stood, Sheriff Tinsley right behind him. "Howdy, Sheriff. Long time I no see, Whit. What you gents drinkin'?"

"Nothing for me right now," Whit said in cold level tones. "I came here to do some talking tonight." His eyes ranged about the room. "A lot of folks in this town have an idea I had something to do with that stage holdup. That, I'm denying right now. I'll admit my father's guilt, but we'll let that pass for the present. He's already paid for his part in that business." Whit paused a moment, then continued: "Sheriff Tinsley, here, has a mistaken idea that I'm planning to rub out the posse that was responsible for my father's death. I'm not, but I haven't felt like talking about that before. I understand the position the posse was in. Its members did their sworn legal duty. I understand three were killed in the course of that duty and more wounded. I'm regretful about that, too, but there's nothing I can do about it—"

"Spoken like a man, Whit," Deputy Talbert interrupted.

Whit ignored the words and went on: "I reckon there's been a lot of talk about my father's pardners in that holdup. Who they were, and so on. One of those pardners killed the coach driver; the other killed the guard. Dad had seen the whole business as a stick-up, nothing more. There wasn't to have been any killing. You men who knew Cougar Gallatin well know he wasn't the sort of man who killed in cold blood or picked on those weaker than himself. The whole fault lies with the two skunks with him who got buck fever, lost their nerve, and pulled their triggers—"

"Seems to me, Gallatin," Rugger Hess growled, "that you know a hell of a lot about that holdup. Besides your old man and the two hombres you claim lost their nerve, there was a fourth man. I've an idea you could put a name to him if you wa'n't scared of your own skin—"

"Hess, you keep your mouth shut," Tinsley ordered sharply, glancing a bit nervously at Gallatin.

"Nobody asked for your opinion, Hess," Deputy Tabert growled. "Keep still and let Whit finish this his own way."

"That's exactly what I'm aiming to do," Whit said coldly. "As to that fourth man, I wouldn't say. It might have been the fellow named Scar Hopkins who lit out of town in such a hurry, but I wouldn't want to state definite. That's whatever. I'll get on with what I know for sure . . . The day of the holdup I'd returned from the Cross-X range where I'd been working on beef roundup. Dad wasn't home when I arrived. As a matter of fact, I hadn't expected him to be, as I got home a couple of days earlier than he'd planned on. I'd been riding pretty hard. My bronc and I were right weary. I took the hawss down to that water hole beyond the hill behind the house and turned him loose. Then I came back to the house and rolled into bed."

Whit paused to let these facts sink in before continuing. "It must have been along toward late afternoon when I was awakened by voices coming from the front room of the house. It was Dad and the other three talking about the holdup they'd pulled that day. There was an argument on. One of the men—it might have been this Scar Hopkins—sounded like he'd completely lost his nerve. He wanted to get his share of the money and leave this section pronto. By that time Dad had commenced to regret the whole business. By listening I learned about the two killings. That part stuck in Dad's craw plenty. He wanted to turn the money back and confess to the whole business. That made further argument. Finally the talk died down, with the four of 'em agreeing not to split up the money until some sort of decision could be reached and the rumpus over the holdup and killings had died down. Until that time it was agreed that the stolen money could be hidden under a loose board in our front room. It's there now, and Sheriff Tinsley can get it any time he wants to go out and go after it."

Excited exclamations burst from the men in the room. Whit held up one hand for silence. "I sort of figured that with time to think things over Dad would have things his way and he'd see that the money was returned. What would be done about the killings I didn't know, but I knew Dad would work that out too. I didn't want him to know what I'd heard, so while the four of 'em were still talking I grabbed my duds and slipped out the back door of the house. I got my horse saddled and figured to ride off and come back the next day, to make it look like I'd just returned home. Well, we all know now that Dad and the other three left our place for town and waited for news of the holdup to arrive. It wasn't but a short time after I came home the following day that Dad's body was brought out to the house. You all know what had happened in town, meanwhile."

"I'd still like to know who that fourth man was?" Rugger Hess rasped. "How do we know you're speakin' truth—"

A thin-lipped, contemptuous smile flitted across Whit's face. "Why you so interested in that fourth man, Hess?" he asked softly. "Taking it for granted my dad was number one, aren't you interested in the second and third—or do you already know them?"

Hess's face flamed dark red, then went white. Before he could voice a reply Whit jerked Cougar Gallatin's twin guns from his holsters and held them, butt foremost, so everyone could see the fresh notches cut in the walnut handles. "The sheriff tells me Dad took three with him when he died. But there were two more he should have taken. Those two were probably hiding from his lead. I've cut those three notches for Dad. Now I'm figuring to cut two more on my own account."

THE MARK OF CAIN

A TENSE SILENCE DESCENDED ON THE BARROOM. Finally Talbert asked, dry-lipped, "Who's the two, Whit?" Hess didn't say anything.

Whit slipped the twin guns back into holsters. "As I see it," he said slowly, "Dad's pardners in the holdup figured to get him killed so they'd have more money for themselves. With Dad out of the way, they likely figured they could come to our place and get that money at their leisure. If they hadn't learned that I was there today they'd probably have gone out there tonight for the cash—"

"Who's the two men?" Talbert asked again. "Did you recognize their voices when you overheard 'em talkin' to Cougar?"

"I recognized two of the three. If the third was Scar Hopkins, I couldn't say. I never knew him." Whit's tones dripped icicles. "But I haven't any doubt about the other two."

"Who were they?" Talbert asked a third time.

Whit Gallatin's face flamed with sudden anger. "You

low-down double-crossing skunk!" he blazed. "Is it necessary *you* ask? *You* know! And so does Rugger Hess! Are you waiting for me to put your names into words? Or are you going to try to deny it with drawn guns?"

For one brief instant the two men hesitated, while others in the room, Sheriff Tinsley included, stood in frozen astonishment. Talbert and Hess realized they were cornered now. Trapped! There was only one thing left to do, one chance that still remained to them: kill Whit Gallatin. With Gallatin's death would die the accusations he had made. After that the others could be bluffed out with the claim that Gallatin had been lying.

Gene Talbert moved first, then Rugger Hess got into action. Whit waited until both men had touched their gun butts before he reached to holsters. A sudden thrill ran through him as his palms closed about Cougar Gallatin's twin six-shooters. The two .45s swept up—out—savage orange lances of fire spurting from their muzzles.

A keen sense of exaltation coursed through Whit's body as he saw his first bullet take Rugger Hess in the chest. Hess spun off balance, bumping into Gene Talbert, causing the crooked deputy to miss his first shot.

Talbert righted himself, threw down for a second try. Whit felt the breeze of the leaden slug fan his right cheek. He thumbed two swift shots, one from either hand, then sent a third winging toward Rugger Hess, who was trying to rise from the floor and get his gun back into the fight. Hess slid forward on his face, the weapon clattering from his grip. An instant later Talbert's body jackknifed and he toppled across the body of his pardner.

Black powder smoke drifted through the air. Everything had happened too swiftly for Sheriff Tinsley to prevent the fight. He spoke sharply to Whit now, but Gallatin had no ears for him. He was backing across the floor, his cold voice coming sharply through the smoke spiraling about the room. "Anybody else want in on this?" he challenged savagely. "Jerk your irons if you're craving to take a hand!"

No one replied. The arms of several men shot abruptly toward the ceiling. Two men commenced to edge frightenedly toward the doorway. Somebody raised his voice: "You can put 'em away, Gallatin. Nobody here wants any part of your game."

Something of disappointment passed across Whit's face. He gave a short nod, then turned slowly toward Sheriff Tinsley, spun the guns in his hands, and presented them, butt foremost, to the sheriff. "I reckon you'll be wantin' my hardware, Bob," he said, hard-voiced.

Tinsley shook his head. "Keep 'em, Whit. Hess and my deputy—damn him—reached first. You was within your rights. I didn't know before how it was. But is it actually true like you told it—"

"Ask 'em," Whit snapped, "if they got enough life left to answer."

The sheriff strode over to the two forms sprawled on the floor. Other men gathered near, while Gallatin stood apart at the bar. Hess was already dead, but Gene Talbert lived long enough to confess the part he and Hess had played in the stage holdup and killing. It was Hess who had killed Trent Ziebold. Talbert had shot the guard. Before he died, Talbert named Scar Hopkins as the fourth man. Hopkins had lost his nerve and fled without even awaiting a division of the payroll money.

Everything was as Whit Gallatin had told it.

Whit swept the room with a scowl, his eyes as hard and cold as ever, then without a word he turned and strode swiftly out to the street. The crowd which had gathered before the swinging doors parted as he approached, then turned to watch him walk with long strides toward the west end of town. A man looking after him muttered, "Well, the Cougar's whelp has tasted blood. Fair and square that fight was, but next time I wonder. Ten to one he turns killer like his old man was."

Sheriff Tinsley had been pushing through the crowd when he heard the words. Roughly he told the speaker not to talk like "an utter damn fool," then he hurried after Whit's retreating form. When he caught up to Gallatin, Whit was standing in the light shining from a restaurant window, carving two fresh notches in his gun butts. He looked up and saw the sheriff just as he replaced his knife in his pocket; his eyes were bleak, challenging, as they met the sheriff's. He said tersely, "I'll be leaving now. You won't be wanting me." It was a statement of fact rather than a question. Young Gallatin was keyed up, nerves tense, prepared to heat his gun barrels at the slightest provocation, something within him even seeking out that provocation and welcoming it if it could be found. Tinsley shivered at what could happen should he try to detain Gallatin now. He faced Whit steadily, saying in a quiet voice:

"I've already told you I wouldn't be holding you for that shooting. You fired in your own defense. I merely trailed you to get some information. You heading for your ranch now?"

"Is that any of your business?" sullenly.

"I figure it is, Whit. If you're going to the ranch, all

right. If you're not, I want more details regarding where that payroll money is hidden. You mentioned it was under a loose floor board. I don't want to have to go all over your house looking for that board."

Gallatin relaxed a trifle. "I won't be going back to the house for a while. I don't know where I'm going, but I've got to get away." He added explicit directions for locating the stolen money.

The sheriff said thanks and went on: "I'll be heading for your place as soon as I can pick up a couple of reliable men . . . Now you listen to me, son; don't be too ready to kill. I know the urge is there, like you got a devil inside that's all the time making your trigger finger itch, but whether you believe me or not, I'm statin' that killin' don't make for an easy life. What you got in your blood is somethin' you're goin' to have to fight and fight hard, if you ever want any happiness in this life—"

"Happiness!" Whit jerked out scornfully.

"I know how you feel, boy. Later, after you've thought things over, you'll see different, I'm hopin'. Deep down, you don't really want to be a killer."

Whit said bitterly, "Do *I* have any *choice* in the matter? It's in the Gallatin blood. I've heard that since I was a youngster. How can I help myself?"

"I never heard of anything like that in your mother's blood, Whit. You've got to keep rememberin' you're only one half Gallatin. Your ma was responsible for the other half of your make-up. Don't ever forget that part, and it will help you fight this other thing. But you'll have to keep fightin'."

Whit laughed. It wasn't a nice laugh. Harsh and ugly, it was the sort of laugh that grated on a man's sensibilities. "Bob, I'll lay aces to tens *you* don't know whether I want to be a killer or not. I'm willing to play the cards as they fall to me, so why should you give a damn?"

Tinsley said quietly, "Why should I give a damn? I could give you a number of answers to that, son, but you ain't in no fit mood to listen right now. You just keep thinkin' what I've said—and keep fightin'. Adios and good luck, Whit."

Gallatin stared at the sheriff a moment, jerked out an angry "Adios," and without giving the sheriff time to say more, he crossed the sidewalk, vaulted over the hitch rack to his waiting horse, climbed into the saddle, and wheeled the pony. Straight down the street he rode, and out of Toyah Wells, urging the horse to the utmost in speed. The sheriff stood gazing sadly after him until the sounds of thundering hoofs had died in the distance and the dust had again settled to the roadway. Then, shaking his head, Tinsley turned and directed his steps toward the Toyah Wells Bar.

SCAR HOPKINS

IT HAD BEEN NOTHING BUT STARK FEAR that had stampeded Scar Hopkins out of town when he had heard his name mentioned the night the news of the stage holdup had been brought to Toyah Wells. He had been standing on the outskirts of the crowd when the whisky drummer, Wagman, told his story, and at mention of the word "Scar" had instantly slunk away in search of his horse. Once in the saddle, he had spurred frantically to get out of town, and only when he was miles distant had some slight reassurance returned to his frightened being. Even then it was with some reluctance he had pulled his weary, foam-flecked mount to a halt at the side of the road and dismounted to sit on the grass and get matters straightened out in his confused mind.

Hopkins was a tall, lean, swarthy-complexioned man with a heavy black beard; his eyes were a washy blue, as though someone had poured a trace of bluing into a mixture of starch and water when they were being formed. The beard had nothing to do with his age but was worn as a disguise. There had been some trouble up in Canada, and the authorities were seeking a smoothly shaven man who had shot another man in the back after a quarrel over a card game. But all this was a year behind Hopkins now, and he felt himself well out of the reach of Canadian law, so much so, indeed, that he hadn't even bothered to change his name when he crossed the line into the United States and worked his way gradually down into the Southwest country.

At present he sat at the side of the road, scowling in the darkness, the cigarette butt in his hand long since gone dead. "Damn the luck," he muttered peevishly. "I don't know what come over me, running away like this. I should have stuck around. There could be other fellers called Scar. If any accusations were made, I had Deputy Talbert and Rugger Hess to back me up. I wonder if they'll go through with the plan to frame Cougar Gallatin into getting killed?"

He finally decided they probably would. He and Hess and Talbert had only wanted Gallatin along on the holdup in case trouble was encountered: Gallatin had plenty of nerve and his guns were fast. An angry curse was torn from Hopkins's bearded lips. "And now with me out of the way, there'll be only Hess and Talbert to split that payroll money. That ain't fair. I'm entitled to my just share. It was me helped think up the plan—even to getting Gallatin put outten the way."

Hopkins rode on after a time, resentment growing within him. He stopped at a small town which lay farther east and spent some hours in sleeping, eating, and thinking. The more he dwelled on the matter, the more indignant his thoughts at losing out on his share of the stolen Angela Mine payroll money. Finally, still uncertain what he planned to do, he bolstered up his courage and turned his pony back toward Toyah Wells, approaching cautiously as he neared the vicinity of the town and keeping well away from the beaten trails leading to it.

That afternoon, on a high ridge overlooking Toyah Wells's dusty street, Scar Hopkins lay on his stomach and from behind a screening tangle of brush viewed the gun fight which ended only when Cougar Gallatin died. Hopkins saw the arrival of the sheriff and, later, the departure of the wagon carrying Gallatin's stiffened form toward the Rafter-G Ranch. "What a tough old bustard that Cougar was," Hopkins mused with some awe. "If I'd had his fighting spirit I'd not run off like I did." He added angrily, "Damned if I do it again. I got to get in touch with Talbert and Hess and let 'em know I ain't to be counted out when that money gets split up."

But as he rode toward Toyah Wells after dark that night, his courage evaporated again; and instead of riding boldly in, he tethered his pony some distance away and sneaked on foot to the rear of the Toyah Wells Bar, where, peering through a dusty back window, he could see plainly the occupants of the saloon. Deputy Talbert stood at the bar, as did Hess and several other men. A short time later Hopkins saw the saloon doors bang open to admit Sheriff Tinsley and another man, who resembled strangely the late Cougar Gallatin.

Hopkins frowned in the gloom, his face almost pressed against the dirty windowpane. "That young feller," he mused, "must be Cougar's whelp I've heard of."

A moment later conversation seeping through the narrowly open rear door of the saloon confirmed Hopkins's surmise. His knees commenced to shake as he caught the import of Whit Gallatin's remarks. Apparently the whelp was wise to a lot of things that had been going on. Then there came the swift detonations of heavy gunfire, and when the powder smoke had cleared away, the prone bodies of Deputy Talbert and Rugger Hess were revealed to Hopkins's startled gaze. A wave of fear swept over him, and he slunk quickly away from the rear wall of the saloon and hurried frantically to his waiting horse. Once more he made his way swiftly from Toyah Wells.

This time, however, Hopkins pulled up a short distance out of town. There was a sick, hollow feeling at the pit of his stomach; cold beads of perspiration dotted his forehead. But through it all a persistent thought kept recurring: with Talbert and Hess out of the way, there'd need to be no split of the money. All that was necessary was to ride to the Rafter-G before anyone else could get there, lift that loose floor board, and seize the stolen payroll money.

It required considerable nerve for Hopkins to make up his mind, but eventually he turned his pony in the direction of the Rafter-G. Even now he wasn't moving fast; his hand trembled on the reins as he directed the horse along a course paralleling the road leading to the Gallatin ranch. He had progressed only a few miles when he heard the swift drumming of hoofs at his rear. Pulling to a halt and drawing back in the brush, he spied the rider who was passing, his mount's hoofs beating a rapid tattoo on the dusty trail.

In the light from the moon Hopkins recognized the grim features of Whit Gallatin as the horse tore past. Then Gallatin rounded a curve in the trail and disappeared. Dust motes swam in the moonlight and finally settled back to earth.

Hopkins shifted nervously in his saddle, shivering a little while he waited for the sounds of the hoofbeats to die away. "Geez! The look on that hombre's face," he muttered. "I'd sure hate to have him riled at me. 'Pears like he's just honin' to find someone to kill."

Another thought intruded: "What in hell is Gallatin in such a hurry to get to his ranch for? I wonder if he's plannin' to get that money and light out. By Gawd! I'll bet that's it. He's headin' for the cash that I worked to get—cash that should be all mine rightly, now that Hess and Talbert are done for. I wonder . . ." Greed overcame some of his fear as he commenced to make plans. "I'd certain hate to face him, though, 'thout I was sure of gettin' the first shot. Nope, I wouldn't want none of his game. Did I say face him? Wait!" A plan began to form in Hopkins's mind. "I got brains. Why don't I use 'em? I could follow along to the Rafter-G, wait until Gallatin had got the money and started to leave with it . . . He'd have to leave; the sheriff knows the money is out there . . . I could wait, hidden near the house, until he come out with the money, then get behind him and pull trigger." Hopkins laughed suddenly. "Face him! Hell! I won't have to face him. It will be easy as rollin' off a log."

He guided the horse into motion and turned it along the road leading to the Rafter-G. Now he put spurs to the animal and hurried it on its way. Before long he spied the ghostly outlines of the Rafter-G ranch house standing dark and cheerless in the bright moonlight.

Hopkins had expected to see light shining from its dust-coated windows, but there wasn't any light or even the slightest movement about the building to be seen.

He had drawn his mount to a walk, but now he dismounted and led the animal by its reins as he made his way around to the rear of the house, half expecting to see Gallatin's horse waiting. But there was no sign of life to be seen here, either.

Hopkins, paused, puzzled. Where was Gallatin? Had he already secured the money and left? Surely he must have come here. There was just a chance, of course, Hopkins admitted, that he hadn't. At any rate, there wasn't too much time to waste. The sheriff would likely be coming out to get that money. "I've got to work fast if I want to learn anything," Hopkins told himself.

Drawing his six-shooter, he stepped softly to the rear door of the house and found it unlocked. He stepped inside. A board creaked under his foot and he stiffened. A new thought struck him. Perhaps Gallatin was someplace within the house and hadn't bothered to light a lamp. He lifted his voice and cautiously called, "Hey, Gallatin." There was no reply.

Hopkins waited a moment, then moved softly to the front of the house. Again he spoke Gallatin's name, and again there was no reply. Hopkins was in the front main room of the house now. Moonlight streamed through the windows. The room appeared to be empty. Hopkins's gaze flitted about the room. He saw a holstered gun hanging with gun belt over the back of a chair. Probably Whit Gallatin's gun. But where was Whit?

Hopkins looked nervously about, turned and quickly inspected a couple of bedrooms with the aid of moonlighted windows and a couple of scratched matches. Both were empty. "Damned if I like this," he muttered. "It seems sort of spooky. Reckon I'd best get back to that front room, grab the money, and light out fast—providin' Gallatin ain't already got the money and sloped." He returned to the front room, then reluctantly holstered his six-shooter. Going quickly to one corner of the room which was in partial shadow, he groped about on the uneven floor. After a few minutes he located the loose board he sought and lifted it out and to one side. Reaching one hand into the opening below, he felt about, but his fingers encountered only air. A curse of frustration left his lips. Had Gallatin already been here and secured the cash?

Throwing himself flat on the floor, Hopkins thrust one arm to the shoulder into the opening, down past cobwebbed joints, his fingers outstretched, feeling frantically about. A sudden sighed relief parted his bearded lips. His fingertips had just managed to brush against the tops of canvas sacks. He tried reaching farther to secure a firm grip on the money sacks, but to no avail: his arm wasn't long enough. Bitter profanity rolled from his tongue as he finally gave up and climbed to his feet.

"Damn the luck," he growled. "I've got to find something long enough to reach down and hook them sacks outten there. If I had a cane or a long pole—something with a curved end . . . It wouldn't need to be very long, neither. All I lacked was an inch or so."

His eyes went quickly about the room. What could he use? There were no tools near the blackened fireplace. There was a clutter of objects on the table, including some old letters Whit had placed there that day. In a sort of feverish haste Hopkins brushed the letters swiftly to the floor as he caught sight of a spur leather. The spur, when he lifted it to his gaze, proved to be rusty and broken. A rowel might be made to catch on a canvas sack, but Hopkins doubted it; the points would probably just turn and fail to hold. He examined other objects on the table—a bit of broken harness, some empty cartridge shells, a cigar box with no cigars in it, a stack of ancient magazines and newspapers, a partly filled Durham sack and brown papers, a whisky bottle long since drained of its contents.

Hopkins swore fervently and left the table. He considered breaking up a chair in order to get a rung or section of curved chair back. Then his eye caught sight of Whit Gallatin's gun hanging on another chair. He crossed the floor quickly across the patches of moonlight and secured the weapon. It might be possible to lower the gun by the barrel and hook the curved gun butt into the sacks ... This idea too, was suddenly relinquished: the gun butt would probably just slip off the sacks.

As he realized the need for hurry a feeling of panic commenced to build in Hopkins. Damn it! He had to get something sharp to lift those sacks. But what? He stood with Whit Gallatin's gun in hand, his eyes darting swiftly about the room. Suddenly an idea came to him.

"What a fool I am," he rasped. "There should be some sort of long-handled fork back in the kitchen. Why didn't I think of that before?"

He had started to turn toward the kitchen when he tensed suddenly, listening. The sounds of drumming hoofs reached the house clearly. Hopkins leaped to a front window as the hoofbeats slowed down, and in the light of the moon viewed through the oak trees, he recognized Sheriff Tinsley and two other men.

A blind rage based on frustration overcame Hopkins's first fear. With the money almost in his grasp, was he to be cheated out of it now? There were only three riders approaching. With steady nerves and quick thinking he could yet win this game. But Hopkins lacked both the requisite nerve and thinking. In addition, rage controlled his movements from now on.

Without thinking further, he lifted Whit Gallatin's gun and knocked the pane of glass crashing from its pane, then cocking and drawing a bead on the sheriff, he pulled trigger. A cooler head might have been successful, but that first sound of broken, jangling glass had warned the approaching riders and they scattered for cover. Almost before the sound of the heavy detonation had died away, an answering fire had come from three different points. Leaden slugs battered against the front wall of the house; one bullet came whining through another window and ricocheted wildly about the room.

A frightened curse welled from Hopkins's throat as he continued to shoot blindly, wildly, toward what he hoped were the points of concealment taken by the sheriff and his men. This maneuver only brought a more savage reply from those outside the house. Sharp lances of gunfire crisscrossed between trees and house.

Quite suddenly Hopkins realized he had been pulling trigger on an empty gun. Whimpering with stark fright, he now had only one thought: how to escape. Throwing the six-shooter to the floor, he turned and made a mad dash toward the rear of the house. Once outside, he leaped to his saddle and plunged in his spurs. He was five miles away before he gathered sufficient courage to draw to a halt and listen for pursuers. There wasn't a sound to be heard. "I—I reckon," Hopkins told himself in shaky tones, "I'd best clear out of this country for good. I can change my name, and there'll be easier pickin's someplace else." He again put spurs to his horse and drove on.

By this time, of course, the sheriff and his two men had entered the house and secured the money sacks. One of the men, called Slim, had possessed a greater reach than had Scar Hopkins, and it was due to his efforts that the stolen sacks of money now stood on the table in the ray shed by a lighted oil lamp.

"I'm damned if I can understand, Bob," the other man, Adams by name, was saying, "why you're so hell-bent on thinkin' that wa'n't Whit Gallatin who was here—"

"That's utter damn nonsense," Tinsley said angrily. "Whit Gallatin wouldn't have run like that. The way that hawss sounded, its rider needed only to be carryin' a feather to be flyin'. Whit wouldn't have run. He don't scare easy."

"But it stands to reason it was Whit," Slim put in. "Look, it was his paw—old Cougar—who worked for this money. Ain't it likely he would come here to get it before he left the country—"

"That's not Whit's way," the sheriff said stubbornly. "If Whit had done that shootin', one of us—maybe all of us—wouldn't be here now, I'm bettin'. That first slug was way wide of my head when it buzzed past. Whit would have hit his target. 'Sides, I just can't see Whit shootin' at me and then runnin' like all the devils from hell was after him."

"He just got plumb scared, if you ask me," Slim said.

"Whit wa'n't the scarin' kind."

"There's a first time for every man," Slim persisted.

"Sure, he got scared," Adams put in. "Just got panicky and run for it. Dropped his letters on the floor—you picked 'em up yourself, Bob—and his gun too—"

"The letters could have been here before," Tinsley said patiently. "And I've already told you—more'n once—that Whit ain't carryin' that gun no more. He took over Cougar's guns—"

"We should have took after him when we heard his horse runnin'," Adams said. "If we'd caught him, you'd seen that—"

"Look," Tinsley said heavily, "we came here to get some money. We got it. And now we'd best stop jawin' and get back to town."

"Ain't you even goin' to get on that feller's trail or nothin'?"

"Why in hell should I?" the sheriff demanded in exasperated tones. "Nobody's been hurt. We got the money. It's my guess that some low-down in Toyah Wells heard Whit say the money was here and come out before us, hopin' to get it."

But Slim and Adams weren't convinced. The following day the story was all over Toyah Wells that Whit Gallatin had been nearly caught stealing the payroll money and that only a stiff gun battle with the sheriff and his men had driven Gallatin off. In time the story grew; people spoke of the men Gallatin had killed before he left. Folks nodded their heads and said sagely that that Gallatin was "a bad one and took after old Cougar." After a while it wasn't just Gallatin they spoke of; it was Killer Gallatin.

Even when Tinsley showed a telegram he had received from Whit, it convinced no one. Practically everyone was convinced that Whit had gone to the bad—gone bronco with a vengeance, as the saying went.

MURDER

WHEN WHIT GALLATIN HAD LEFT THE SHERIFF at the hitch rack in Toyah Wells and driven his pony furiously out of town, he had cared little where he was headed: the thought uppermost in his mind had been to get away. Killer, was he? And again that harsh ugly laugh had left his lips. Killer? Well, why not? There were men who paid good money to hire a fast gun. Whit laughed some more. Louder. The tones became high-pitched while the horse tore madly along the hoof-chopped, wheel-rutted road stretching west under the bright moonlight. Something insane entered Whit's laugh until it careened off at a hysterical angle and suddenly changed to a half sob. Reaction had commenced to set in after the strain under which be had been laboring the past twenty-four hours and more.

He fell silent, still driving hard in the saddle, his face drawn in taut grim lines, thinking of his father. Tears welled in his eyes, and he brushed them impatiently away as he pulled the pony to a slower gait. There was a hard lump in Whit's chest that hurt—hurt like hell. God! If he could only do something to relieve that pain. The horse went on, the dusty road now unreeling more slowly beneath the horse's steady hoofbeats.

Overhead the moon rode serenely through a thin scattering of wispy clouds. Far to the west, low down on the indigo horizon, a handful of stars showed above the distant hills. Whit was thinking hard now, so hard he failed to notice that his horse had passed the Rafter-G ranch house and was ascending one of the slopes lifting beyond the house. After a time it was gradually borne in upon him that the moonlight beneath which he had been riding was now broken and was shining down through the widespread limbs of live-oak trees, shining also on the graves of his father and mother a few feet away, where the horse had come to a stop of its own volition. Whit lifted his head and brought the animal to a halt, while he stared at the twin mounds of earth, one covered with grass and a roughly hewn slab of lettered granite; the other of freshly disturbed earth. He hadn't realized where the pony was bringing him. Slowly Whit slipped down from the saddle and stood gazing soberly at the graves.

He was remembering now what the sheriff had said: he was only half Gallatin; the rest of his heritage had descended from his mother. The thought affected Whit profoundly. He recollected the message from his father, brought by the sheriff: Cougar Gallatin hadn't wanted his son to be a killer, to have the taste of blood continually on his lips. There was something else the sheriff had said: "It's the mark of Cain, a thing in your blood you'll have to fight." A thing in his blood he'd have to fight. Killing, that was it. Well, he'd killed, already lived up to that old Gallatin tradition. It came back to Whit now, how Hess and Talbert had looked when they crashed down. Viewed through the hot red haze of smoke and blood, it hadn't seemed particularly evil to pump leaden slugs into other men—especially when they deserved such treatment. But considered later, in the cold light of reason, it wasn't at all pleasant to look back upon—those two crumpled and dying human beings who had once been men and whose greatest sin was that they had been too weak to act honorably toward other men.

A question rose in Whit's mind: could he have handled the business in any other way? Viewed from some angles, those killings had been almost as bad as murder. Talbert and Hess and one other—Scar Hopkins?—had been responsible for his father's death, even if only indirectly. Hopkins, no doubt, had been privy to their plans; he also carried his share of that responsibility. But there were man-made laws to cover such contingencies. It might have been better to have invoked those laws . . . Something in his blood he'd have to fight . . . A sudden feeling of revulsion set in. Abruptly Whit Gallatin realized he hated himself. He felt his body shudder from head to toe. Nerves, that was it, nerves tightly strung like high-tension wires. Taut. Ready to snap. The sort of nerves that would have to be kept completely in control or there'd be more killings, more mad moments blurred with the crimson haze of spilled blood and gun smoke.

Whit knew now he didn't want to be a killer, ever, if it could be avoided. Ah, there was the rub: if it could be avoided. There was something in his blood he'd have to guard against day and night, something he'd have to fight continually—an evil over-powering thing that could rise, swiftly and unannounced, to sweep away all clear thinking and in the space of one insane moment completely dominate a man's better instincts and turn him into a beast which acknowledged only the urge to kill. It was a thing that couldn't be easily mastered.

"But I'll lick it, so help me God I'll lick it," Whit promised himself fervently. "I'll fight it until it's finished once and for all time." He turned back to his horse and climbed into the saddle, then rode quietly on. No doubt about it, Bob Tinsley had been right in his advice. "I reckon it's due Bob to let him know how I feel," Whit mused as his horse moved beneath the moon-dappled shadows of oak trees. "First chance I get

I'll send him word."

Whit had traveled some distance away when he heard faintly from his rear the sound of gunfire, apparently coming from the vicinity of the Rafter-G ranch house. For just a moment he paused, half inclined to return. Then he set his jaw stubbornly. "It's nothing to do with me now," he told himself. "I'd best keep going before I get that urge to heat my gun barrels again."

He put spurs to his pony and pushed on. He hadn't heard any more shots. Three days later he sent a telegram to Sheriff Bob Tinsley, knowing the message would have to be relayed by stagecoach mail from the telegraph station nearest Toyah Wells. The telegram bore but few words:

YOU WERE RIGHT, BOB. THANKS FOR TELLING ME. I'M FIGHTING IT. WHIT GALLATIN.

For three years Whit roamed the Western country from the Canadian line to the Mexican border, spending most of his time in the Southwest. At the back of his mind was some vague idea of someday encountering the man known as Scar Hopkins and bringing him to justice for the part he had played in Cougar Gallatin's final downfall. Whit was firmly resolved that when and if he did find Hopkins he would turn the man over to legally constituted authorities; he was determined not to kill the man if it could be avoided. Whether, when the time came, Whit's determination would be equal to the test, he had no way of knowing. However, at the end of three years of travel Whit could pridefully state that he had never fired on any man. He had picked a rough and rocky road for himself but adhered to it strictly. And it wasn't easy. As Cougar Gallatin's son he had inherited his father's reputation, and for a time many were the fabulous tales that leaped into circulation concerning "Killer" Gallatin, as Whit came to be known.

Would-be badmen, thinking to enhance their fame, more than once had tried to pick quarrels with Whit. Each time he had managed to bluff his way out of such scrapes through one method or another of overawing his opponent. It mattered not that he never thumbed lead any more. Through the breadth of the Western country his reputation spread. Legends sprang into being concerning the notches cut in his .45 butts. It was said that those butts had been cut so often they now resembled corrugated washboards. As a matter of fact, Whit never carried more than one of those famous guns nowadays, but the real truth of the matter was never related or, if it was, was never given credence.

Was he not Killer Gallatin, son of Cougar Gallatin, famed exponent of gun battles? Were there not many, many notches cut in his gun butts? Folks never believed that only two of those notches represented Whit's share of the killings—and those two cut in self-defense.

But there was a certain strain living as Whit did. His face became set in harsh lines. On more than one occasion he had abruptly left towns rather than stay and go through with some fight that couldn't otherwise be avoided. People never gave him credit when such things happened. Instead it would be rumored about that Killer Gallatin had an important job someplace and lacked the time to stay when better-paying killings were to be found elsewhere. Often it required every bit of Whit's will power to restrain the quick draw that would result in some less skillful gun fighter's death. Men would note his face set in hard, tigerish lines, never realizing Whit was fighting the demon within himself. He would be standing well balanced on the balls of his feet, arms slightly held out from sides, challenging some opponent to draw. Then the enemy's gaze would shift to Whit's burning eyes and he would remember certain stories in circulation relative to Killer Gallatin's incredible speed in drawing and accurate shooting. Always such enemies backed down with muttered apologies.

When this happened Whit would breathe an inner sigh of relief, thankful that once more his bluff had been successful. Then he would hurry off at the first opportunity, feeling more than ever certain that all the world was set against him, insistent on trying to drive him into the situations he was most anxious to avoid. No, it wasn't easy, the life he lived; that thing in his blood that kept urging him to kill and kill and kill made life that much more difficult too. It would have been so much simpler, when danger threatened, to go through those swift motions of taking life—the quick draw, the sudden jolting burst of smoke and flaming lead, the thrill of exultation that would run through his being, as it had once before, could he see a lifeless opponent pitch to the floor.

For it must be remembered that these things could have been accomplished with ease: Whit Gallatin was far faster than the average gun fighter when it came to shaking lead from his gun barrels, and his way of life demanded continual practice with his six-shooters—a practice that was carried out by shooting at tin cans and other objects.

There had been instances—just a few—where some man with more courage than the general run would accept Whit's challenge and start to reach for his gun. That was when it was most difficult for Whit to restrain the killer instinct. At such times he would bring into play the long quirt that dangled from his left wrist. It was really more whip than quirt, probably twelve feet long and made of woven strands of rawhide. The end tapered to a fine, wire-interlaced lash that could sting, when necessity arose, like the fangs of a diamondback rattler—except that there was no poison in its bite.

One thing Whit had discovered at the end of his three years of roaming: as time passed, the temptation to kill grew less, and each day brought a firmer check on his emotions. He developed a sort of harsh, bitter humor; often his remarks carried all the sting of the quirt at his wrist. It didn't help things either when he commenced to be blamed for various robberies and other similar crimes. Lazy sheriffs, failing to catch the bandits responsible, became prone to lay the jobs at Killer Gallatin's door; and though no one was ever to prove anything of the sort on Whit and he escaped being jailed, it made his way just that much harder, the continual strain of such a life giving him the appearance of a man at least thirty years old when he was, in reality, much younger.

His roaming had taken him down into Mexico, and early one morning on his return to the States he had passed through a narrow canyon—he was by this time hundreds of miles from Toyah Wells—which slashed a twisting course through the Encontrón Mountains. On either side rose sheer sandstone walls. Far above Whit could see a narrow curving ribbon of turquoise sky; beneath his pony's hoofs the way was cluttered with broken rock. There was little vegetation to be seen; what there was, was dry and twisted, its roots clinging tenaciously to sparse patches of shallow sandy soil. Gradually, as Gallatin's buckskin gelding progressed, the narrow trail—if trail it could be called—widened;

the bluffs on either side sloped more gradually. A short time later Whit Gallatin found himself emerging into open country, and in the softer going he spied the marks of horses' hoofs, though he judged they'd probably been made the previous day.

Ahead lay a broad rolling vista covered with bunch grass, and some distance to the left Gallatin spied a small bunch of white-faced cows, though they were too far off for him to read the brand. He pushed on, his pony taking easily the gentle slopes that rolled ahead. To the north and west it looked like good grazing country, but to the east the terrain took on a semi-desert appearance. Paloverde trees and an occasional saguaro cactus rose above the greasewood and mesquite. These, in turn, gave way to a broad alkali flat, shimmering brightly in the morning sunlight, which stretched nearly to the mountains and ended in a sort of broken and gashed "badlands" region which terminated only when it encountered the serrated-peaked range running at Gallatin's rear. A hot, persistent breeze swept down from these rocky slopes.

"Reckon I'd best keep straight on north," Whit mused. "Looks mighty warm off there to the right." He glanced down along the trail he was following. "Unless I've missed my guess, this should bring me to some town called Palomas. Can't be much of a town—at least this isn't much of a trail. I figure it's just used by folks wanting to cut through the mountains to *mañana* land." He lifted his gray eyes toward the sky. Some distance ahead a group of soaring buzzards made slow-moving patterns above the tops of the mesquite and other growth. "Must be something dead up ahead," Gallatin mused. "Likely some beef animal pulled down by a coyote is attracting those scavenger birds."

Nevertheless, he touched spurs to the pony and quickened pace. Ten minutes later, rounding a tall clump of prickly pear, Whit saw what had drawn the birds, which by this time had winged to higher levels but were still circling about, as though reluctant to desert the vicinity. Gallatin pulled to a halt, dismounted, and dropped the reins over his mount's head; then, walking carefully, he approached the spot, just off the trail, where the dead man lay sprawled on the sandy earth, one knee drawn up, the other outstretched. The body lay on its stomach, face buried in the sandy soil, the right arm twisted beneath, the left hand reaching out, fingers wide, as though extended to break the fall when it had come. A small hole, darkly stained, showed just beneath the left shoulder blade on the back of the dead man's vest.

The dead man had been possibly fifty or fifty-five years of age, with iron-gray hair. A battered black sombrero lay a couple of yards off where it had fallen; the remainder of the corpse's togs showed he had been a bowman. A Colt's six-shooter was still in its holster. Gallatin moved away from the body and commenced to scrutinize the surrounding earth. There were a great many hoofprints to be seen, but they were so superimposed and the ground so chopped that it was difficult to determine how many horses and riders had halted at this spot. The only bootprints in view led to the dead man and must be his. Had he arrived here on foot? Unlikely, Gallatin concluded. Whoever killed him had probably taken the horse off, or at least driven it away. There seemed to be no signs of an ambush, so it was likely the dead man had known one or more of the men who had participated in his death.

"Maybe," Whit mused, "he'd been riding with the

others and a quarrel broke out. Or they might have been enemies that he come across, running off his cows. Still, I don't see any cow sign hereabouts. That part don't matter so much anyhow. What does matter is he was shot in the back and his gun is still in his holster. He never had a chance. That looks like murder to me."

He continued to scrutinize the ground without making further discoveries, and gradually worked his way back to the body. Here he knelt down and felt the dead man's outflung left hand, then lightly touched the back of the neck. The flesh was marble-stiff and surprisingly cool, considering the heat of the Southwest sun.

"It's my guess"—Whit frowned—"that this happened sometime last night, or very early this morning, though it would take a doctor to tell for sure on that point."

He was about to rise again when another imprint caught his eye: there, traced faintly in the sandy soil, was the outline of a man's palm, with fingers outspread. Someone, doubtless the murderer, had braced his weight on one hand while he stooped down to examine his stricken victim. Lines of thought creased Whit's forehead. "Must have been enough dew last night to moisten that sand. Now it's blowing away fast. That print will be completely gone in another hour. It's too damn bad such things can't be saved until some murdering scut's hand can be found to fit the print. Someday I'll bet folks will know how to save such prints—" He broke off. "No use of me dreaming about things like that . . ." He studied the print some more and noticed now there was a definite line running directly across the palm. It was more like a thin channel than a line and could perhaps denote some sort of narrow ridge on the palm of the man who had made the print. Whit scowled. "It's like the fellow might have had a cord tied around his hand—but why? I suppose there's a number of answers to that question, but I don't know any of 'em. Maybe it doesn't matter anyway. The thing for me to do is get on to that town of Palomas and report this to the sheriff, if there's one there."

He returned to his horse and procured a blanket with which he came back to the dead man. Spreading the blanket over the corpse, he weighted the corners with small chunks of rock to prevent its being blown away. Then he remounted. "Lucky the coyotes haven't found that body yet," he told himself. "Now if they'll just stay away a few hours longer, until somebody can come after this body . . . " He didn't finish the thought but kicked the buckskin in the ribs, starting the pony in a long, ground-devouring lope that carried its rider swiftly along the trail.

SUCKER-BAIT

WHIT GALLATIN CLATTERED OVER A PLANK BRIDGE above the shallow Palomas River—it was more creek than river—and found himself entering the town of Palomas. It wasn't, to tell the frank truth, much of a town. It consisted of one narrow winding street flanked on either side by buildings constructed of rock and adobe and, in some instances, timber, with high false fronts. There had been some attempt to create another street, parallel with the main street, and a couple of cross thoroughfares, but little had come of the effort. Mostly the residences seemed to have been flung down in a sort of helter-skelter fashion with paths leading to the so-called business section.

Along this main thoroughfare ran an almost unbroken

line of hitch racks on either side. There were several saloons, a small brick bank, a couple of general stores, and various other buildings of commercial enterprise. Here and there a cow pony stood slumped on three legs, or a wagon waited at a hitch rack. There were not many people abroad; the plank sidewalks oozed resin. A hot dry wind blew in from the semi-desert country spread at the foot of the Encontrón Mountains.

Whit drew rein before an adobe-and-rock building with a wide wooden awning that stretched across the sidewalk. To one of the uprights supporting this awning was a sign that read: "Sheriff's Office, Clarendon County." The sign looked as though it had been painted fairly recently; the other signs in town, Whit had noticed, were sun-faded and cracked. He dismounted from his pony, walked around the end of a hitch rack, and tried the door of the office, which proved to be closed and locked.

A couple of men in cowman togs came striding along the walk. Whit stopped them to ask if they knew where he could find the sheriff. Neither could supply the answer, one saying, "If he ain't in his office, you might locate him in the Shamrock Saloon, pardner." The words were followed by a gesturing thumb which pointed across the street. Whit said "Thanks," and the men strode on.

A watering trough stood before the Shamrock bar. Whit led his pony across the dusty street, then loosened the animal's saddle cinch and stood waiting while it drank. Two or three men passed, eyed the tall figure in the corduroys cuffed at ankles, noted that he was a stranger in town, nodded briefly, and went on their way. If they wondered about Whit at all, their thoughts had to do with the long, loosely looped quirt or whip he carried in his left hand, rather than with the six-shooter slung at his right thigh. While he waited for the pony to finish drinking Whit gazed at the Shamrock Saloon, hearing voices from inside floating above the double swinging doors, and noting the dusty windows on each side of the entrance with the large green shamrocks painted on their glazed surfaces.

A few minutes later Whit pushed his way through the batwing doors, his spurs clanking on the rough board floor as he made his way to the bar stretching along the right-hand wall. There were a number of customers drinking at the bar; at a table on the opposite side of the room four men sat playing seven-up. Light entered from dust-encrusted windows at the back and one side. At least, Whit noticed, the mirror over the back bar was clean and free of flyspecks; the pyramided glasses and bottles below fairly glistened. A neat sign over the mirror gave the information that Barry Flynn, Esq., was owner and sole proprietor of the Shamrock Saloon. An instant later Flynn, a short skinny man with a pleasant grin, brick-red hair, and the map of Ireland on his face, came along the bar to request Whit's pleasure. His voice, when he spoke, carried a pleasant touch of Celtic brogue.

Whit gave his order, and the bartender set out a bottle of lukewarm beer and a glass of tepid water, apologizing for the lack of chill in both. "Comes the day I could be gettin' of a bit of ice in here, mister, it's dealin' more fairly with my customers I could be. But with no ice and the weather what it is"—a shrug of skinny shoulders—"I can do only what I can do."

"So long as it's wet, I'm not kicking," Whit said.

"It's a tolerant man you are." Flynn smiled. "I'd be glad could I say so much for all my customers."

Whit downed the water at a gulp. Flynn instantly refilled the glass, then moved down the bar to attend to the needs of other customers. Whit sipped his beer in silence, gradually becoming aware that a definite quiet had settled over the barroom. There'd been a falling off in the noisy conversation that had filled the place when he entered. He glanced along the bar. Most of the men were engaged with their drinks, but two or three were staring frankly in his direction. A couple of whispered remarks at the far end of the bar caught Whit's ear, but he couldn't distinguish the words. Oh well, it didn't matter if he couldn't hear what was being said. He knew without being told, or could at least guess at the import. Things were falling into the old pattern; this had happened numerous times before. Whit knew that someone in the Shamrock had recognized him as Killer Gallatin. Mentally he braced himself for any trouble that might come. The thing to do was to locate the sheriff, tell him of the dead body he had found, and then get out of Palomas as soon as possible.

Whit continued to sip his beer, and after a few minutes the buzz of conversation rose once more. At the far end of the bar three men were talking in louder voices than the others, probably because of an over-indulgence in alcohol. Whit followed their conversation and caught snatches of words here and there. One man, he discovered, was known as Calgary Rhodes; the other two were apparently brothers named Tiernan, Tack and Bat Tiernan.

Rhodes was a lean, swarthy-complexioned man in overalls, high-heeled riding boots, cotton shirt, and calfskin vest. A six-shooter hung in his well-worn holster. A bright crimson neckerchief was knotted at his throat, and a slouch brim sombrero covered his unkempt black hair. He looked as though he had not shaved for a couple of weeks. The two Tiernan brothers were also in range togs and had the appearance of being hard-bitten individuals.

Whit beckoned to the bartender. Flynn came hurrying along the bar. "Would you be wantin' another beer?"

Whit shook his head and placed some money on the counter. When he had received his change he asked, "Where can I find the sheriff?"

Again silence had descended over the room. Before Flynn could reply, Calgary Rhodes broke in: "Maybe I could tell you, mister. What you wanting the sheriff for?"

Whit replied evenly, "I'll tell him when I see him." He saw the flush mount to Rhodes's face before he turned back to Flynn and repeated his question.

"It's Sheriff Brandon you'll be wantin'?" Flynn said.

"I don't know his name. I stopped across at his office, but he wasn't there."

"Dan Brandon was after ridin' to Curtisville yesterday," Flynn went on. "He should be back any minute now. He told me, so he did, he'd not be returnin' later than noon today, and Dan Brandon is no man to be breakin' of his word."

Whit consulted the old gold watch he carried. It wasn't yet quite eleven o'clock. He replaced the watch, shoved some money back on the bar. "In that case, I'll wait. Another bottle of brew will help pass the time."

Whit occupied himself with the second bottle while conversation again filled the room. A tall, spare, grizzled man with keen blue eyes and wide white mustaches pushed through the swinging doors and paused a moment within to adjust his gaze to the dimmer light. His glance swept swiftly along the bar and finally came to rest on Calgary Rhodes.

"Humph!" the man grunted disgustedly. "Had a hunch I might find you here, Rhodes." He swept off his Stetson and mopped his brow with a bandanna. "How in hell long do you figure we should wait for the mail? You left the outfit two days ago, recollect? I told you to ride straight back. You'd best understand once and for all there ain't no place on the 2JD for loafin' cow pokes. Where in the devil have you been since you left day before yesterday?"

"Sorry, Mr. Dawson," Rhodes said silkily, though he failed to make the tones sound apologetic. "I wasn't really loafing. It's just that—well, to tell the truth"—he forced a sheepish smile to his swarthy features—"I ran into these two friends of mine"—gesturing toward the Tiernan brothers—"and I reckon I took on too much to drink—"

Jeff Dawson snorted. "Never even got around to pickin' up the mail, I suppose?"

"Matter of fact, I didn't," Rhodes admitted. "Just thought I'd best get sobered up before ridin' back to the ranch. I aimed to bring the mail with me, though, and these two friends"—again gesturing to Bat and Tack Tiernan—"hoping you might see your way clear to finding some work for them."

"Have you lost your wits, Calgary?" the older man asked in withering tones. "We told you last week there was no place on the 2JD for your pals. And that's final. You're forgettin', too, that we only took you on at a time when we happened to be a mite short of help. We ain't really been needin' you for a couple of months now, but we've tried to do the square thing and let you keep your job. But there's no place on the outfit for boozers and loafers, so unless you make up your mind to straighten out a mite, we're liable to cut down our payroll some."

All other conversation in the barroom had ceased while customers listened interestedly to the quarrel. Rhodes's features had taken on an angry red flush. One of the Tiernan brothers said something to him in an undertone that made the flush deepen.

Rhodes swung back toward Dawson. "All right, you've made yourself clear, Dawson. If that's the way you're feeling, you can take your job and stick it. I've managed to get along for quite a few years without any help from the Dawson brothers. I can do it again. It's no prime pleasure for me, working on your 2JD spread." He repeated, "You can take your job and stick it—see?"

Angry words rose to the old cowman's lips, but he checked them, and his reply was spoken calmly. "Suits me right down to the ground, Rhodes." He drew some coins and bills from the pockets of his faded Levis, separated them, and placed Rhodes's money on the bar. "There y'are. You and the 2JD are quits, Rhodes. Get your stuff out of the bunkhouse as soon's possible. After that I'm askin' that you don't poke your nose around there again."

"And supposing I do?" Rhodes queried insolently, picking up his wages. "What could you or anybody else on the 2JD do about it? Just because you and your brother happen to be running the biggest herds in this neck of the range is no sign you can run everybody else the way you like too."

The words brought sneering laughter from the two Tiernan brothers.

Old Jeff Dawson glanced quickly at the Tiernans, whose gaze quickly dropped before that of the cattleman. A contemptuous smile touched Dawson's lips, then he turned back to Rhodes. "Supposin' you do, Calgary?" he repeated softly. "Well, hombre, in that case I'm plumb likely to burn your hide for you. I hope I'm makin' that clear."

The eyes of the two men locked for a moment, then Rhodes laughed harshly. "You're scaring me to death, Dawson, but don't get any idea that this ends things between us. You and your brother have run this country long enough. Someday you'll learn other folks have ideas, too—and they might not fit in with yours." Again that short, harsh laugh.

"That sounds like a threat, Calgary," Dawson said calmly.

Rhodes shrugged. "I'm not responsible for what you happen to think. Take it any way you like. Me, I don't give a damn . . . All right, Dawson, we're quits. I'll be out to the ranch this evening to get my gear." He swung abruptly away from the old cattleman, feeling he had been bested in the verbal encounter, feeling also that something was necessary to re-establish himself in the eyes of the Tiernan brothers. He pushed some money out on the bar. "Set 'em up for the house, Barry. Calgary Rhodes is buying."

Barry Flynn eyed Rhodes a moment, then shrugged his thin shoulders. "If you'll be after naming your poison, gintlemin, the Shamrock will be serving it."

There came a shuffling of feet as men straightened at the bar. Flynn moved along, taking orders and setting out drinks.

Jeff Dawson had taken up a position a few feet from Whit at the bar. When Flynn took the cattleman's order Dawson added, "I'll be payin' for what I drink, Barry. I'm not drinkin' on Rhodes's money."

Flynn set out a bottle and small tumbler, then passed

on to Whit. "Count me out," Whit said. He had taken a dislike to Rhodes and felt disinclined to partake of his hospitality.

Finally everyone was served. Rhodes hadn't failed to hear Dawson's and Whit's refusals. Dawson's he could understand, but angry lines settled in his swarthy face at Whit's refusal. He stared steadily at Whit a moment, then nodded, as though confirming something in his mind. Here was an opportunity, he concluded, to gain further prestige in the eyes of the Tiernan brothers, in all Palomas for that matter. Palomas? In the whole Southwest country!

Rhodes lifted his drink, downed it at a gulp, wiped his mouth with the back of one hand, and swaggered down the bar to confront Whit. "You, stranger," he accused harshly, "you refused to drink with me."

A long sigh left Whit Gallatin's lips, and the thought ran through his mind, *Here it comes again.* A sudden not understandable hate for Calgary Rhodes coursed through his whole body. An instant before he had merely felt a dislike for the man; now his feeling had changed to a violent hatred. He glanced over his shoulder at Rhodes, saying in a quiet voice that belied his inner turmoil, "Yes, Rhodes, I did."

"That could be a mistake on your part, mister," Rhodes growled.

"Lots of folks make mistakes," Whit replied calmly. "Maybe you're making one right now. Maybe if you'd had a mite less to drink you'd not be so careless."

Rhodes swore. "Nobody's telling me how much I should drink!"

Whit smiled thinly, "And nobody's telling me *when* I should drink."

"Don't be too sure of that, mister," Rhodes snapped.

"You're a stranger in Palomas. I went out of my way to include you when I invited my friends to drink. Hombres hereabouts generally drink when Calgary Rhodes buys, unless they got a damn good reason."

"I had that reason," Whit said quietly. "The same being that I didn't feel like drinking—just now."

"Oh," For the moment Rhodes couldn't for the life of him think what to say next. The clatter of bottles and glasses along the bar had ceased as the others paused to listen to the conversation between Rhodes and Whit Gallatin. Flies droned lazily in the momentary silence. Whit had swung around, back to the bar, waiting for Rhodes's next words.

Rhodes tried a new tack: "I ain't sure I like your reason, mister. Sa-a-y"—as though just thinking of something—"haven't I seen you someplace before?"

A faint smile twitched at Whit's lips. "It could be. I've been there."

Rhodes said, "Where?"

"Someplace."

Rhodes growled, "Oh hell! Fool talk." He paused. "By Gawd, I've got it! It was in El Paso—nigh onto three years back. You're Killer Gallatin!"

At the mention of the name a certain tension tightened through the barroom. Most of the customers stood as though frozen, their eyes glued on Whit. Jeff Dawson studied Whit with new interest. There was a quick shuffling of feet at Whit's left, and a man moved abruptly across the barroom, as though anxious to leave Killer Gallatin's immediate vicinity.

"I hit it!" Rhodes repeated triumphantly, "You're Killer Gallatin!"

Whit replied in the same even tone: "A heap of folks have called me by that name, but you, Rhodes, you never saw me live up to it, did you?"

Rhodes laughed harshly. "I knew I was right. No, I never saw you kill anybody. I'm commencing to wonder if anybody has. That time in El Paso, I saw you bluff out a two-bit tinhorn who didn't have the guts to reach for his gun. But that was in Texas. Over this way we don't bluff so easy."

Whit was thinking fast, remembering now the particular El Paso incident Rhodes had mentioned. The man he had bluffed out on that occasion had been anything but a "two-bit tinhorn." The fellow had, in fact, been considered one of El Paso's fastest gunmen. Whit considered. Undoubtedly Calgary Rhodes was better than average when it came to gunplay. His very confidence in approaching Killer Gallatin as he had denoted that much. But speed in a gun fight wasn't everything. There were other elements to be taken into consideration: the psychology of gun fighting, how much nerve a man possessed, the luck of the break as it was called. For a moment Whit was strongly tempted to carry through the business with a flaming gun. Something within him urged him strongly in such direction. With an effort he steeled himself against such action. There had to be, there simply had to be, another way.

Rhodes said again, sneering. "Over this way we don't bluff so easy."

"I don't remember," Whit said evenly, "asking you about the folks over this way."

Foolishly Rhodes gained additional confidence from Whit's easy manner. "You don't, eh, Gallatin?" he spat. "Well, I'm telling you—see?—whether you ask or not." He backed a pace, expecting to see Whit take up the challenge.

Whit laughed softly. "Rhodes, you've had too much to drink. That being the case, I can't somehow take much interest in your remarks. Let's talk this over some other time if you still feel the same way." Abruptly he turned back to the bar.

A sneering smile slashed Rhodes's dark features. He felt confident now that Killer Gallatin was trying to avoid a fight with him. That much was true, but Rhodes misunderstood Whit's attitude, the reason behind Whit's action. "Gallatin," he snapped, "I think we've been hearing wild tales about you being bad."

Whit again turned to face the man. He said in rather weary tones, "You sure have, Rhodes, you sure have."

Rhodes nodded. "I figured it that way. Somebody's been spinning a heap of windies, and a lot of folks has just let their imaginations run away with 'em."

"Some folks sure have," Whit said evenly. "And some folks are sure likely to find a heap of trouble that way, too, Rhodes." He added pointedly, "A mistaken imagination, Rhodes, can prove to be heap bad medicine for a man sometimes. That's something else you might ponder on a spell."

Something in the quiet tones caused Rhodes to pause. His eyes narrowed suddenly. Was Killer Gallatin hoorawing, kidding, him? No, it couldn't be. Rhodes's gaze fell to the long whip curled in Whit's left hand. "What do you do with that leather snake, Gallatin, go fishing?"

Whit smiled lazily. "Uh-huh. Sometimes I catch polecats and suckers. Aren't nibbling, are you, Rhodes?"

Rhodes's face suddenly flamed with rage. He *was* being kidded and hadn't realized it. Now, however, it was too late to back out. Moreover, Calgary Rhodes prided himself on his gunwork. He was certain he was faster than Gallatin.

Quite suddenly Rhodes threw discretion to the winds. "It's my guess you use that whip to drive sheep," he jerked out.

"Right again." Whit laughed. "Better start moving, Rhodes. This is cow country."

A series of laughs rose in the Shamrock Saloon. Rhodes glanced quickly around the barroom, noted that the Tiernan brothers were grinning with the rest. Rhodes suddenly saw red. "Damn you, Gallatin, I got a good notion to whip you out of Palomas with that oversized quirt of yours. I got a hunch you're just a big bluff."

"You're not the first man to make that mistake." An edge had crept into Whit's voice. "Was I you, I wouldn't repeat that statement."

"I'll repeat it when and where I choose," Rhodes rasped, entirely missing the steel in Whit's smooth tones. "I'm repeating that you're a bluff, living on your old man's reputation. For that matter, Cougar Gallatin was all bluff too—"

"That's enough, Rhodes!" Whit's words fairly crackled.

But Rhodes didn't even hear the interruption as he continued:—"a lousy bluff, a two-bit, tinhorn, slab-hoofed bluff that—"

"I said that was enough!"

Rhodes had commenced backing away as he talked. One hand was already moving down toward his holster. "Enough, is it?" he grated. "Damn right it's enough. For you it's too much. But I'm repeatin' that Cougar Gallatin was a sway-backed, back-shootin' son of a—"

"You'd better pull that gun and go to work. Rhodes!"

Every one of Whit's words cracked like reports from

a Winchester. Here was the answer to Calgary Rhodes's challenge. Already Whit had gone into a half crouch, poised on the balls of his feet, right hand hovering above the walnut butt of the six-shooter in his holster. The batwing doors of the Shamrock banged open as two men scurried from the reach of expected bullets. Other occupants of the room backed from the vicinity of Whit and Rhodes, their eyes wide. This was the sort of thing they had heard of Killer Gallatin, and he was apparently about to live up to his reputation.

Whit's face was a twisted mask of hate, his eyes thin flaming slits of rage. Now as never before since the night his father had died did he feel the urge to kill. The fingers of his right hand, savagely eager to close about his gun butt, quivered expectantly. Through his whole being coursed a sudden feeling of exultation.

Rhodes had backed two more steps, realizing now for the first time he had pushed Gallatin too far. He thought recklessly, *All right, it's a showdown. I'm faster than he is.* His narrowed eyes were watching Whit's right hand. Abruptly his own hand swept toward his holster, the palm closing securely about the butt of the six-shooter.

And in that same moment Whit regained control of his emotions. Even as Rhodes's gun cleared leather Whit's left arm flashed up, unloosing the curled black whip. The wire-woven lash, moving with the incredible speed of a striking rattlesnake, flashed through the air between the two men and wrapped itself tightly about the rising gun in Rhodes's fist.

Instantly Whit's left arm snapped back. Even before Rhodes could tighten his forefinger about the trigger he felt the weapon being ripped from his grasp. All the blood drained from his features as his unbelieving eyes saw the six-shooter go clattering to the pine floor boards some distance beyond his reach. Rhodes stared blankly at his empty hand, stunned by his sudden disarming. A weakness assailed his knees as he raised dull, incredulous eyes to the weapon he had clutched only a split instant before.

A deft flick of Whit's left wrist released the lash from the six-shooter. A second similar movement brought the long whip leaping back through the air like some live thing, to fall into even coils in Whit's hand. Rhodes took one uncertain step toward his gun on the floor.

"Don't try it, Rhodes," Whit said sternly. "Remember, I've still got my gun. Don't make me use it."

"My God," Rhodes muttered hoarsely, "you wouldn't shoot an unarmed man, would you?"

Slowly Whit shook his head. A long sigh went up from the customers in the Shamrock. Tiny beads of perspiration stood on Whit's brow. A sudden sense of relief ran though his being. He had won an even greater victory than the clients of the Shamrock realized. Whit went on: "Rhodes, you said some mighty harsh things about my father a spell back. Feel like taking 'em back?"

"Hell, yes," Rhodes said quickly. "I was all wrong in what I said about Cougar Gallatin. I'm plumb regretful. I—I—" He paused, groping for further words.

A thin smile crossed Whit's face. "That's enough, Rhodes. From now on just remember about this whip being good sucker-bait for catching polecats. Maybe that's wrong, but I reckon you catch my meaning."

Rhodes's face flushed crimson as a sudden laugh from the saloon customers relieved the tension. Now that the moment of danger had passed and he was still alive, Rhodes commenced to regain his nerve. "I'll remember all right, Gallatin. I won't make the same mistake—next time." There was a veiled threat in the words. "It will be a long time before I forget. If you're wise, you'll remember something too—that it was your whip, not your gun, that stopped me. Just a trick, that's all. Oh, I'll not be forgetting—"

Whit interrupted with a sort of bored "Cripes! Let's forget it." He hadn't missed the implication in Rhodes's words. He felt instinctively that he wasn't yet finished with Calgary Rhodes. He turned toward the bar. "Barkeep, I'll be around town. When the sheriff returns, tell him I want to see him, will you?"

"I'll do that, Mr. Gallatin." Barry Flynn smiled.

"Thanks." Without another word Whit strode toward the doorway and out to the street. The batwing doors swung to a stop behind him.

Immediately conversation sprang up. "Whew!" one of the customers whistled. "Killer Gallatin must have a job of lead slinging along the border someplace—"

"Meanin' just what?" Jeff Dawson demanded shortly. His eyes had been on Calgary Rhodes, who was occupied in securing his six-shooter from the floor.

"Well," the speaker replied, "don't it stand to reason? From all I've heard, Gallatin don't let an enemy escape so easy. But if he'd shot Calgary when Calgary didn't have no gun, Gallatin might've got tangled with the law here. If he was detained here by the law, he couldn't get on about his job. Right lucky for Calgary—"

"Shut your damn mouth," Calgary said angrily, "or you might not be so lucky."

The man shrank back. "Cripes! I didn't mean nothin'—"

"And you didn't say nothin' that made sense neither," Jeff Dawson broke in. "Wilkins, you just ain't got the brains that Gawd give you. You're just a plain jackass—and I'll apologize to the jackass."

And with that Dawson turned and hurried through the doorway in search of Whit Gallatin.

WHIT CO-OPERATES

IN FRONT OF THE SHAMROCK, Dawson paused in the shade of the wooden awning stretching above the sidewalk. Whit Gallatin was standing beyond the hitch rack near his horse, mopping his face with a bandanna. He paused a moment and scowled toward the front of the saloon. Then his gaze fell on the old cowman. Whit's scowl deepened. Dang old fool. Probably come out to have another look at the famous Killer Gallatin.

With a muttered exclamation of wrath Whit turned to his pony. Setting one booted foot against the beast's side, he seized and tightened the cinch until the buckskin gelding grunted with indignation. Then he stepped up into the saddle, intending to ride out of town for an hour or so.

Dawson hadn't missed the easy grace of Whit's movements as he mounted. Gallatin was a rider, no doubt of that, was the thought that passed through the grizzled cowman's mind. Whit was turning the pony away from the hitch rack when Dawson spoke.

"Just a minute, Gallatin."

Whit turned a hard, scowling countenance on the elder man. "Well?" he demanded ungraciously, pulling the horse to a halt.

Dawson stepped out to the edge of the walk. "I'd like to see you a minute."

"You can see me from there, can't you?"

Dawson chuckled. This Gallatin sure tried to make folks believe he was wilder'n a bobcat. "Why didn't you finish Rhodes when you had a chance?"

"That's my business," Whit said shortly.

"I always heard tell your business worked the opposite way."

Whit's eyes bored into Dawson's. "Meaning what?"

"The way I hear it, your business is *killin'*."

"Do you always believe everything you hear?" Whit asked stiffly.

"Nope," Dawson stated dryly. "Only about ten per cent. But I've been wonderin'. There was three-four times you should have plugged Rhodes. So I'm still wonderin'. Are you sure enough Killer Gallatin?"

Whit said bitterly, "That's what folks call me."

Dawson didn't miss the implication in his tone. He said, "Humph!" and considered Whit a moment, then, "I'd like to buy you a drink."

"Why?"

"I want to talk to you."

"Why?" Again the single cold question.

Dawson said wearily, "Oh, for Gawd's sake, don't be so dang suspicious. You act like you haven't any friends and mebbe don't want none, nuther."

"Maybe I don't," Whit said sullenly.

"Now that's a damn lie and you know it," the old cowman said mildly. "Everybody wants friends. Look here, if you won't let me buy you a drink, how about you buyin' me one?"

"I don't know any reason why I should—" Whit commenced. Something humorous in the situation appealed to him. His lips curled at the corners. "All right, I'll buy you a drink. I don't want to go back in the Shamrock right now, though." He got down from the pony, flipped reins over the tie rail, and joined Dawson on the sidewalk.

"Shamrock's the best saloon in Palomas—" Dawson began, then paused as he heard voices at his rear. Turning, he saw a group of heads watching from above the batwing doors of the saloon. "C'mon, this is too public. T'tell the truth, I don't think either of us wants a drink right now. We'll find a place to *habla.*"

Neither spoke as they strode along the sidewalk until Dawson had led the way up the steps to the porch of the Palomas Hotel, a two-story frame building standing on a corner. A row of chairs lined the porch railing, and they sat down. The old cowman was first to break the silence. "I'm Jeff Dawson. Me 'n' my brother John run the 2JD outfit west of here. It's a nice spread; we've a good crew. We pay a mite better wages than the other ranches hereabouts."

Whit said coldly, "I don't remember asking you for this information." His eyes were fixed glumly on a couple of pedestrians strolling along the opposite side of the street.

"Ain't said you did," Dawson said cheerfully. "I'm just offerin' it—free gratis. For nothin'." He paused. "We could use you on our pay roll if you're lookin' for work."

Whit's features hardened. "My gun isn't for sale to any man," he said shortly, "popular opinion to the contrary."

Dawson chuckled, procured from an upper vest pocket a stogie of prodigious length, reached for a match and scratched it, then bit off one end of the stogie. He puffed out a few clouds of gray smoke and chuckled again. "Just as I expected," he said softly, as though speaking to himself. "Gallatin don't want a job on the 2JD." Further clouds of smoke issued from his lips. "Course mebbe he's got money. There's other ways of makin' a livin' 'sides punchin' beef animals. I figure he might be makin' a mistake. But if he don't want to work for us, why, he just don't. That's all there is to it."

"Dammit, no, I don't want to take a job with you," Whit said testily. "I've just tried to make it plain to you my gun isn't for hire."

"Why, you danged young fire-eater," Dawson snapped back, removing the stogie from his lips, "who in the tarnation hell said anythin' about your rusty, broken-down, hammerless, misfirin', cracked-butted, sightless, stiff-triggered, powder-pitted, antique ol' gun? Huh? Have I said anythin' about hirin' a gunman? You know dang well I ain't! I may be old, but do I look like I'd shuck out good coin of the realm to somebody to do my fightin' for me? Huh, do I? Have I mentioned your lead-slingin' ability or how many ounces of .45 slugs you could shake outten your weapon in a given time? Huh? Did I? Who in the name of Aunt Maria's old black tomcat brought up this subject of guns? Was it me? What in hell do I care about your gun? I'm lookin' for a cow hand." He drew hard on the stogie. "You got the lines of a puncher, or I miss my guess. But your gun is the farthest subject from my mind." Dawson's keen blue eyes twinkled.

In spite of himself Whit grinned. "I'm begging your pardon for mentioning my gun," he said politely.

Dawson jerked a second stogie from his vest pocket. "Here," he ordered, "stick this in your face. 'Tain't as black as it's painted. Pure broad leaf, seasoned just right. Light 'er up."

Whit "lit 'er up," puffed quietly a few moments, and

found the stogie surprisingly mild. Then he removed it from his mouth and scrutinized its astounding length. "Sometime back," he drawled, "I seem to remember something was said about fishing."

Dawson chuckled. "That see-gar might be a fish pole at that—but not for catchin' polecats or suckers. I figure I might have a cow hand nibblin', though."

"You might have one interested, at that," Whit admitted.

"You've worked cows." It was a statement, not a question.

"Plenty." Whit nodded. "Got an outfit of my own back home—that is, land. No cows. I keep my taxes paid. Someday I'm going back and stock it. Yes, I've worked for a lot of outfits from the Canadian line to the Mexican border."

"I'd like to see you drawin' wages from the 2JD."

"I'll tell you later. I've got to see the sheriff when he shows up."

"What you wantin' to see Dan Brandon about?"

"I'll tell Brandon when I see him."

"Damn if you ain't tight-mouthed."

"Probably. I've just learned not to make unnecessary statements. Very few men get into trouble through keeping their mouths shut." Whit changed the subject: "I heard you tell Rhodes there wasn't much to do on your outfit at present."

"That's right." Dawson nodded. "We took him on when we were shorthanded last year. When things went slack we hated to lay him off. But he just got lazier'n all get out. He'd leave the ranch and not show up for a couple of days at a time. Done a lot of unnecessary drinkin' too. But come beef roundup, there'll be plenty of work again. There's always room on the 2JD for a good man."

"I'll let you know when I've seen the sheriff."

"I don't know what difference that'll make."

"There might be some trouble. I might be involved in it. You wouldn't want to find your new hand in trouble right off the bat—"

"If you ain't the damnedest!"

"Maybe I am . . . What do you know about Calgary Rhodes?"

"Not much. He hit this section about a year back. Like I say, we took him on. Why you askin'?"

"You don't know where he come from or anything?"

Dawson shook his head. "I don't know as I ever heard him say. He's mentioned various places through the West, but never anythin' definite." Dawson said again, "Why you askin'?"

Whit stared moodily into the roadway. "I've been looking for a certain man. I feel as though I'd seen Rhodes before someplace, but his face isn't familiar. He spoke of my father—Cougar Gallatin—as though he might have known him one time."

"Cougar Gallatin's name was known all through the Southwest," Dawson pointed out, "just like—" He paused abruptly.

"Just like mine is," Whit finished bitterly.

"Oh hell, forget it," Dawson said. "I didn't mean anythin'—" He broke off. "Here comes Sheriff Brandon now."

Whit glanced in the direction of Dawson's pointing finger and saw a broad-shouldered man in tan corduroys and battered sombrero approaching on a gray horse. Dawson raised his voice. "Hey, Dan! Come up here a minute,"

Brandon lifted his head, caught the direction of the

shout, then reined in toward the sidewalk. He mounted the steps to the hotel porch, a tall man with sandy-gray hair and tight lips. He was smoothly shaven and wore on his open vest the badge of office.

"Hi yuh, Jeff. Say, it's damn hot."

"You called the turn. Dan, this is a friend of mine, name of Gallatin—" He turned to Whit. "Say, what is your first name?"

"I was named Whitlock. Some folks call me Whit."

"That's it—Whit. This is Sheriff Brandon."

The sheriff shook hands. "No relation to Killer Gallatin, I hope."

Whit stiffened. "I've been called Killer Gallatin."

The eyes of the two men locked. The sheriff's mouth was like a straight length of string; his eyes had hardened.

Dawson said, "Now look here, Dan, don't you get any wrong ideas. I've seen Whit in action—"

"A lot of men have seen Killer Gallatin in action," Brandon cut in. "A good many of them didn't live to tell it—"

"That's a lie," Whit said evenly.

Brandon glared at him. "Gallatin," he said finally, "men don't throw that word in my teeth without—"

"Men don't throw that Killer word in my teeth either," Whit said evenly, "without me asking for proof. Have you ever seen me kill anyone? Or have you just listened to a pack of lies?"

"You got Whit all wrong, Dan," Dawson said earnestly. "Now just hold your hawsses a mite and let me do the talkin'. A short spell back Whit could have killed Calgary Rhodes easy as rollin' off a log, but he didn't do it. He had plenty justification too—"

"Rhodes? What about him? What's that would-be

tough hombre been up to now? Can't I leave town overnight without some sort of fracas breaking out? Jeff, I never could understand how you kept Rhodes on your pay roll so long—"

"If you'll just shut your trap a minute I'll tell you what happened to Rhodes," Dawson interrupted. He told the story. Brandon listened in silence. When the old cowman had concluded, the sheriff cast a glance at the long whip curled in Whit's hand and said, "That Rhodes has been building trouble for himself for some time now. Too much drink and he thinks he's tough. Gallatin, under those circumstances, I wouldn't have blamed you any if you'd plugged him. If I've got the wrong idea about you, I'm sorry. But I've heard a lot about you. I'll admit I never took the trouble to check the stories that came my way. But you understand how such things go—"

Whit said, hard-voiced, "Forget it. I'm asking no favors." He was about to say more when Dawson interrupted:

"Dan, did you see anything of my brother when you were in Curtisville?"

Brandon shook his head. "I saw John when he passed through here early yesterday morning. Told him if he'd wait a couple of hours I'd make the ride with him, but he was anxious to be on his way. Once I hit Curtisville, I had so much to do I didn't get around town much. He ain't back yet, eh?"

Dawson shook his head. "He'll probably come through here this afternoon. That sawbones he goes to see always takes a hell of a time to treat him—"

"Look here, Sheriff," Whit broke in impatiently, "I stopped off in Palomas on purpose to see you."

Brandon shifted his gaze. "So? What's on your

mind?"

"I found a dead man on the trail. I figured it should be reported."

Dawson blurted, "T'hell you say!"

Brandon's frame stiffened. "Dead man, eh? Who was he?"

"I haven't any idea. He'd been shot. In the back. It looked like murder to me."

"Tell me what you know and make it fast," Brandon snapped.

Whit related his story. When he had finished the sheriff considered, then asked, "You didn't see anyone on your way through Torchido Pass or on the way here?"

"Torchido Pass?" Whit said.

"That's the name of that twisting canyon through the Encontróns," Brandon explained. "If you were in Mexico last night that's the only pass you could get here by."

"I didn't see a living soul after I left Mexico," Whit said.

"You're sure this dead man wasn't a Mexican?" Brandon pursued.

"Didn't look like it. I gave you the description as near as I could tell. I didn't move the body, of course."

Brandon directed a glance at Dawson. "You any idea who it could be, Jeff?"

Dawson shook his head. "There's a number of men the description might fit around Palomas, my brother John among 'em, of course. But I ain't heard of anybody around Palomas being missin', and John is northeast of here, while Torchido Pass is southwest. Probably some stranger cuttin' through the pass, just like Whit did this mornin'."

"Probably." Brandon nodded. He turned again to Whit. "You say you spent last night at Nuevo Cesto. How were things there?"

Whit looked surprised. "All right, I reckon. It's just a sleepy little Mexican town, like most you see along the border. Adobe shacks and some stores, and chickens scratching in the road. A few big houses—"

"I know Nuevo Cesto," Brandon said impatiently. "Been there dozens of times. I mean did you see anything unusual there, any signs of trouble?"

Whit shook his head. Then he frowned. "No-o, I didn't see any signs of trouble. Now that you mention it, though, there did see more people around than you'd expect in a town of that size. Men seemed to be meeting in little clusters and talking seriously about something. I slept in a little *posada* there. Come to think of it, they didn't seem too anxious to take me in. But what difference does the town make? What's that got to do with the dead man I discovered?"

"I don't know." Brandon sighed, half lost in thought. "I wish I did." He roused himself. "Well, I'd best ride out and see what's to be seen. Gallatin, I'll want you to ride with me—"

"Meaning I'm under suspicion?" Whit asked.

"I didn't say that," Brandon replied testily. "I'm just making sure you don't leave Palomas until I give the word."

"Now look here, Dan," Dawson commenced, "Whit didn't kill this feller—"

"You don't know who killed him any more than I do," Brandon snapped.

Whit demanded, "Would I be likely to report it if *I'd* killed him?"

"You might," Brandon said coldly, then his tone

softened. "Look here, I've not said you killed him, but you're a witness. I'm asking that you stick around for a spell. Please note that I said 'asking.' Now are you going to co-operate or aren't you?"

Whit nodded. "I see your point. I'll ride with you."

Dawson glared angrily at the sheriff. "Reckon I'll ride along too."

Brandon shrugged his shoulders and descended from the hotel porch. Dawson and Whit rose and went to get their horses.

IDENTIFICATION

WHIT AND DAWSON WAITED before the Shamrock Saloon while the sheriff entered to announce that a dead man had been found on the Torchido trail. He asked questions of the customers at the bar and repeated the description of the dead man as Whit had given it to him. No one, apparently, could throw any light on the matter. The sheriff emerged from the saloon grumbling, "Dammit! I no sooner get back here than I have to go out again." He sent a man hurrying to the livery for a fresh horse, then called after him, "Zeke, you'd best get a wagon and team you can drive too. The corpse might be too stiff to make easy loading on a horse's back. Get back here soon's possible."

They stood waiting. In a short time the man named Zeke returned with another horse for the sheriff and a wagon to which was hitched a pair of bay animals. Brandon switched his saddle to the fresh mount. Some dozen men, among whom were Rhodes and the two Tiernans, drawn by curiosity, announced their intention of accompanying the sheriff. Within a few minutes the riders and wagon got under way, raising clouds of gritty dust along Palomas's main thoroughfare.

Barry Flynn stood on his porch watching them depart. The small cavalcade was only a block away from the saloon when Jeff Dawson, riding at Whit's side with the sheriff, turned and shouted, "Barry! If John comes through before we return, tell him to wait for me and we'll ride to the 2JD together."

"I'll be takin' care of it, Jeff," Flynn called back.

Horses and men settled down to the trip across the sage- and greasewood-dotted range. Whit, Dawson, and the sheriff rode ahead, the wagon a few yards behind. The other riders were spread out around the wagon and to its rear. The animals moved at a steady trot. Ahead, seeming nearer than they actually were in the clear air, rose the jagged peaks of the Encontróns, now bright in the midday sun. The steady wind, blowing down from the mountains, carried a fine sandy grit that worked itself into eyes and throat and nostrils. The riders weren't moving fast, just fast enough to stay with the wagon.

Brandon reined his horse around a tall saguaro cactus, then again fell in at Whit's side. The sheriff glanced resentfully past Whit and said to Dawson, "Did you have your dinner?"

Dawson shook his head. "Neither did Whit."

Brandon snapped, "Gallatin had to come with me. You didn't."

"Mebbe I felt it was necessary," the old cowman said.

"Yeah," Brandon sneered. "You just wanted a ride and some fresh air, I suppose."

"Put it like that if it suits you," Dawson said mildly.

The sheriff swore. "Dammit, Jeff, you've known me long enough to know that Gallatin will get a square deal from me no matter what comes up."

"If you take time to think things over, yes," Dawson replied. "But I've seen you jump to some mighty bad conclusions in the past, too, Dan. I just ain't takin' chances."

Brandon reddened. "Blast that memory of yours," he growled. "Just 'cause I once arrested the wrong man—and that was ten years ago—you think I'm li'ble to make the same mistake again?"

"It could happen," Dawson said imperturbably. "You was right proddy when you first met Whit. Not only that, Rhodes and them two Tiernans come along with us. Why?"

"Morbid curiosity, I calls it—like the rest of them bustards trailin' after us."

"You ain't no proof of that," Dawson snapped. "I was in the Shamrock when Rhodes made his play. You wa'n't. No tellin' what them scuts has got in mind."

"Look here, you two," Whit broke in, "no use you getting into an argument on my account. I can take care of myself."

"I've heard you could," Brandon said testily. "I don't know what all the fuss is about, anyway. I ain't put you under arrest."

"And for a dang good reason," Dawson flared. "You ain't got no proof agin Whit. But the very fact you mention 'arrest' shows how your mind's workin'. That's why I come along."

The sheriff said tiredly. "Oh hell . . . I'm going to drop back and talk to Rhodes and those others. I'd like to learn from them just what happened in the Shamrock." He pulled his horse to a halt off the trail and waited for those in the rear to catch up.

Dawson and Whit rode on in silence for a few

minutes. Finally Whit said, "Much obliged."

"For nothin'." Dawson chuckled. He drew out another of his stogies and lighted it, shielding the match flame from the wind in his cupped, gnarled hands. He drew out a second stogie and offered it to Whit. Whit refused with thanks, saying he'd roll himself a cigarette. The two men smoked in silence while their ponies kicked up dust beneath their hoofs. A jackrabbit scurried frantically from the trail and darted for the security of a clump of prickly-pear pads sprouting nearly ripe fruit. Whit glanced back over his shoulder and saw the sheriff in conversation with Rhodes and some of the other men. The sheriff looked angry. Now and then the wheels of the wagon at Whit's rear gave forth a protesting squeak, attesting the lack of grease.

Dawson broke the silence with another chuckle. "Dan mentioned somethin' that happened ten years back. He was new in this county then. Had his first job as a deputy and was eager as a beaver at a new stream. 'Bout that time the 2JD was havin' some trouble with cow thieves. I happened to be out on the range one day and was brandin' a stray I'd come across. I'd just put down my iron when out of the brush pops Dan Brandon and allows as how I'm under arrest; claimed he'd been followin' me for two hours and now he had the evidence he wanted. We was strangers at that time, him never havin' seen me before—didn't know me from Adam's ghost. I tells him who I am, but he won't believe me. Puts me under arrest and holds a gun on me all the way to town. The boys sure hoorawed him plenty 'bout that when the truth of my identity come out. Most folks has forgot it now, but every time I want to get a rise outten Dan I needles him about jumpin' to conclusions."

Whit laughed. "Offhand I'd say he was right efficient

on his job."

"Oh, no doubt of that. There ain't much crime in Clarendon County. Dan will put up with a lot of windjammin' such as Rhodes, say, does, and pay no attention. But once let a man get outten line and Dan will put the quietus on him pronto."

"What's this Curtisville town you mentioned a spell back?"

"Biggest town in the county—county seat, in fact. My brother John rides there once a month to see a medical specialist that's tryin' to cure him of a lame wrist which has bothered him for a year now. He broke it, and it never did seem to get right again, to hear John tell it. I've told him a hundred times that old bones don't heal like new, but he won't realize he's gettin' on in years. Specialist don't seem to be doin' much good, nuther. We got a sawbones in Palomas that done John just as much good. But it's my opinion that John likes an excuse to get to Curtisville more'n anythin'. He's been plumb restless since his wife died two years back. Got a nice daughter, too, Laura—that's my niece. You'll like her."

"When you figuring I'll be meeting your niece?"

Dawson's eyes widened innocently. "Ain't you plannin' to work for the 2JD? I thought we had that all settled."

Whit grinned. "You know dang well we didn't decide definitely."

"*I* did, anyway. You wouldn't want to change my mind, would you?"

"Let's wait and see how I come out with your sheriff, Mr. Dawson—"

"Mister be damned! I'm Jeff to my friends. That includes them on the 2JD pay roll too."

Whit changed the subject: “I should think Brandon would have his office at the county seat.”

“He used to. Then about six-seven months back he switched his deputy up to Curtisville and set up his sheriffin’ office in Palomas.”

“How come?”

Dawson paused uncertainly. “We-ell, you see, we’ve been hearin’ rumors for some time that a revolution is buildin’ up over in Mexico. Don’t know if there’s any truth in it or not. That’s why Dan was interested in your opinion of Nuevo Cesto—whether it was quiet and so on. Dan claims he heard the revolutionists’ headquarters was there.”

“Why should a revolution in Mexico—if it comes—induce Brandon to change his office to Palomas?”

“Revolutions mean gun battles. Whatever side loses is due to be executed if it don’t escape. Losin’ revolutionists always head for the United States for safety. Sometimes the winners are right on their tails. Torchido Pass is the only way through the Encontróns for a good many miles. Should a bunch of Mexes come spillin’ through the pass into Clarendon County there might be some trouble. Brandon aims to be as close as possible to the pass if trouble comes—and he figures it’s his responsibility more than his deputy’s to watch for said trouble.”

Whit nodded. “I don’t just see one sheriff standing off a bunch of fighters boiling out of that pass, but I respect Brandon’s attempt to preserve law and order. Take a few hundred revolutionists, desperate and hungry, drop ’em into Palomas, and hell sure might break loose.”

“You get the idea.” Dawson nodded. “Brandon just prefers to be on the job himself rather than trust the business to one of his deputies.”

At that moment the sheriff spurred alongside Whit again. Whit said, "Did you get the story?"

Brandon nodded, his eyes smoldering. "Rhodes claimed you tricked him—that he could have beaten you to the shot—"

"Hell's bells!" Dawson burst out. "I told you that Rhodes was tricked. He was watchin' Whit's gun hand and entirely overlooked the whip. But I doubt he could have beat him to the shot, anyway."

"Will you keep your mouth outten this, Jeff?" Brandon snapped. "I'm not through talkin' yet." He went on: "The two Tiernans back Rhodes up. They tried to give me an impression that Gallatin took some sort of unfair advantage of Rhodes, that Rhodes wa'n't lookin' for trouble a-tall."

"You got my word for what happened," Dawson said huffily. "What did them others back there say?"

"Not much," Brandon said disgustedly. "They're too afraid of Rhodes and the Tiernans to say much. But they weren't over-enthusiastic about backin' up Rhodes, either. Their reluctance sort of makes me think you gave me the correct version, Jeff."

"Never knew me to lie to you, did you?" Dawson said in hurt tones. "I don't take kindly to you checkin' up on my story that-a-way, Dan." He winked at Whit. "I'm commencin' to think mebbe you've hurt my feelin's. I'll have to ponder it a mite—"

"Oh, you go to hell," Brandon said good-naturedly.

Whit said coldly, "If there's any doubt in Rhodes's mind that I got the best of him, fair and square, I'll be glad—"

"No, you don't," the sheriff said quickly. "None of that, Gallatin. The matter is settled now. I don't want it opened again."

"Suppose Rhodes wants it opened? What do I do, just wait like a dummy until he's plugged me?"

The sheriff was silent. Finally, "We'll meet that problem when it arises. If I'm not there at the time, you'll have to use your own judgment."

"That's all I'm asking," Whit said quietly.

The mountains were nearer now. Across the tops of the greasewood and mesquite Whit could see the opening between ridges that denoted the entrance to Torchido Pass. It wasn't more than a mile or two farther on that he had found the body. He glanced toward the sky. Here and there he could see floating black specks drifting about and soaring in wide arcs against the vast turquoise expanse, though none of the buzzards was lying low.

Dawson said suddenly, "Rider coming." He raised his arm.

Whit and the sheriff followed with their eyes the pointing finger. Coming through the sea of greasewood and mesquite, approaching at an angle, was a man on a black horse. After a moment the sheriff grunted, "Looks like Lowendirk." Dawson said he reckoned it was Lowendirk too.

Whit asked, "Who's Lowendirk?"

"Calls hisself Drake Lowendirk." Brandon supplied the information. "Rich dude from Denver. As he tells it, he owns some sort of factory there. Got to working too hard. Health broke down. His doctor shipped him out here for his health. Advised him to do plenty riding. Which same he does. He rented a small house in Palomas but don't mix with us common citizens too much. Oh, he's always polite and all that, but sort of standoffish all the same. Probaby figures we ain't in his class, speakin' financially. Which same we ain't."

Whit commented. "He seems to ride all right."

"Hell," Brandon growled, "he's been in Palomas seven-eight months now. If a man can't learn to ride in that time, he might as well give up. And before he come here I understand he was up in Jaboncillo County someplace for a spell. That's just north of here. Anyway, that's his story."

"You got any reason to doubt it?" Whit asked.

Brandon's eyes widened. "Why should I doubt it? I don't know of any reason for not believin' what he says. I just never paid much attention to him. He ain't my sort. I never had the money to mingle with rich dudes."

He fell silent as Lowendirk rounded a tall paloverde tree and turned into the trail ahead. Whit saw now that the man's clothing—Levis, flannel shirt, fawn-colored sombrero—had none of the worn appearance that comes from hard toil. Even the six-shooter in its bright yellow holster looked as though it had seen little use, if any. Lowendirk was a big man with wide shoulders, growing a bit paunchy about the middle. He had dark hair and eyes; his long jaw had that bluish appearance seen on men with heavy beards even when cleanly shaven.

The sheriff and his companions stopped as Lowendirk pulled his horse to a halt. "Afternoon, sheriff," Lowendirk greeted. "You and your friends out enjoying this invigorating air?" There was something brusque, at the same time mocking, about the man, as though he were sure in his own mind that these people before him were his inferiors.

"Too much dust and sand in this breeze for me to find any invigoratin'," Brandon stated tersely. "Not to mention the heat. If you think this is a pleasure trip—" He broke off. "Didn't see anything of a dead man along this trail, did you, Lowendirk?"

"Covered with a blanket," Whit put in.

Lowendirk's dark penetrating eyes shifted momentarily to Whit, then moved back to the sheriff. "Dead man? No." He glanced at the other riders, nodded shortly to Dawson, and came back to Brandon again. "No, I haven't seen any dead man. I've not been following this trail. Just been riding sort of aimlessly about, exercising this horse. And myself. Who died?"

"Murdered," Dawson put in.

"Sounds rather nasty," Lowendirk said. "Any idea who it is?"

"Not yet," the sheriff replied. "Maybe you'd care to come along and help identify the body."

Lowendirk shook his head. "I don't think I'd be interested. Anyway, it's not likely I'd know this murdered man. I'm a stranger in this section, as you know. Where'd you hear about this?"

Brandon jerked one thumb toward Whit. "Gallatin says he came across the body early this morning on his way to Palomas. Mr. Lowendirk, this is Gallatin."

Lowendirk acknowledged the introduction with a nod and a brief curving of the lips. "Gallatin? The name sounds familiar. Where have I heard it before? . . . Ummm...Isn't there some gun fighter in the Southwest by that name? Killer Gallatin, I think he's called?"

"My name happens to be Whit, though I've been called Killer."

Lowendirk's dark eyes narrowed. "Oh, I'm sorry. No offense intended."

"No offense taken," Whit said quietly.

Lowendirk said, "I'm glad to hear that. It would certainly be a serious mistake to get off on the wrong foot with a man of your reputation, Gallatin."

Dawson put in dryly, "It certainly would, Lowendirk."

Lowendirk shifted his attention briefly to Jeff Dawson, "I'm sure you're correct, Dawson." He gathered his horse's reins. "Well, I mustn't detain you any longer, Sheriff Brandon."

"You're sure you don't care to come along with us?" the sheriff asked.

Drake Lowendirk shook his head. "To make a rather grisly joke, well, dead bodies aren't quite to my taste on this bright day. I'll be getting along. Good day, gentlemen."

He spurred his mount on its way, and the sheriff and his companions moved once more along the Torchido trail.

Fifteen minutes later Whit said, "Slow down, Sheriff, it's right along here someplace." He moved a couple of yards farther on his horse, then pulled to a halt and dismounted. Pushing past some greasewood bushes, he saw the blanket-draped figure as he had left it. "Here you are."

The other men dismounted. Brandon jerked over his shoulder, "You hombres stay where you are. I don't want this ground messed up until I've had a chance to read 'sign.' "

The others pressed along the edge of the trail as the sheriff moved up to Whit's side. Stooping, he drew aside the blanket. There was a sudden exclamation at Whit's shoulder. He turned and saw that Jeff Dawson had joined them. The old cowman's eyes were wide; the color had fled from his seamed features.

"Great God!" Dawson exclaimed. "That's my brother John."

The sheriff nodded, standing beside the body, blanket

in hand. "It's John Dawson, all right."

"All *wrong*, I'd say," Calgary Rhodes put in. "Dan, I figure it's up to you to arrest Killer Gallatin for John's murder. Ten to one you'll find Gallatin's footprints around this body somepace. Fit 'em to his boots—"

"You're talking like a damn fool, Calgary," Brandon snapped. "Why wouldn't his footprints be hereabouts? He found the body. It's his blanket he left here—You, Gallatin! Don't start anything."

Whit paused. He had taken a quick angry step in Rhodes's direction. Now he halted, shrugging his shoulders, and turned toward Jeff Dawson, who stood as though stunned, staring with wide eyes at the silent form sprawled on the earth. "I'm plumb sorry about this, Jeff," Whit said softly.

Dawson swallowed hard, nodded dumbly. Then he turned and half stumbled toward his horse, followed by one of the other riders who was offering expressions of sympathy. Whit joined the sheriff, who was rapidly going through the dead man's pockets. A quantity of money was found. "Twa'n't robbery, anyway," Brandon grunted. "Plumb through the heart, I'd say. Likely died almost instanter." His eyes glanced about the earth. "Looks like there'd been at least a dozen riders hereabouts when it happened."

The other men had commenced to crowd in again, but Brandon warned them back. "You too, Gallatin, I want to look this earth over careful."

Whit retreated, but not before he had had an opportunity to look for the handprint he had seen earlier that day in the sand. There was no sign of it now, the wind having blown away all traces of it. Even the hoofprints looked much shallower, more blurred than they had before. The other riders who had accompanied the sheriff were scattered through the brush, looking for any other evidence that might be found.

Whit joined Jeff Dawson at his horse. The old cowman's eyes looked moist. There was a grim touch to his straight lips. "I reckon I know how you feel, Jeff," Whit said. "There's nothing I can say to help, I reckon."

"Not a thing," Dawson said. He had better control of his emotions now. "Thanks just the same, Whit." He gulped and brushed the back of his hand across his eyes. "Look here, I'm askin' again that you take a job with us—with me. I'd like you to stay around until this business is cleared up, son."

Whit nodded. "I'll stay," he promised. The two men stood in silence.

After some time Dawson said, "I can't understand what John was doin' way over here. He should have been in Curtisville when this happened. There ain't nothin' I know of could have brought him to this neck of the range. I just don't understand it."

There was further silence. After a time Whit saw Brandon and a couple of the other men lifting the dead man into the wagon. Again the blanket was used to cover the body.

Brandon strode over to where Whit and Dawson were standing. He said briefly to Dawson, "No important sign to be found, Jeff. It's a mystery to me. Maybe something will come out later to give us a clue as to just what happened." He turned to Whit. "I sort of hate to do this, Gallatin, but I reckon I'll have to put you under arrest. Are you coming quiet, or—"

"I'll come quiet, of course," Whit said evenly, "but I don't get the idea. I never knew John Dawson. I had no reason for shooting him. Is this the penalty a man receives in this part of the range for reporting what he found?"

"I know, I know," Brandon broke in, "but I don't see what else I can do. Your rep is against you. Rhodes and some of the others insist you should be held. I don't say I agree with them, but—"

"Are you or Rhodes running this county?" Jeff Dawson demanded angrily.

"I am, of course," Brandon snapped. "But after all, even if he's not guilty, Gallatin is a material witness."

"All right, he's a witness," Dawson said coldly. "I'll agree to that. Whit won't be runnin' away. He's goin' to work for the 2JD. I'll be responsible for him, or I'll put up bail if you insist on arrest, but by Gawd, Dan, you're not goin' to frame anythin' against a 2JD hand. Now does my word mean anythin' to you or not?"

Angry words rose to Brandon's lips. "Who in hell said I was aiming to frame—" He broke off, growling, "Hell, Jeff, if you put it that way, there won't be any arrest. Your word is good with me. C'mon, we'd best get started back. This is no time for you and me to be arguing."

"No, it ain't, Dan," Dawson said grimly. "My argument is due to run in some other direction when—" He paused, and unconsciously one hand crept toward the gun at his hip and his eyes rested on the blanket-covered form in the wagon bed. He turned and climbed up to his saddle. "Like you say, it's time to get started back. Whit will be on hand when you want him."

A DRIVING URGE

THREE WEEKS PASSED. An inquest had been held, but no new evidence was produced. The jury returned a verdict to the effect that John Dawson had been killed by someone unknown, and Dr. Breen, Palomas's medical man, acting as coroner, had directed Sheriff Dan Brandon to take the necessary steps to apprehend the murderer. The following day Dawson had been buried in the Palomas boot-hill cemetery, the funeral being attended by a large number of people throughout Clarendon County.

During the days following the funeral Whit Gallatin had become firmly established as one of the crew on the 2JD Ranch, with its old rock-and-adobe ranch house and wide front gallery, surrounded by ancient cottonwood trees. Back of the house were corrals, the bunkhouse, a barn, blacksmith shop, and the tall windmill. There had been a definite slacking off in work following John Dawson's death, and Whit had been able to get well acquainted with the various members of the crew.

First in order came the foreman, Whitey Laidlaw, a slim towheaded man around forty years of age; then came leathery-faced Bob Corbett, Button-Eyes Cobb, Shorty Farran, Red Maguire, and Dutch Vander. The 2JD cook, Skillet Potter, was an individual of considerable tonnage, being built pretty much on the order of a beer keg, with thinning hair and a round face. All the crew had worked for the Dawsons for some years and were loyal to the core. It was rather a new experience for Whit to find himself accepted by men like these, and he was enjoying it. He had no way of knowing, of course, that Jeff Dawson had told the crew as much as he knew of Whit Gallatin and had threatened to fire instantly any man who referred to him as Killer Gallatin. The men had met him as "Whit," and Whit was the name he went by. No one mentioned his past life. Gradually, in such friendly surroundings, Whit was losing his cold defensive attitude.

Laura Dawson, too—Jeff's niece—he had met, though he had seen only little of the girl. Following her father's funeral she had stayed indoors much of the time. She was a slim, boyishly built girl with thick hair the color of a polished chestnut and gentian-hued eyes with long black lashes. Her mouth was generous; her chin had in it the same determination found in her uncle Jeff's jaw.

Whit was sitting on a bench in the sunshine just outside the bunkhouse one morning, soaking up the early warmth and smoking an after-breakfast cigarette, when he saw Whitey Laidlaw approaching from the direction of the barn. Through an open window of the mess house, which was attached to the bunkhouse, came the clatter of pots and pans as the hefty Skillet Potter washed the dishes.

Whit got to his feet as Laidlaw came up to him. "Hope you've got a job for me at last, Whitey." Whit smiled.

"I was talking to Jeff up at the house a spell back," Laidlaw replied in a slow drawl. "He mentioned about seeing you later on. You might throw your rig on your bronc."

"That sounds good."

"Getting restless, Whit?"

"Some. Why shouldn't I be? Ever since I've been

here I've been doing nothing but sit on my tail and eat and sleep."

"I seem to remember a coupla days when you were instructing the boys in the use of your whip." Laidlaw smiled. "Just where did you pick up that whip business, anyway?"

"An old cowman up in Montana taught me about two years back. I had a job running down broomtails with him. You can believe it or not, but I've seen him pick a fly off a horse's hip with his whip more than once when we were running in a bunch of animals. He was good! He'd come to this country from Australia when he was a young man. From what he told me, they use whips like mine down there quite a bit."

"I'd say he was a mighty good teacher. You seem to know your business. From what Jeff says, you sure tangled Calgary Rhodes's gun plenty."

Whit frowned. "Probably so—but Jeff didn't put me on the crew just to give lessons in whip-snaking." He paused. "I'd feel a heap better with some regular work to do. I know horses and cows. I see you handing out jobs to the other boys—"

"Not too many of 'em, you haven't," Laidlaw cut in. "John Dawson's death was a body blow to the whole outfit. There hasn't been too much to do around here, anyway. You should know how it is this time a year. Later there'll be plenty work—"

"I still think," Whit pursued, "I should have had my share of such work as there was to do."

Laidlaw hesitated. "To tell the truth, Whit, you should have. But Jeff give me orders. Said you was just to lay around and get acquainted with us and that he had something in mind for you. He'll tell you about it when the time comes."

"That still don't explain just why he hired me."

"Maybe I can give you a hint," Laidlaw said. "Jeff told me that any man who could keep himself in check and not lose his temper, the way you did against Calgary Rhodes that day, was well worth hiring. I'm inclined to agree with him."

Whit said, "Thanks, Whitey."

Laidlaw said, "*Por nada, amigo.* No thanks necessary."

He strode on his way, and Whit went to saddle his buckskin. Within a few minutes he returned to the bench and rolled another cigarette. The back door of the ranch house slammed, and Jeff Dawson came walking toward the bunkhouse, the inevitable black stogie in his mouth.

Whit got to his feet. "Hear you got a job for me."

"There's no rush. Sit down a minute." He sank on the bench at Whit's side. "I ain't had no real chance to *habla* with you since John's death. Didn't want to talk to nobody for a spell, and then there was those trips I had to make to the county seat to get the will settled and so on. Court business moves slow, but it's all settled at last. Then the result had to be put into the newspaper; how I was the biggest ranch owner in this section. Lot of nonsense, if you ask me."

"I suppose. Still, it's something for you and Miss Laura to be known as wealthy ranch owners. A lot of folks would like that."

"I don't care one way or t'other, son. Laura don't have anythin' to do with the ranch, of course."

"Didn't Laura's father leave her his half of the ranch?"

Dawson shook his head. "I get his whole half share. John—he was a mite younger than me—but he could look farther ahead. He always had an idea that I might marry someday, and he got to thinkin' that maybe a strange woman comin' into the house might make things difficult. Sometimes, y'know, women don't get along. So he fixed it in the will; if he died first I was to get his share. In return, I settle a sum of money on Laura, so she won't be the loser. In addition I pay her a share of the profits each year. In that way Laura is free to move out any time she likes, but she says she never will so long as I'll have her here. That's forever, far's I'm concerned."

"She might marry sometime."

"I've thought of that. Her man will be welcome here." Blue smoke curled from the stogie and mingled with the gray puffs Dawson blew into the sun-filtered air. "You know, I'm still wonderin'."

"About what?" Whit asked.

"It's still a puzzle to me why you didn't shoot Rhodes that day you had a chance. You had plenty provocation."

Whit scowled. "Maybe I didn't want to kill him." The answer was short and to the point. Whit started to continue, then stopped.

Noticing the younger man's hesitation, Dawson said, "Look here, Whit, you don't have to tell me if you don't want to. But I just can't understand you roamin' around the country, workin' up a reputation as a killer. But it's none of my business, so we'll say no more about it. I shouldn't have—"

Whit cut in abruptly, "Jeff, I think I do want to tell you about it. You've been a real friend. You're the first man in three years who offered me a job that didn't want to hire me because of my reputation. Would you believe me if I told you I wasn't really a killer?" He paused. "Aside from having it in my blood."

"I mentioned that day I met you," Dawson reminded dryly, "that I only believed about ten per cent of what I heard. I reckon I'll include your statement in that ten per cent. I could see you was rarin' to let daylight through Rhodes that day, but for some reason you was holdin' yourself in check. You was like a prize fighter fightin' under wraps, as the sayin' goes. You was entitled to shoot him. It wasn't that you was afraid—"

"That was just it," Whit broke in, "I was afraid. Wait, let me explain. You see, my father was a killer. Killing is something that's in the Gallatin blood. Dad didn't want me to be like him. He went out, gun-fighting. I had to kill the two men who were responsible for his death. Otherwise they'd have killed me first. And there was a third man—" Whit paused. "Anyway, after I'd cooled off I commenced to see things different. Good law enforcement won't ever come so long as men insist on taking the law into their own hands . . . "

From that point Whit continued and told his whole story—how he was believed throughout the Southwest to be a killer of the worst sort, and how for three years he had continued to fight the demon in the Gallatin blood. When he had concluded there was a long silence.

Finally Dawson said unbelievingly, "And do you mean to say you haven't killed a man since you downed this Talbert hombre and Hess?"

Whit shook his head. "I've not even fired on a man since then."

Dawson looked bewildered. "Damme if I understand it—with your reputation—Say, how in hell do you keep outten fights?"

"You saw me take care of Calgary Rhodes."

Dawson nodded. "Yes, but does that whip trick of yours always work?"

"Not always. Sometimes I don't have to use it. Occasionally I can bluff a man out of drawing his gun. So long as I don't make the first move to draw and force a man into something, he may have enough time to change his mind. There've been times when I was lucky enough to get my gun out first—"

"Lucky enough!" Dawson snorted.

"—and that has a way of making a man change his mind too. More than once, to avoid trouble, I have stayed away from towns where I knew gunmen were hanging out. Not that I was afraid of 'em—" Whit broke off, eying Dawson defiantly. Dawson chuckled. A slow flush crept into Whit's cheeks.

The oldler man read the thought in Whit's eyes and hastened to apologize. "I wa'n't laughin' at you, son. Hell's bells! I never thought for a minute you were afraid. It's—it's just that you're so dang in earnest about this business of not wantin' to kill. Nobody's doubtin' your nerve. But if you don't aim to shoot anybody, why do you pack a gun?"

Whit looked embarrassed. "There'd be less chance of me having to face gun fighters if I didn't wear a gun. I've got to lick this blood taint while I'm packing a six-shooter. I don't dare make it easy for myself."

"By Gawd, you're not, either."

Whit frowned. "It's sort of hard to explain, Jeff, but the longer I can go on—that is, meeting gun slingers every so often and making them back down without me having to shoot—the better grip I'm getting on myself. Do you see what I mean?"

"I see what you mean all right." Dawson shook his head slowly. "But you're sure not takin' any easy trail in your crusade. That's what it is—a crusade—like in the old days, fightin' against the powers of evil—"

"Aw, cripes!" Whit looked impatient. "You're making too much of the business. It hasn't been so hard the past year. As my reputation as a killer grew I found less and less men inclined to pick quarrels with me. And as far as carrying a gun is concerned, the time might come when right would be on my side and I'd have to shoot, whether I wanted to or not. And so I have to keep practicing all the time. There are snakes to shoot and fence posts and tin cans."

"I'm commencin' to understand." Dawson looked thoughtful. "You mentioned this feller Hopkins that made the plan against your dad with Talbert and Hess. Why do you keep lookin' for him? You aimin' to shoot him?"

Whit scowled. "Jeff," he said slowly at last, "I—just—don't—know. Something's kept driving me on to look for the man for three years now. Somehow he's got to be brought to justice. What will happen when I do meet him face to face, I can't say. Maybe I'll be strong enough not to shoot. Maybe I won't. Maybe he'll be too fast for me. But so long as there's that doubt in my mind, I've got to keep looking for him. I just can't seem to help myself."

"Damned if you ain't the persistent one," Dawson said, something of awe in his eyes.

"It's not me!" Whit exclaimed. "It's something inside me that keeps pushing me on. I got to find out, that's all."

"Son, you sure got a drivin' urge behind you." Neither man spoke for several minutes. Within the kitchen Skillet Potter was breaking up kindling. A flour sack thumped on a table. Dawson finally said, "Whit, did Whitey mention a job you could do?"

"He didn't say what it was, just told me to saddle my

bronc. I'll be glad to get busy."

"Don't be in a rush. Your job today will be to ride in to Palomas with Laura." Whit looked startled. Before he could speak Dawson continued: "I didn't intend to, but maybe I have hired you for your gun reputation. It's this way: there's somethin' damn funny goin' on in this country. With John gettin' killed, and all, I don't like it. What it is, I can't say, but I just sense that somethin's mighty wrong. I'll feel safer from now on if Laura has someone to ride with her—"

"In other words," Whit said slowly, "I'm being put on your pay roll as a bodyguard."

"Put it that way if you like."

"Why wouldn't one of the other 2JD men do as well—better, in fact? She's acquainted with 'em, and—"

"The other men haven't your reputation with a gun."

Whit scowled. "So here I am back to the old reason for being hired." Dawson interrupted to say that it wasn't quite the same. Some of the tense lines died from Whit's face. He said, "All right, maybe it isn't the same thing, but it's ended up that way. But I'm willing to pass over that. The thing is, I don't know much about girls. I've never known but a few, and them not too well."

Dawson snorted. " 'Bout time you got acquainted with a girl then. You'll like Laura, and if I don't miss my bet, she'll like you."

"But she knows nothing about me—"

"She'll take you at face value. She doesn't care what's in your past. Take my word for it. I know that girl."

"We-ell, if you put it that way," Whit said reluctantly.

"I do put it that way. There'll be more to your work. You won't be ridin' with Laura all the time. You're a stranger here, and folks won't think too much about it if you ask questions."

"What sort of questions?"

Dawson hesitated. "If I or one of the crew started questioning folks, people might think it was funny. You, bein' a stranger, can't be expected to know all that goes on around Palomas. You can throw in a question here and there—"

"What sort of questions?" Whit asked again.

"To tell the truth, I'm not sure. What I'm getting at, I want to know who killed my brother John. If he'd been robbed I'd be inclined to think some bandits done it, but the fact that he wasn't makes it look mighty queer. Why was he killed? He didn't have any enemies—that is, nobody that hated him enough to do a killin'. He had no recent serious disagreements with anybody so far as I know. When I was in Curtisville I did a lot of questionin' around. I learned that he got there all right that day, but he never did get to see that doctor he was supposed to visit. What changed his mind and sent him ridin' way off toward Torchido Pass? If we could learn what was back of that move we might have a clue to his killer."

Whit looked dubious. "What you need is a good range detective."

"Maybe so. But I don't know one, and it would take a spell to dig one out. I should have thought of this nearly three weeks ago, of course, but I've felt sort of stunned ever since John was killed. I ain't been usin' my head the way I should. But I got a hunch you may be able to help. You're smart—" Whit had raised one protesting hand. Dawson went on: "Of course you're smart. Any hombre that can play the lone-wolf game the way you have the past three years and not get killed—or even kill anybody—has got to be smart. I don't see it any other way. I'm not asking too much, just that you keep your eyes open. No tellin' what you might notice that other folks hereabouts would miss."

Whit thought of the imprint of a man's palm he had found beside John Dawson's dead body. He had never mentioned this to anyone. It occurred to him he might tell Jeff about it. Then he hesitated. Jeff might build too much expectancy on such a discovery, or he might mention it to someone else. Whit decided to keep still. Instead he said, "All right, Jeff, I'll take a whirl at it."

"Fine, son. I hoped you'd see it my way. There won't be too much ridin' with Laura to do. Aside from that you're a free agent. You can come and go as you please, with no questions asked. If you discover anything you think I should know I'll be glad to hear it . . . Laura will be ready to start in about an hour. She's aimin' to visit a friend of her mother's in Palomas today. You can take her there and call when she wants you to ride her home. In between, your time is your own . . . Oh yes, Calgary Rhodes never did show up here to get his junk. It don't amount to much; some clothing and so on. You might shove it in a burlap sack and drop it off at the Shamrock Saloon for him to pick up." Whit agreed. Dawson continued, "While you're waitin' for Laura you might saddle up her pony."

Whit nodded, and Dawson strode off toward the house, leaving Whit to ponder which would be the tougher job of the two: escorting a girl he didn't know, or running to earth the murderer of John Dawson. Whit had about decided the latter might be the easier. "Still," he mused, "maybe not. The other might pan out all right."

RANGE DETECTIVE?

WHIT BROUGHT THE HORSES UP when he saw the girl approaching from the house. Laura Dawson wore riding boots, a divided riding skirt of soft doeskin, and a mannish flannel shirt. A bandanna was knotted below her throat, and her reddish-brown hair was tucked beneath a well-worn black Stetson with a flat crown. Even while Whit was wondering if he should help her up to the saddle the girl said, “Morning, Whit—you see, I’m going to call you Whit,” placed her left foot in the stirrup, and swung easily up on her pony’s back.

Whit said, “Yes’m,” and mounted an instant later. Stirrup to stirrup, they rode out of the ranch yard and headed along the trail to Palomas. The trail was well defined and marked with wagon-wheel ruts and hoofprints. Now and again it dipped into a hollow or lifted across a slight elevation. Occasionally it twisted around an outcropping of reddish sandstone, then straightened out again.

The two loped their ponies steadily for a time, then pulled them in to a slower gait. The girl could ride all right, Whit had long since decided. On either side of the road grass appeared plentiful. Mingled through it was the ever-present greasewood, mesquite, and an occasional yucca. Now and then small bunches of white-faced cows, branded with the 2JD symbol, would be seen scattered along the way.

“The beef stock looks to be in good condition.” Laura broke the silence at last.

“Yes’m, they do.”

“Mostly our herds stay pretty close to Palomas River—it’s rather ridiculous to call it a river when you consider it's only about twenty feet across at the widest. Back where it heads it's a lot narrower and doesn't commence to spread out until about twelve miles from town. But it runs all the year round, until it reaches the badlands country southeast of Palomas. There it just sinks into the sands and disappears."

"Yes'm, I reckon it would."

Laura glanced sharply at her companion, her red lips tightened. Another half mile was negotiated in silence. Finally the girl said, "Look, don't you like to talk? I've heard of these strong, silent men, but I never expected to be found riding with one."

A smile twitched the corners of Whit's mouth. "I don't ever remember laying claim to being strong, Miss Laura."

"But you are silent." The girl eyed him with some exasperation.

Whit shifted uncomfortably in his saddle. What did a fellow talk about to a girl, especially one whose father had recently been killed? He hadn't even been sure she'd feel like talking under the circumstances. Finally he said, "The 2JD seems to be a right big spread."

"It's all of that," Laura agreed. "Shall we talk about acreage for a while?"

Whit made an effort. He turned in his saddle and gestured toward a range of mountains running north at his rear. "Do those mountains have any particular name?"

The girl smiled. "You're showing some improvement, I think. Yes, they're a continuation of the Encontrón Range. You see, the Encontróns run along the Mexican border for miles, then turn sharply north. From here they're like an inverted L. The Mexican boundary and the southern boundary of the 2JD are the same. The line runs along the top of the mountains. The ranch holdings comprise all that land lying in the pocket formed by the angle of the L."

"Phew!" Whit whistled. "That is a spread!"

"Best grazing land in these parts. There're a few other outfits to the north that do tolerable well, though. The ranches to the east are small, and then south of Palomas the land just peters out to desert and badlands—cactus, heat, sand, alkali, and rattlers."

"I noticed that when I rode toward Palomas that first day I hit this country—" Whit stopped short, thinking of the discovery of John Dawson's body and knowing the girl was thinking the same thing.

Silence again fell between the two riders, broken only by the soft thud-thud of the ponies' hoofs as they stepped through the sandy soil of the trail. Finally the girl said, "Well, shall we talk about the weather now?"

Again that grin touched Whit's lips. "The sun's mighty bright. There doesn't seem to be a cloud in the sky. Warmish, but not too warm."

"Look, Whit," Laura said, "we've got to do better than this. You don't have to be so stiff and standoffish. Dad is dead. We both know it. There's nothing much can be done about it now. I'm not forgetting anything. My memories of Dad are pretty precious. But if you think I've concluded to live a life of silence and grieving, you're all wrong. Did you ever know a woman who didn't want to talk?"

Whit considered. "Nope, I can't say I have—" He broke off in some consternation.

Laura laughed. "Well, let's hope that breaks the ice. Did Uncle Jeff tell you you were to act as a bodyguard to me?"

Whit nodded. "Yes, whenever you wanted to ride."

"I thought so! Darn him. He wouldn't admit it to me. Just said he wanted me to go riding with you so we'd get acquainted. What's he afraid will happen?"

"I'm not sure," Whit said. He felt the color rising in his cheeks. "And now I've given him away. Maybe I should have stayed silent."

"Pshaw! From all Uncle Jeff tells me, you've been staying mighty silent and to yourself for a number of years now . . . Yes, he told me your story. Now there's no use of you acting bothered about that. I don't care who you were or what you were before you came here. Killer! That's the most ridiculous thing I've ever heard. And this silly business about having killer blood in your veins! You got half of your blood from your mother, you know. I doubt there was any killer strain there."

"There wasn't," Whit said. "You know, a friend of mine, Bob Tinsley, once said something just like that."

"Friend. I thought you claimed you didn't have any friends."

"He died about a year back. That's what I heard, anyway." Whit remained silent a moment, then went on: "There's a tradition that all the Gallatin men—"

"I know," the girl interrupted. "Uncle Jeff told me all about that. You've gone three years without killing anyone. Bang! There goes your tradition."

"There were two men in Toyah Wells—" Whit commenced weakly.

"You were forced to kill them, Whit, in self-defense. Maybe you'll kill again. I don't know. But that's no sign you have to drag yourself through life thinking you're a killer by instinct and that you don't dare have friends. Personally, if I had your attitude toward life I think I'd take up something sprightly like grave digging."

Whit laughed. He found himself admiring the girl

more all the time. There was a sort of husky quality in her voice that he thought fascinating. He began to wonder if there were more girls in the world like Laura Dawson. He doubted that, though. They talked on other subjects, and he was surprised how often the girl inclined toward a man's viewpoint in certain things.

Laura gestured toward the coiled whip that generally was carried in Whit's hand but which now he had hung over his saddle horn. "I wish you'd teach me to use that long quirt of yours sometime."

He looked at her, astonished. "Why?"

"I think it might be fun—not snapping it at people, but at inanimate objects. I can ride. I carry a gun which I know how to use. I like to learn new things."

Whit colored with pleasure. "I'd sure enjoy teaching you when we can find the time."

The talk turned on various subjects. Almost before he realized it the horses were clattering across the plank bridge over Palomas River and then pushing on into town. It wasn't yet ten o'clock. There were a number of pedestrians on the street. The usual cow ponies and wagons were scattered along at hitch racks. Laura spoke to two or three acquaintances. Near the center of town she led the way up a dusty side street, then turned right until they came to a small white cottage surrounded by a picket fence and shaded by a huge cottonwood tree.

"This is Dr. Breen's house," Laura said. "It's his wife I'm going to visit. She was my mother's best friend before Mother died. I won't ask you to come in. The doctor is likely out, and I'd hate to see you caught"—her blue eyes twinkled beneath the long lashes—"between two women. I believe we mentioned something about women liking to talk."

Whit laughed and left her dismounting from her pony.

After promising to return for the girl at four o'clock, he turned his mount back toward the main thoroughfare.

A few minutes later he was entering the Shamrock Saloon. Only a pair of customers stood at the bar near the front end. Barry Flynn had just finished serving them, and now he came down the long counter to learn Whit's needs.

"The mornin's mornin' to you, Whit," he greeted. "And how go things with you this day?"

"Never better"—Whit smiled—"unless you could improve matters with a bottle of beer."

"I can be doing exactly that, my bucko." The beer and a glass were placed on the bar beside the burlap sack Whit had brought in from his horse. "And what would that be?" Flynn asked, pointing one finger toward the sack.

"Calgary Rhodes's gear. He never did come out to the 2JD to pick it up. Jeff Dawson asked me to bring it in. He asked that you tell Rhodes it's here."

"I'll be glad to oblige Mr. Dawson—though I can't be sayin' as much for the Rhodes spalpeen."

Whit sipped his beer. "Rhodes is still around town, I suppose."

"He's in and out—him and them two Tiernans. It's a fine kettle of fish them three is. I'd be trustin' of them no farther than I could throw a brick house."

"What do the Tiernans do for a living?"

"If I was to guess, I'd say they cut honest men's throats to steal the money off them. But I couldn't say for true. They holed up in a shack to the east of town. Rhodes has took to bunkin' in with 'em." Whit asked another question. Flynn shook his head. "No, I couldn't be tellin' you where they come from. They settled on Palomas nearly a year since, but it's no work I ever heard of them doin'." Somewhat irritably he jerked the sack of Rhodes's. belongings from the bar and set it someplace beneath. "The sooner he is takin' his junk away, the better I'll be pleased. And if he'd be after takin' his ownself clean out of this town I wouldn't lose any sleep. Him and a few more that's commencin' to look up to Mr. Rhodes like he was a leader."

Whit studied the beer in his glass. Finally he asked, "Barry, what enemies did John Dawson have hereabouts?"

"Enemies, is it?" Flynn shook his head. "There's none that I know of. Everyone liked John. He was a gentleman."

"But someone hated him enough to kill him."

"That is possible. Or mayhap John Dawson was mistaken for another man. It's happened before, such accidents."

Whit nodded, unconvinced. They had been holding their voices low so as not to carry to the customers at the other end of the bar. "I was just wondering," Whit said at last. "I'd got to thinking that maybe you'd heard of, or remembered, someone who had quarreled with John Dawson before he was murdered."

"Every witness at the coroner's inquest was asked practically that same question," Flynn reminded. "And nothin' came of it—"

"Except," Whit said, "it was brought out that John Dawson had once given Calgary Rhodes a dressing down for abusing a horse."

"And that over five months back," Flynn pointed out. "Are you after thinkin' Rhodes would have waited this long had he been holdin' a grudge?"

"I don't know," Whit said slowly, and again, "I just don't know. I'd like to know where Rhodes was the night before Dawson was killed."

"And that's somethin' else you heard at the inquest, was you listenin'. Rhodes was at the Tiernans' shack, and the three of 'em drunk as lords."

"And who swore to that statement?" Whit asked.

"Rhodes—and both Tiernans—Bat and Tack, both. They alibied each other."

"And who else swore to it?" Whit persisted.

"Who else could be swearin' to it?" Flynn demanded. "There was no one else there to—" He paused suddenly.

"That's what I mean," Whit said.

Flynn looked steadily at Whit. "Would you be doubtin' their sworn statements?"

"I'd feel like a fool if I didn't."

"I think, b'Gawd, you're correct. But what have you to go on?"

"Not a solitary, blessed thing," Whit admitted. "I've just got a hunch in that direction."

"Perhaps it's because you have no likin' for Calgary Rhodes."

"That could be," Whit conceded.

"Perhaps you should be takin' of your suspicions to Dan Brandon."

Whit shook his head. "I'd have to produce some sort of proof, and that I haven't got, Barry. The sheriff might think I was just trying to throw him off the track. You see, I'm the only one who hasn't an alibi for the time at which Dawson was killed. I suggested to Brandon that he could check up on my previous night's activities at Nuevo Cesto—"

"I remember." Flynn nodded. "And Brandon said you could purchase alibis or anythin' else in that town, and that he could put no faith in anythin' that come out of Nuevo Cesto. I think he was wrong."

"And everybody else who ever had anything to do with John Dawson had an alibi for that night." Whit frowned. "What's the sheriff been doing, have you any idea?"

"Nothing you could put your finger on, as I see it. He walks the town and asks questions. And learns nothin'. And his temper isn't improvin' with such work—"

Flynn broke off and glanced toward the entrance. Whit followed his glance and saw the batwing doors swinging slightly. "Somebody must have started to come in and then changed his mind," Whit commented.

Flynn nodded. "In the bit of a glance I had, it looked like Mr. Lowendirk, though I'd not be sayin' with certainty."

Whit spilled the remainder of the beer from the bottle into his glass, finished it off, and started to roll a brown cigarette. He scratched a match, fanned his lungs deeply with the smoke, then asked, "Barry, what do you know of Lowendirk?"

"A little." A frown had come over the Irishman's face. "He's a wealthy man from Denver, come to Palomas for his health. He rides a great deal—"

"Where?"

"That I'd not be knowin'."

"Where does he live?"

"He rented a house south of here. It's surrounded with paloverde trees, and there's a corral at the back to keep his three horses."

"How far south?"

"Just outside of town."

"He lives there alone?"

"So far as I could be tellin'."

"A wealthy man," Whit speculated, "usually brings along a servant to cook and so on."

“I’ve seen or heard nothin’ of any servants. Twice now I have seen Mr. Lowendirk eatin’ of his dinner at the hotel.”

“Does he have any friends in town?”

“That, too, I couldn’t be sayin’. I’ve heard of none. From what I hear, he keeps to himself. Standoffish, as the sayin’ goes.”

A couple of cow hands from the Z-Bar-Y outfit strode in, nodded to Whit, and took up positions midway of the bar. Flynn went to serve them and within a few minutes left them to their drinks and returned to Whit. Whit said, “You haven’t told it all, Barry. You sort of frowned when I mentioned Lowendirk’s name. What are you holding back?”

“I was intendin’ to get to it; there was no holdin’ back. But it’s a queer business that I couldn’t be puttin’ too much stock in. It happened in this wise: Yesterday afternoon Calgary Rhodes and Bat Tiernan was in here, drinkin’ my stock and forgettin’ to pay until I pressed ’em for the money—they was that far along, they was, with their talk gettin’ maudlin and their tongues thick with the moss that too much alcohol lays on a man’s innards—”

“In short,” Whit broke in, “they were getting soused.”

“That’s the word exactly. And sudden, between drinks, they started questionin’ me about Mr. Lowendirk and askin’ what I knew of him. And I told ’em no more and no less than I’ve told you. And with that Bat Tiernan makes a silly gigglin’ sound and announces he knows a detective—a range dick, he called him—when he sees one—”

“A detective—Lowendirk?” Whit asked, eyes narrowing.

“I’m tellin’ it as I got it.”

"What else was said?"

"Bat Tiernan no sooner spills what he says than Rhodes turns ugly and tells Tiernan not to talk so much. I questioned Rhodes some, and he finally admits that he had heard rumors that Lowendirk was a range detective, but he won't say where he heard the rumors. He threw out some hints that led me to suppose someone in town—mebbe one of Rhodes's loafin' followers—had recognized Lowendirk from seein' him some other place. Tiernan acted inclined to talk some more, but Rhodes got the subject twisted to somethin' else."

Whit frowned. "But what would a range dick be doing here? Have you heard of any of the outfits losing stock to thieves, Barry?"

Flynn shook his head. "There's not been much rustlin'. Dan Brandon keeps cow thievin' down pretty well. Of course there might be somethin' in that line and me never hear a word of it."

"I was talking to Jeff Dawson just a few days ago on the subject," Whit said, "and he told me the 2JD had no troubles beyond the natural losses that come to every herd."

"Maybe it's not cow thieves that brings Mr. Lowendirk here," Flynn speculated.

Whit nodded. "He might be following on the trail of one of Rhodes's buddies. To tell the truth, I sort of sensed something odd about Lowendirk the first day I met him—"

"Shhh!" Flynn said. "There's himself comin' in now."

Whit turned his head and saw Lowendirk just pushing through the swinging doors of the entrance.

SKILL DEMONSTRATED

WITHOUT BEING ASKED, Barry Flynn set another bottle of beer before Whit and then turned to Lowendirk, who had just taken up a position at the bar a few feet away. Lowendirk nodded to Whit and ordered a shot of whisky. Flynn pushed a whisky glass and a bottle of Old Crow bourbon before Lowendirk. The man poured a neat three fingers of liquor, took a sip, and set down the glass. Flynn recorked the bottle and replaced it on the shelf behind him along with a number of other bottles of various brands. Lowendirk took another drink of his whisky and, turning, asked after Whit's health. Whit thanked him and said he was feeling fine and poured some beer into his own glass.

Lowendirk said after a few minutes motioning to the whip curled in Whit's left hand, "I understand you're quite clever with that long black thing."

Whit smiled and said continual practice brought such cleverness as he possessed. He added, "Where've you been hearing about my whip?"

Lowendirk smiled, his dark eyes carrying a look of amusement. "A great many people have told me about it here in Palomas. I hear you put the quietus on that Rhodes fellow when he was about to pull his gun on you."

Whit nodded noncommittally. "That was probably better than getting into a gun fight."

"Certainly it was—for Rhodes," Lowendirk said. "However, from what I've heard of you, Gallatin, you're no stranger to gun fighting."

"You shouldn't," Whit advised coldly, "believe everything you hear."

Instantly Lowendirk was contrite. "I'm very sorry, Gallatin. I shouldn't have mentioned the matter. It was just—well—" He paused, as though embarrassed. "I've sort of felt under obligation to you. That likely led me into a friendly feeling—I'm not making myself clear, am I?"

"Does it matter?" Whit asked in even tones.

"It matters a great deal to me," Lowendirk said earnestly. "I've wanted to be friends with you. You—you see, the first time I saw Calgary Rhodes I took a dislike to him. He's blustering, obnoxious; he's too ready to threaten people with guns. When you took him down a peg I felt as though you'd done me a personal favor. It was something he deserved. I think every honest man in Palomas feels the way I do." He looked anxiously at Whit. "Am I clearing this up a bit, Gallatin?"

Whit smiled. "You're making a greater fuss about the matter than it deserves, Lowendirk. Let's forget it."

"Gladly. I was commencing to feel as though I'd put my foot into something that didn't concern me. It's good of you to overlook my clumsiness." He took another sip from his glass, replaced it on the bar, and continued: "Regardless of what's been said, I'm still curious about your whip. I'd give a great deal to witness a demonstration of your skill."

Whit's eyes twinkled. "Perhaps you'd like to take part in a demonstration. You could enact the part Rhodes had three weeks back and start to draw on me."

Lowendirk's dark eyes widened. "You—you mean challenge *you*? Heaven forbid!" He glanced at the weapon holstered at his right hip. "Firearms are completely out of my line. I don't know why I wear this six-shooter, only everybody out here seems to wear a gun. I like to conform. I've only fired it twice, and then at a target. No, I know very little about guns."

"I guess we'll have to pass up the demonstration, then"—Whit laughed—"so long as you refuse to draw on me."

"I guess we will," the man replied reluctantly.

Other customers had entered the bar—townspeople and a few punchers from various ranches. Barry Flynn's forehead was dotted with beads of perspiration as he strove to catch up with the requests from his patrons.

Whit and Lowendirk stood side by side, occupied with their drinks. Finally Lowendirk tossed off the remainder of his whisky. He said, "Could I buy you a drink?"

Whit refused with thanks. "Some other time, perhaps. Right now I've still got better than a half bottle of beer."

"Well, I can use another drink anyway." Lowendirk glanced down to the far end of the bar. "Flynn, I say, Flynn! How about a little service?"

There was a great deal of conversation in the Shamrock, and the bartender failed to hear Lowendirk's call. Lowendirk looked annoyed and again started to raise his voice.

Whit checked him. "Wait a minute. Maybe I can get what you want. What brand are you drinking?"

"Old Crow. But there's no need of you going around the bar—"

"I don't intend to." Whit's gray eyes twinkled. "Maybe Barry will flay me alive for this; but you've been asking for a demonstration—"

Without finishing his remarks Whit ran his gaze along the shelves of bottles until it fell on the Old Crow. Quickly he measured off the distance and then moved back, shaking out his long whip as he moved. Some of the other customers noticed him and wondered what he intended to do. Whit moved back two more paces, paused an instant . . .

His left arm, drawing the whip behind it, came slowly back over his shoulder, then flashed forward and instantly back again in one smooth, eye-defying motion. The lash of the whip sang through the air as it darted straight for the Old Crow bottle, wrapped itself around the neck, tightened, and then jerked the bottle off the shelf from between its companion containers. Like some live thing the bottle came flying through the air to land in Whit's waiting right hand. A deft flick of his left wrist untangled the lash and, laughing, he set the bottle on the bar before Lowendirk. "Now it's up to you to draw the cork and pour—" he commenced.

Barry Flynn had looked around just in time to see his whisky go hurtling through space. His mouth gaped open in astonishment before he found his voice. "Holy Mother of Gawd!" He came hurrying along the bar. Other men who had witnessed the feat set up a cheer.

Lowendirk's dark eyes widened. "Clever—very, very clever," he murmured. "I've never seen anything so adroit, Gallatin."

Barry Flynn eyed Whit with some exasperation. "It's the long arm you have, my boy, to be reachin' across my bar in such fashion and jerkin' of bottles off my shelf. But suppose you had missed and jangled my bottles this way and that and banged them against my mirror? What then?"

"In that case, Barry, I'd have been in your debt for some broken and spilled stock." Whit laughed.

The exasperation died from Flynn's eyes. He turned to the others. "Never in all my days have I seen the like. That whip of his was like a trained snake, the way it reached across and brought back my bottle."

Cries of "Do it again!" filled the saloon. Whit shook his head. "I'd probably miss the next time"—he grinned—"which same would send me into bankruptcy."

Lowendirk had poured himself a drink and lighted a cigar. "A very impressive performance," he commented. "It's too bad everyone here couldn't see what you were doing. You're sure you don't care to do it again?" Various other customers amended Lowendirk's request.

Whit shook his head, "Let me try something else next time."

"Sure, go ahead!"

"Give us a show, Gallatin!"

"What other tricks do you know?"

These and other cries filled the barroom. More customers were drawn in from the street by the noise emanating from the entrance. The saloon was fast filling up.

Flynn shook his head. "It's the fool I am, criticizin' you for your whip business, Whit. It's drawin' in trade you are. Sure and I'm not mindin' if you lift all the bottles from my shelves." He smiled broadly. "Now if your whip could be drawin' of the corks as well, I'd hire it on for a bartender."

Lowendirk put in, "Gallatin, you mentioned something about trying something else. What did you have in mind?"

Whit said, "How good is your nerve?"

Lowendirk hesitated. "Do you figure to make me part of your act?" Whit nodded. Lowendirk looked reluctant. Someone in the back of the crowd laughed contemptuously. Abruptly Lowendirk said, "I think my nerve is good enough. What are you going to do?"

Whit didn't explain but asked the crowd to clear a space the length of the barroom. Then he asked Lowendirk to take up a stand at the far end. Lowendirk complied. Whit said, "Stand sidewise, please, and hold very still."

Lowendirk turned until his profile stood clearly out against the wall. Somewhat nervously he asked, "I don't know what you intend, but will my cigar interfere in any way?" He puffed jerkily on the cigar while he talked, as if something in the smoke bolstered up his courage.

"Don't worry about the cigar." Whit smiled. "You won't be smoking very long."

He took two quick backward steps, raising his left arm as he moved. There came a sharp cracking sound like the report of a rifle. Almost faster than the eyes of the spectators could watch it, the wire-woven lash hissed through the air and came back once more to Whit's hand.

Lowendirk looked around in some bewilderment. "That was pretty close for comfort," he said. "I could feel the wind of the lash mighty close to my nose." He drew on his cigar, then paused and removed it from his lips. Suddenly it occurred to him what Whit had done. "By God," he exclaimed, "you cut the fire right off my cigar without jerking it from my mouth! What deft accuracy!" He smiled. "And I stood there expecting you were about to snake my hat off or something of the sort."

Exclamations of admiration filled the saloon. Men begged Whit to give further demonstrations of his skill. For the next half-hour Whit was kept busy. Now there was no lack of assistants to aid him in his stunts. Seeing Lowendirk come through unscathed gave the others courage. Whit instructed one man to rush on him, fist upraised, as though in attack. In an instant Whit's long lash had tightened about the man's ankles, spilling him to the floor. He used the whip to show how playing cards could be picked from the band of a man's sombrero, then went further and, with one of the assistants holding up various cards, used the vicious wire-woven lash to rip the pips from the pasteboards. Finally, laughing, wiping perspiration from his forehead, Whit called a halt while the crowd continued to clamor for more.

"There's a limit to everything." Whit grinned. "You hombres don't realize this is work." Reluctantly they allowed him to quit and pressed drinks on him, which he refused.

Lowendirk said, "I'm sure everyone here has enjoyed your whip as much as I have, Gallatin." He added meaningly, "You once had a nickname which I'd suggest be discarded. Instead—well, your friends call you Whit, but I think you should be called *Whip* Gallatin."

A new voice cut in: "That might make a better name."

Whit glanced up and saw Calgary Rhodes and the two Tiernan brothers among the crowd. "What you hinting at, Rhodes?" Whit asked, quiet-voiced.

"Just what I said," Rhodes sneered. "You've proved that you're entitled to the name Whip, but I still can't see where you ever got a right to use that nickname Mr. Lowendirk said should be discarded. I never yet heard of a man being killed with a whip."

"It can be done," Whit said, holding a firm check on his temper. "Oh, I can assure you it's possible, Rhodes. Would you like me to prove it to you?"

Some of the color faded from Rhodes's swarthy features. He backed away a step. "I'll take your word for it," he said hastily. Laughter and jeering remarks filled the saloon. Rhodes's face grew red now. "What I meant," he continued, "was that your whip work is just a bag of tricks. When it comes right down to it, there's nothing like a six-shooter if a man finds himself in a really tight spot. And it's not every man who knows how to handle a six-shooter. A lot of folks get by on bluff."

Whit smiled thinly. "You should know, Rhodes," he said softly. "You should know." He hesitated a moment, then said, "You wouldn't want to put it to the test, would you?"

Before Rhodes could reply Tack Tiernan cut in, "No use of you two hombres gettin' proddy. Calgary don't want no trouble. It's just that we understand you're right good with a gun. Well, Calgary ain't no slouch, neither, when it comes to throwin' lead—I mean shootin' at some sort of target, y'understand?"

"I understand," Whit said evenly. "But what's all this leading to, Tiernan?"

Rhodes again took up the conversation. "It's like this: I've got a stunt I do with my gun that Tack and Bat think is right good, and we got to wonderin' if you could do it."

"I wouldn't know," Whit replied quietly, "until I'd seen your trick."

"I'll show you." Rhodes turned to the bar. "Barry, let me have some poker chips."

The Irishman spilled a handful of chips out on the bar with the warning, "If you're goin' to do any shootin', I'll not be havin' it in here. You can be puttin' on your act out in back of the Shamrock, where you'll find plenty of open air."

Rhodes grabbed the chips and pushed through the

rear door of the saloon, followed by the Tiernan brothers and Whit Gallatin. Drake Lowendirk was among the crowd that streamed after them. At one side of the rear doorway a stack of empty beer cases was supported by the building wall; on the other side grew a tall clump of prickly-pear cactus. Some short distance off a number of cottonwood trees shaded a cluster of adobe houses. The crowd collected at the back of the saloon, eyes on Calgary Rhodes.

Rhodes said to Bat Tiernan, handing him the handful of red, white, and blue poker chips, "Here, I'll keep one of these. You hold the rest." He turned to the others, grinning confidently as he moved away from them. "Now you hombres watch close and you'll see something."

In his left hand he held a red poker chip; his right rested on his gun butt. Suddenly he tossed the poker chip high in the air. His gun flashed out, roared. The chip continued to ascend. The first shot had missed. The chip reached the top of its flight and started to drop. Again Rhodes fired. The chip instantly shattered, the pieces flying in all directions. The crowd applauded.

Rhodes turned with a smirk. "I should have got it with my first shot, but my hand was sort of stiff. Hurt it one time and—"

The remainder of his words was lost in laughter as the collected men advised him not to make excuses. Bat Tiernan exclaimed, "Hell's bells! Calgary don't have to make excuses for a shot like that. I'd like to see Gallatin do as well." The men instantly switched their attention to Whit.

Whit smiled lazily. "Well, I don't say I could do exactly like Rhodes did—"

"Damn right you can't," Bat Tiernan cut in.

"—but anyway I can give it a try," Whit finished, ignoring the interruption. He strode over to Bat Tiernan. "Let me have some of those chips."

Lowendirk called out, "Gallatin, would you like me to hold your whip for you?"

Whit shook his head. "I can make out, thanks." He turned back to Tiernan and selected five poker chips from the man's hand, picking all white ones.

"Hey," Tiernan objected, "you ain't supposed to have but one chip to work on."

Rhodes was quick to protest, "*I* only had one. With luck, any fool can throw a handful and have a chance of pluggin' one."

Whit laughed softly. "Making it tough for me, eh, Rhodes?" He stood a moment as though in doubt, juggling the five chips in his right hand, the long whip still curled in his left. Finally, "Well, I can give it a try, anyway," he announced.

Abruptly he tossed the five white chips into the air. Sunlight glinted on their turning surfaces. Then his right hand streaked down, came up holding his six-shooter, muzzle lifted toward the spinning chips. Five detonations blended almost into a single flaming report as the five chips dissolved, as though by magic, into something that resembled a miniature snowstorm and the shattered bits went flying off through the drifting black powder smoke. Well before the last piece had fallen to earth Whit had holstered his gun.

For a moment no one spoke. The echoes of the shots died into silence. Then Whit chuckled. "Dang it, I've never been able to do that trick with less than five ca'tridges—"

A wave of laughter went up, followed by cheers and yells. "That's shootin'!" a man exclaimed. "Calgary,

Gallatin made your stunt look like a kid's trick."

Lowendirk moved quickly to Whit's side and drew his own six-shooter. "Would you care to examine my gun, Gallatin?" he asked, a meaning look in his eyes as he pressed the weapon into Whit's grasp.

Whit said "Thanks" and glanced toward Calgary Rhodes.

Rhodes was just holstering his gun, his face clouded up like a thunderstorm. The Tiernan brothers wore an air of dejection. Rhodes said grudgingly, "That was good shootin', Gallatin. But I'm not admittin' you could do it a second time. Luck enters into such tricks, and shootin' at a target and shootin' at a man are two different things. As you may learn someday."

"Do you figure to be on hand to teach me?" Whit asked quietly.

Rhodes said, "Oh hell," and forced a harsh laugh. "All right, I'll admit I was licked. That bein' the case, the drinks are on me. Everybody up to the bar."

The crowd turned and pushed in at the rear entrance. Whit spun the cylinder of Lowendirk's gun and handed it back. "Much obliged" he said. "That's a nice Colt gun, Lowendirk." He drew out his own weapon and commenced to reload.

"I hope I didn't presume," Lowendirk said. "It was just that you had emptied your gun and Rhodes hadn't. I thought you'd want to be armed if Rhodes tried anything."

"I knew what you had in mind." Whit nodded and said "Thanks" again. "With all that crowd around, I didn't figure he'd start anything, though."

"You can't always tell, can you?"

"No, you can't always tell," Whit agreed.

Abruptly Lowendirk changed the subject. "Have they

found any clues yet to the Dawson murder?" he asked.

Whit looked steadily at the man for a moment. "If so, Sheriff Brandon hasn't announced it."

"You personally know of none, eh?" Lowendirk asked.

"What gives you the idea I would?"

Lowendirk hesitated. "I can't say with any certainty. I just had an idea that Jeff Dawson might have hired you to run down the murderer of his brother."

Whit smiled. "For a businessman just here for his health, you seem to be taking quite an interest in the Dawson affairs."

"Under some circumstances that could be natural."

"Look here, Lowendirk, what do you know of John Dawson's death?"

"As to who killed him? Nothing."

"Any idea as to why he was killed?"

"I'm not prepared to say," Lowendirk said bluntly.

"You do know something about the business, then?" Whit persisted.

Lowendirk glanced toward the open rear door of the saloon. From within came the clinking of bottles against glasses and the buzz of voices. "I think we'd better go back into the saloon. Somebody might think it queer if I remained out here talking with you."

"Lowendirk, you've said too little or too much. Why not make yourself clear?"

"I don't think this is the time or place for it, Gallatin. Do you know where I live?" Whit said he could find the place Lowendirk continued, "Why not ride out and see me to night?"

"Why not now?"

"I'd just as soon no one knew you were visiting me."

Whit noddcd. "Tonight, then."

Lowendirk gave directions for locating his house, and the two men returned to the saloon, where they found Sheriff Dan Brandon had just arrived to inquire the reason for the shooting he had heard. Brandon heaved a sigh of relief when he learned Rhodes and Whit had only been shooting at poker chips. He scowled at the two men. "It wouldn't bother me any if you two left Palomas," he observed darkly.

"Maybe it can be arranged"—Whit smiled—"for one of us to leave. That satisfy you, Sheriff?"

Calgary Rhodes shot a look of hate toward Whit but didn't say anything. A minute later Whit said something about it being well past his dinnertime and left the saloon.

TWO-GUN MAN

JEFF DAWSON MET LAURA AND WHIT when they rode into the corrals. "You two get acquainted?" he asked.

Laura laughed, stepping down from the saddle. "We did better coming back than going in," she said. "Whit's kept to himself so long that I think it's going to take a while for him to get accustomed to talking to strangers."

Whit grinned. "I can't say I figure you as a stranger, Miss Laura. Not any more," he said, dismounting.

"I don't imagine Palomas will look on you as a stranger, either," Laura put in.

Jeff Dawson said, "How come?"

Laura supplied the information. "Dr. Breen came home just before I left. He gave me quite an account of Whit's doings. It seems Whit put on a whip and shooting demonstration for the benefit of the Shamrock Saloon. Though when we were coming home Whit didn't mention the matter until I'd pumped it out of him. He's still pretty tight-mouthed, Uncle Jeff."

"Whip and shootin' demonstration?" Jeff Dawson looked blank.

"Nothing that amounts to much," Whit said. "I'll tell you about it later. Miss Laura, I'll unsaddle for you if you want to go on to the house."

"Thanks, Whit. I'd like to get cleaned up and get supper started."

Jeff Dawson turned to the girl. "I got the table all laid, Laura. 'Bout all you have to do is make coffee. I had Skillet bring some fodder from his kitchen. Figured you might be late gettin' back. He made us a pie too. You run along. I'll come about the time you're ready to set down to table."

Whit and Dawson unsaddled the two ponies and turned them into the corral, Whit meanwhile talking about the events of the day. The two men leaned against the pole corral, smoking. Whit concluded his story. Jeff Dawson swore. "I'm sure glad you could give that Calgary Rhodes his comeuppance. Dang decent of Lowendirk to slip his gun into your hand when your gun was emptied. Of course, him bein' a stranger hereabouts, he likely didn't realize Rhodes wouldn't have dared start anythin' with so many people around. Still, we can give Lowendirk credit for good intentions."

Whit said, "There's a rumor in Palomas to the effect that Lowendirk is a detective. I don't know how true—"

"Detective! Who in time would be bringin' a detective in here?"

"I've no idea. Perhaps you have." Dawson said it was a puzzle to him, and Whit continued, "I understand there's been no particularly bad cow thieving going on."

Dawson shook his head. "We've never been bothered

much with rustlers in this country—no more than what everybody has in any section. There's always some rustlin', of course, no matter where beef animals are raised."

Whit frowned. "I've been sort of putting two and two together. Lowendirk—who maybe is a range dick—comes here. Some months afterward your brother gets killed. Is there any connection?"

"You mean Lowendirk killed him?"

"I didn't say that at all. What I'm wondering, could your brother have brought Lowendirk here?"

"Why should he?"

Whit said, "I'm asking you. Did he have any trouble? Did he fear some enemy?"

"I knew of no trouble—nor enemy. I can't think of one solitary thing that bothered John. Leastwise, he never gave me any indication he was worried about anythin'. Only thing I knew to fret him a-tall was the rumors of a revolution buildin' up across the border. He was always a mite leary some Mexes might come swarmin' through Torchido Pass and raise hell hereabouts. But even that didn't give him much concern."

"I shouldn't think there'd be much to bother you in that direction. Torchido Pass is partly on 2JD holdings, I understand. It's narrow. Why not just block it up?"

"It may be narrow, but still and all, that'd be quite a job."

"I know you couldn't block it completely, but a few charges of dynamite placed correctly could sure tumble a heap of rock down and make it tough for horses to get through fast. Or you could hire some men with guns to stand guard. A handful of men could stand off quite a number of riders, with proper barricades—"

"I know," Dawson cut in. "John and I considered it one time but decided against it. It would look sort of unfriendly toward the Mexican Government, for one thing. Another, there's a lot of decent Mexes come through that pass from Nuevo Cesto to buy supplies from the merchants in Palomas. The merchants would lose trade if we blocked off Torchido. Somethin' else—a heap of folks from this side of the line find the pass convenient for gettin' through to Mexico. It's nearly one hundred miles to the east—even farther to the west—before an easy way through the mountains can be found. Nope, Torchido Pass is a convenience for people; it would be mighty inconsiderate to close it off. Fact is, like I say, we talked about it one time, and a heap of folks around Palomas didn't take it kindly. So we just dropped the idea."

"I reckon it doesn't matter much anyway," Whit said.

"It ain't vital, I figure." Dawson came back to Lowendirk. "If he is a detective, what do you reckon he's doin' here?"

"Maybe I'll find out tonight. He asked me to come and see him."

"You don't say! Why?"

"I haven't the least idea. But I figured it couldn't hurt anything to see what he had to offer. I'll tell you more after I've talked to him."

Dawson frowned. "I'm not sure I like the idea, Whit. Supposin' he did have somethin' to do with John's death? For all we know, he might be schemin' to do you some harm. I reckon I'd best go along with you."

Whit shook his head. "If what you say was so, Lowendirk would know that I'd tell you where I was headed when I left here. He'd realize that you'd be on his back if I showed up dead."

“I reckon you’re right,” Dawson conceded. “But if you ain’t back here within a reasonable time tonight I’ll gather the boys and we’ll ride in to learn why. For all we know, Lowendirk might have some sort of tie-up with Calgary Rhodes.”

Whit shrugged his shoulders. “Anything’s possible, of course. Speaking of Rhodes—just as Laura and I were leaving town we spied Rhodes and the two Tiernan brothers riding in the opposite direction. They had bedrolls on their saddles—”

“You mean they’re leavin’ town for good?”

“I couldn’t say. Certainly it looked as though they expected to be away for some time.”

“I hope so,” Dawson said fervently. “Let’s hope that Rhodes has figured that Palomas ain’t big enough to hold you and him both and has decided to look for other huntin’ grounds—”

He broke off as Laura’s voice sounded from the rear door of the ranch house. “Be right with you, girl,” Dawson called back. He added an explanation to Whit: “Me, I’d sooner eat with the boys, but John and Laura and I always et at the house. I reckon it would be sort of lonesome for her if I let her set alone now.”

Whit nodded. “Probably so. Well, I’ll see you later.” He left Dawson starting for the house, while he turned his steps in the direction of the bunkhouse. Passing through the bunkhouse to the adjoining mess house, Whit found the 2JD crew had already started supper.

Skillet Potter stuck a scowling countenance through the door of his kitchen as he heard Whit greeting the other men. “ ’Bout time you learned, Whit,” Skillet growled, “that I like my diners to be on time.”

Whit said insultingly, though his eyes twinkled, “On time for what, Fat? The sort of food you spread always makes me approach with reluctance. I can just barely drag myself to the table."

The other hands broke into laughter. "Whit certainly called the turn." Laidlaw grinned. "I'd have hired a new cook long ago, only Skillet has sort of been pensioned off on this job, and there don't seem no way to get rid of his carcass."

Whit found a place on one of two benches that flanked the long table on either side. Before him were spread platters of steaming food, steaks, potatoes, biscuits, stewed tomatoes. Coffee cups were filled from a huge pot at one end of the table.

Whit forked some food onto his plate. "Maybe Skillet is too fat to move far," he said solemnly. "Might be Jeff could bring a derrick out here sometime and sort of nudge him off the place."

"I dunno," Button-Eyes Cobb said seriously. "After all the time Skillet has weighted down this section, any sudden move might upset the center of gravity and start landslides or somethin'."

Skillet Potter waddled in from the kitchen and slammed another steaming platter onto the table. "Trouble with you cow nurses," he said complacently, "is you don't recognize good food when you eat it. Show me another cook on this range that serves the variety you hombres get."

"Show you?" Bob Corbett said sarcastically. "If we could even see another cook Whitey would have hired him."

"Variety?" Shorty Farran snapped. "What variety? I could stand some variety in the breakfast you serve—every mornin' the same. Beans, biscuits, sow bosom, and some muddy stuff called coffee. Look, Skillet, why can't we have some ham and aigs sometimes?"

"Ham and aigs!" the cook said indignantly. "You hombres talk like you was millionaires. You'll be askin' next for ginny hens and crepes suzy-ettes!"

"If anybody gets crepe around here, it'll be hangin' on a certain fat cook." Red Maguire chuckled.

"What's crepe—whatever you call 'em?" Dutch Vander inquired.

"How would Skillet know?" Shorty Farran said insultingly. "He's just been pickin' names at random from some cookbook."

"I doubt that," Corbett sneered. "I'm bettin' aces to tens that Skillet ain't never been near a cookbook."

"The hell I ain't," the fat cook protested. "There's a lot of fancy dishes I could give folks what would appreciate 'em. Tell me! I didn't cook ten years in a big city hotel for nothin'."

"You must've," Laidlaw insisted. "Nobody would pay you for spoilin' good food the way you do."

Dutch Vander put in, "I'm still tryin' to get Skillet to answer my question. What's them crepe things? I think he's just bluffin' and don't know himself."

"I do too," Skillet said, his face reddening. "They're—they're sort of like a pancake with liquor poured on—"

"Oh, my Gawd!" Button-Eyes Cobb made gagging sounds. "Pancakes with liquor on 'em. What next will Skillet experiment with? It's a wonder to me we ain't all been poisoned."

"I never said I made 'em," Skillet said defensively. "I only explained what they was, but I never made you none."

"I can believe that," Shorty Farran put in. "Any liquor you got would never reach us."

The cook retreated before the barrage of laughter and

reappeared a minute later with another platter. "You hombres want more biscuits?"

"I could use a few," Bob Corbett said, straight-faced. "Come risin' season in Three Sisters Creek I want to go fishin'. These biscuits would make good sinkers. Leastwise, they always have."

Skillet appealed to Whit: "Don't you believe that, Whit."

"I'll say the same, Whit," Red Maguire put in. "Ain't a word of truth in it. Nobody ever fishes in Three Sisters. There's no fish in that piddlin' little trickle. But, molded down to size, Fat's biscuits would make mighty fine bullets—"

"You know why there's no fish in Three Sisters?" Cobb said. "Cause they was all poisoned. Skillet thrun a batch of his sour dough into the creek one time. At that, the fish was lucky. They died. Us poor cow hands has to continue to suffer from Skillet's cookin'."

"Not by a damn sight you don't," Skillet howled. "I'm quittin' just as soon as I've redded up the kitchen. I don't have to take no such criticism of my meals." He turned and waddled indignantly back to his kitchen.

Laidlaw chuckled. "Bout once a month Skillet threatens to quit, but he never stays mad long enough to leave—thank Gawd."

The cook returned five minutes later as though nothing had happened, bearing more coffee, a couple of pies, and various other items. Conversation slacked off, andl a partial silence descended, broken only by the sounds of eating utensils scraping against crockery. Cigarettes were rolled and lighted. One of the men rose and touched flame to the wicks of the kerosene lamps swinging overhead.

Jeff Dawson entered the mess shanty. "Maybe you

hombres will be glad to hear," he announced, "that Calgary Rhodes has pulled out of Palomas. Or maybe Whit told you about it."

Interested faces turned toward Whit. Questions were asked.

Dawson continued, "Didn't he even tell you how he out-shot Calgary today? Calgary was so plumb mortified, I reckon he just up and decided to pull stakes."

"Tell us about it, Whit," Laidlaw said.

Whit shook his head. "I think Jeff is using his imagination. Besides, I haven't time now. Jeff can tell you after I've gone."

He rose from the table and left the mess shanty for the bunkhouse. Here he secured his whip, then after a moment decided not to take it. Instead he fumbled under his bunk in the half-light shining through the bunkhouse windows and dragged out his bedroll. Unrolling it, he quickly removed his other six-shooter and cartridge belt and then strapped both weapons about his middle. He was about to leave the bunkhouse when Jeff Dawson entered. Together they walked down to the corral.

Dawson watched Whit rope out his buckskin and saddle it in silence. Finally he said, "I note you're wearin' two guns, son."

Whit nodded shortly. "They're a matched pair. They belonged to my dad. He passed 'em on to me."

"That don't explain," Dawson said, "why you should wear both of 'em when you've just packed one gun for a long spell. You're expectin' trouble." It was a statement of fact rather than a question.

"No more than I have for years. Don't ask me why I strapped on this other gun tonight. I'm not sure. Just had a hunch it might be a good idea—"

"Why?"

"I want to avoid trouble. Generally, when a hombre wears two guns, he can use 'em. That makes troublemakers shy clear of starting anything in a good many cases. Funny thing is, a lot of men who pack two guns can only shoot with the right hand and just carry one as an extra."

"Can you shoot with the left as well as with your right?"

Whit shrugged his lean shoulders. "Offhand I'd say I was a mite more accurate with the right, though I can get by with the left if necessary."

"You're really not expectin' trouble tonight?"

Whit laughed softly. "This wearing two guns is some more of my bluff. I've got a rep as a gun fighter. All right, I'll try to look as much like a gun fighter as possible, in the hope that people will leave me alone."

"What people?"

"That's something I don't know."

Reluctantly Dawson watched Whit climb into the saddle and turn his pony. "You mind what I tell you now; don't run any risks, son. And if you're not back when you should be, I aim to rush the crew into Palomas and take that town apart—and when I say town I take in all the surroundin' shacks—includin' Mr. Lowendirk's."

"That's good to know, but don't go off half cocked, Jeff. I've a hunch I can take care of myself."

He put spurs to his pony and moved out of the ranch yard.

STRAIGHT SHOOTING

THE MOON WAS RISING OVER THE EASTERN HORIZON by the time Whit reached Palomas. Instead of entering the town by the main street, he swerved slightly to the south, where scattered houses, lights gleaming from their windows, were spotted among the semi-desert plant growth. Somewhat isolated and surrounded by tall paloverde trees and mesquite, Lowendirk's house came into view. It was a squat building of adobe structure. At the back stood a corral with three horses within its bars. A lamp in one window—there were two windows, one on either side of a closed doorway, painted blue—cast a rectangle of light on the sandy soil before the house, where some previous inhabitant had struggled to raise a small geranium garden outlined with chunks of white-washed rock. Needless to say, the geraniums had long since died.

Lowendirk opened the door as Whit was dismounting. "Thought I heard you ride up," he said.

"You've got good ears," Whit complimented. "I was walking my pony, and in this sandy soil a horse's hoofs don't make much noise."

"Sometimes it pays—in my business—to have good ears." Lowendirk smiled. He closed the door as Whit entered.

Whit said, "Just what is your business?"

"We'll get to that in a few minutes. Sit down." He pushed a rocking chair in Whit's direction and settled himself near a table on which stood a bottle of whisky, glasses, and a box of cigars. Whit looked about the room. There was a cot with neatly folded blankets at one side. The floor was of bare planks. Through an open door in the back wall he had a view of a darkened kitchen. Lowendirk rose after a moment and carried the lamp from its position on the recessed window sill to a place on the table. He poured two glasses of whisky and shoved one across to Whit. Whit lifted it to his lips and had to admit it was very smooth bourbon. Lowendirk flipped back the cover of the cigar box. Whit refused with thanks and said he'd roll a cigarette. He got out Durham sack and brown papers, quickly twisted his smoke, and then rose to light it above the top of the lamp chimney. Before he sat down again he moved his chair to one side, out of line of either of the front windows. There were no windows in the side walls.

Lowendirk noticed the move and smiled. "You figuring that somebody might shoot through a window?"

Whit shook his head. "Not figuring. Just not taking chances."

"While we're on that subject," Lowendirk said, "I heard today that Calgary Rhodes and the Tiernans had left town. I'm afraid you've scared them out." He cast a glance at Whit's extra gun but didn't mention it.

Whit shrugged. "I doubt that...We were talking a minute ago about your business," he hinted.

"For popular consumption," Lowendirk said, "I'm a businessman from Denver down here for my health."

Whit smiled. "I've never had consumption—popular or otherwise. I'm still asking."

"You've heard of the Redmondton outfit?"

Whit nodded. "Detective agency."

"Let's say I was brought down here," Lowendirk replied.

"All right—let's. But who brought you down?"

"John Dawson."

"Why?"

"I'm not just certain," Lowendirk said, frowning. "There was something in Dawson's past life that he refused to explain. All he told me was that he feared a certain man, named Nick Starkey, was going to try and kill him. He didn't know where Starkey was, but he feared—had heard, in fact—that Starkey was headed for Palomas. Dawson hired me to find Starkey when he got here and spike his guns." Lowendirk drew a deep breath. "Well, I failed. Starkey apparently found Dawson first."

"And you don't know what caused the murder—why Starkey killed Dawson?"

"I've not the slightest idea. He refused to state how he had incurred Starkey's enmity. Whit, what brought you here?"

Whit looked surprised. "My horse. I'd been wandering down through Mexico and cut through Torchido Pass to reenter the States. On my way I found John Dawson's body."

"Is that all?"

"Isn't that enough?"

"I mean—were you hired to come here?"

"Who would hire me?"

"I thought perhaps John Dawson had grown impatient with my work and maybe had brought you here to act as a guard for him."

Whit shook his head. "I'm afraid you're hitting wide of the mark."

"Probably so." Lowendirk hesitated, then, "Why did John Dawson make monthly trips to Curtisville?"

"Jeff told me he went to visit a doctor—"

"Yes, I know all that. I've checked, and he did visit a

doctor there. But couldn't that just have been an excuse? Perhaps Dawson saw someone else too."

"He could've. I wouldn't know."

"He didn't meet you there and hire you to come here by way of Mexico?"

"Dang it, no," Whit said. "I've told you John Dawson never hired me. Don't you believe it?"

Lowendirk looked disappointed. "If you say so, I suppose I'll have to take your word for it. On the other hand, if John Dawson swore you to secrecy, I could respect the fact that you had given your word and—"

"Cripes, let's forget it." Whit frowned. "You say you did some checking up on Dawson in Curtisville. Did you hear anything of this Starkey hombre there?"

"Yes, I did, but I never did meet him face to face. I did learn this much: Two days after Dawson was murdered, Nick Starkey left for California. He's in San Diego now."

"How do you know this?"

Lowendirk smiled. "How does any detective learn such things? I can't tell you more without violating some confidences. That part doesn't matter anyway. What does matter is the fact that I know where Starkey is. I also know he's planning to return here eventually and make more trouble."

"What sort of trouble?"

"I can't say with certainty. He killed John Dawson. He may be planning the same fate for Jeff Dawson. Or his niece."

Whit stiffened. "How come you never took all this up with Jeff?"

"When John Dawson hired me I was sworn to secrecy. I haven't left like revealing to Jeff what I know—yet."

Whit took another sip of his whisky. His cigarette had gone out and he scratched a match. "Why are you telling me all this? What do you want from me?"

"I hoped that you'd discovered something I could use. I'm willing to exchange information with you, but apparently you know nothing." Lowendirk blew clouds of smoke from his cigar. "To tell the truth, Whit, after seeing you in action today—your shooting and so on—I'm impressed with your ability. We could make a profitable thing of this."

"In what way?"

"By joining forces. Once Nick Starkey has been caught, I can go to Jeff Dawson with the story of what I know. Dawson is a wealthy cowman. He'd pay my fee and no questions asked. I'd be willing to split my fee with you if you'll agree to work for me."

"What would you want me to do?"

"I want you to go to San Diego, find Nick Starkey, and bring him back here."

"Even if I found him, do you think he would talk or come with me?"

Lowendirk smiled meaningly. "Considering your ability with a six-shooter, I don't see how he could help himself."

"In other words, you want him dead or alive?"

"I'm not particular, so long as you get Starkey's confession to Dawson's murder first."

Slowly Whit shook his head. "I'm afraid we can't do business, Lowendirk."

"I don't know why. I could guarantee you at least a thousand dollars."

"My guns aren't for sale."

"Oh hell! I think you're being foolish, Whit. I might even be able to raise the anti—say fifteen hundred."

"My answer is still the same."

Lowendirk sighed. "This is a great disappointment, Gallatin. I'd hoped we'd be able to work together. But if you can't see it my way, you just can't, of course. I'll have to continue to work alone. Can I give you another drink—or a cigar?"

"No, thanks." Whit got to his feet, retrieved his sombrero from the table, and put it on. "I've got to be getting back to the ranch."

He started toward the door. Lowendirk stepped past him and opened it. A cool breeze swept in from outdoors. Lowendirk said, "Well, good night. I'm sorry you can't see your way clear to going to California for me, but if we can't do business, we can't."

"That's the way it has to be," Whit replied.

For just a moment he was silhouetted against the lighted interior of the room as he stood there gazing out across the moonlight-bathed range. Then he took a quick step to one side toward his waiting pony.

Seventy feet distant a blaze of orange fire erupted in the brush surrounding the house. Simultaneously a leaden slug thudded into the doorjamb. An exclamation of alarm left Lowendirk's lips and he cried, "Come back inside—quick!"

Whit ignored the words as his right hand stabbed down and came up holding his six-shooter. He threw a quick shot at random in the vicinity of the spot where he had spotted the explosion.

A running figure broke frantically from cover, sombrero pulled low on forehead, and commenced a crouching, zigzagging retreat through the greasewood and mesquite. He fired one wild shot that flew high overhead as he ran. Whit was in full pursuit now, six-shooter clutched in either hand, but holding his fire until an opportunity presented itself for a clear shot at the fellow. From some distance to the rear Whit heard the sound of snapping branches and thudding footsteps across sandy soil as Lowendirk came dashing through the growth.

The unknown assailant appeared suddenly, streaking past a tall mesquite, and started across an open stretch bright with moonlight, seeking the shelter of a high wide clump of prickly pear. Fire and smoke burst from Whit's right hand and blended with the report from his left. The speeding man crossing the clearing faltered in mid-stride, as though some invisible, gigantic force had abruptly swept his legs from under him, then crashed down in a heap on one shoulder. Moonlight glinted on his weapon as it spun crazily from his hand to land in the nearest patch of brush.

Whit closed in fast, thinking, *I brought him down without killing! I didn't aim to kill!* He could see the man trying to raise his body from the earth, both arms braced before him. Whit caught a glimpse of panicky eyes from beneath the low-drawn sombrero brim and heard the fellow's frightened voice: "Don't shoot again, Gallatin. Don't shoot! I'll tell you anything you want—"

The abrupt roar of a six-shooter cut short the words, and the man slumped on his face. Whit had already turned and saw Lowendirk, gun in hand, pushing through the waist-high brush. He joined Whit, and they stood looking down on the quivering form on the earth. After a moment the quivering stopped. Lowendirk said coldly, "One of us got him, anyway."

"I reckon it was you," Whit said quietly, "though I could wish you'd held your fire. We might have learned something."

"Maybe so," Lowendirk returned in a grim voice,

"but any time a man throws lead at me I go out to finish him as soon as possible."

"At you?" Whit's gray eyes narrowed. "I figured he was shooting at me."

"Why should he be shooting at you?" Lowendirk demanded.

"That's what I wanted to ask him."

Lowendirk shrugged. "You fired after his first shot, then twice more. I had to race back into the house to get my gun or I'd have been right with you. I fired once. Who's to say which bullet did the most damage?"

"I'd bet on yours," Whit said. "I fired for his legs and brought him down."

"Your first shot might have hit him and he maybe still kept on running—"

"Let's see who he is. It could be he's not dead yet," Whit proposed.

The two men stooped over the silent figure sprawled in the clearing, holstering their guns as they moved. The man was already dead when Whit turned him on his back. A quick examination showed him to have been struck three times. There was a bullet through each thigh, and a third bullet had entered his head just below the left eye. Blood oozed from an ugly purple hole at that point. The man's eyes were wide, staring, already growing glassy.

"Know him?" Lowendirk asked.

Whit nodded. "It's one of the Tiernan brothers—the one they called Tack."

"Sure enough, that's who it is. I didn't recognize him at first." Lowendirk gave a short harsh laugh. "That hole in his head probably made identification difficult." Whit looked at Lowendirk and saw that the man's face looked hard, relentless, in the light of the moon. Lowendirk went on, "I think this proves it was me Tiernan was gunning for."

"What makes you think that?"

"Do you know of any reason he'd want to shoot you?"

"Nothing in particular," Whit admitted.

"I heard today," Lowendirk went on, "that he and his brother and Rhodes had been spreading a rumor to the effect that I was a detective. Tack Tiernan has probably seen me someplace. He likely had an idea I was after him for some job he'd done and figured he'd better stop me before I got him."

"It's possible," Whit conceded. "Well, I suppose we'd best go look for Sheriff Brandon and tell him what's happened."

"That's the best thing to do. And regardless which of us fired the shot that killed Tiernan, I think it's something he had coming."

"The way I look at it," Whit replied, "whether he had it coming or not, it was your shot that finished him. I fired for his legs."

"There's no use arguing that now, Gallatin. We'll throw the problem in Brandon's lap."

Twenty minutes later they found the sheriff in the Shamrock Saloon and told their story. The customers in the saloon gathered around and listened, wide-eyed. When the story had been concluded, Brandon said, "You're both using .45s. It's going to be right hard to figure whose bullet killed Tiernan."

"If Gallatin said he aimed for the legs," a customer broke in, "I'd say he hit the legs. I saw him hit five poker chips today—"

"Nobody asked you for your opinion, Wilson," Brandon growled. "Go get an extra horse and come with us. We'll go out and fetch that body."

An hour later Tack Tiernan's body had been brought into the local undertaker's, and the sheriff, accompanied by Whit and Lowendirk, had visited the shack where the Tiernans and Calgary Rhodes had lived. The house proved to be empty of all but some crude furniture, and lighted matches showed that all personal belongings had been removed.

"Looks like they've cleared out for good," Brandon said, "but why did Tack come back?"

"To kill me, I suppose," Lowendirk replied promptly.

"Did he have any reason to kill you?" Brandon demanded.

"I'm not sure," Lowendirk said slowly. "I've heard that he was circulating a foolish rumor to the effect that I was a detective. Maybe he thought I was after him, but I don't know why—"

"Are you a range dick?" Brandon asked bluntly.

Lowendirk smiled contemptuously. "Isn't that rather a ridiculous question, Sheriff Brandon?"

"Yeah, I reckon it is," Brandon growled. "Still, I can't understand—Oh hell! Let's get back to the Shamrock. I need a drink."

Ten minutes later the three men drew their horses to a halt before the Shamrock tie rail. Lights from a few buildings shone along the street. Occasionally a passer-by clumped on high heels over the splintered sidewalks. None of the three made a move to dismount.

"Offhand," Brandon spoke at last, "I'd say that Tack Tiernan had been gunning for Gallatin."

"I feel certain he was shooting at me," Lowendirk insisted.

"That could be," Brandon conceded, "but so far as I know, he never even spoke to you, Mr. Lowendirk. On t'other hand, if he thought you were a detective . . ." The sheriff let the remainder of the sentence dangle in mid-air, then said more directly, "For a man who hasn't had much to do with firearms, you certainly showed some straight shooting tonight, Lowendirk."

"Maybe I just made a lucky shot," Lowendirk said quickly.

"Maybe you did." The sheriff shrugged. "I don't know as there's much more to be said. You both shot at Tiernan, but he shot first, accordin' to your story—"

"Do you doubt it?" Whit asked quickly.

"I didn't say that," Brandon growled. "As things stand, all we know is that one of you killed him. His legs were broken, but it was the shot in the head that finished the job. I don't know as it matters too much who fired that particular shot. Tiernan went asking for trouble and he found it. I don't even see any reason for holding an inquest, unless Breen demands it. Tiernan ain't no great loss to the community. And for that same reason I'd be a fool to arrest either one of you. Unless something new crops up, the business is finished so far as concerns the law in Clarendon County." He stepped down from his saddle. "I'm going to get a drink. Either of you care to join me?"

Whit said he was heading back to the 2JD at once. Lowendirk remained behind. When the sheriff had disappeared through the swinging doors Lowendirk said quietly, "Whit, I told you certain things in confidence tonight—regarding my status here and John Dawson and so on. I'm asking that you keep those things to yourself."

"I've never been known for loose talk," Whit said, and before Lowendirk could speak again, he had turned his horse and went loping off down the street.

Whit had just clattered across the plank bridge covering Palomas River when he saw a body of riders approaching. As he drew nearer he recognized Jeff Dawson and the 2JD punchers. Jeff hailed him with a certain relief in his tone as the horses drew to a halt. "Anything much happen tonight?" he added casually.

"Tack Tiernan got killed," Whit said, then went on and told what had happened from the time he had started to leave Lowendirk's house. When the exclamations of surprise had died down Button-Eyes Cobb blurted out, "What were you doing at Lowendirk's house, Whit?"

"Just visitin', that's all, just visitin'." Whit smiled.

"In other words, Button-Eyes," Whitey Laidlaw jeered, "it ain't none of our business. Don't ask questions that don't concern you."

"Well, we can turn around now and get back home," Jeff Dawson said.

A chorus of protests greeted the words. "Cripes, Jeff," Red Maguire said in hurt tones, "it was you suggested that we all go in to town and get a coupla drinks. Course we realize now that you must have had somethin' else in mind."

"Maybe I did," Dawson grunted. "All right, you hombres ride on in, but don't stay too long. Whit and I will get started back."

The punchers proceeded toward town, while Dawson and Whit continued toward the 2JD, their horses traveling at a walk. Whit said, "What's the matter, Jeff, did you get overanxious?"

"Been anxious ever since you left the ranch," Dawson said. "What did Lowendirk have to offer?"

"He admits he's a Redmondton operative. He offered me a job with him. Jeff, who's Nick Starkey?"

"Starkey? Nick Starkey?" The old cowman frowned. "Don't know him. Never heard the name. What about him?"

"According to Lowendirk, he might have murdered your brother." Whit hesitated at Dawson's exclamation of incredulity. "I'll give you the story as Lowendirk told it to me. But don't say I told you. Lowendirk asked me not to repeat anything . . . " From that point on Whit repeated what he had learned. When he had finished:

"By the seven bald steers of Moses Mountain!" Dawson blurted. "I never in all my days heard the like! So John hired Lowendirk to protect him from somebody named Nick Starkey! And I don't even know Starkey! Never heard of him even."

"You're sure your brother just went to Curtisville to see a doctor?"

"That's what he told me." The old cowman seemed bewildered. "Damn! I don't even know when he could have met this Starkey. Except for a short time, we was together practically every day."

"When weren't you together?"

"Hell! That goes back to when he wa'n't even married yet. We'd talked a heap about wantin' to raise cattle, but neither of us had any money. He suggested we go to minin' in Colorado, but I couldn't see it. Anyway, he went prospectin' and run onto a little pocket of gold. It petered out quick, but he dug hisself about eight thousand dollars first. Meanwhile I'd hit Curtisville, and one night in the Golden Buck gamblin' hall I took a whirl at roulette. I was lucky, and from a small start run my winnin's up to better'n six thousand. So John and me pooled our money and started the 2JD. We was successful. Later John went to sparkin' a girl up to Curtisville and they got hitched. Then Laura was born. Now you got nigh the whole history of the Dawson family—far's I know."

"He never mentioned any trouble he'd had in Colorado, did he? With this Starkey or anybody else?"

"Nary a word, Whit. All the years I've knowed him he never acted worried or anythin'. Dang funny he'd take his troubles to a range dick 'stead of confidin' in his brother. Do you suppose you 'n' me had better light out for San Diego and see can we locate this Starkey hombre?"

Whit hesitated. "Suppose we let that wait for a spell? Something else may turn up to give us a clue."

They spurred the horses to a faster gait. Beside him Whit could hear Dawson muttering from time to time: "Starkey . . . Nick Starkey . . . I just can't seem to recollect the name."

RHODES RETURNS

THE DAYS DRIFTED ON TOWARD THE END OF SUMMER. Now, at night, there was a certain chill tang in the air. Dust had settled more thickly on the greasewood, and the brush grass had taken on a sere and weathered appearance. Before many more weeks passed the 2JD would be starting its wagons and *remuda* for the beef roundup grounds. No complications had arisen from Tack Tiernan's death; Dr. Breen bad agreed with Sheriff Brandon that an inquest was unnecessary. Both Whit and Lowendirk had been absolved of all blame in the man's killing. The consensus of opinion was that Tack had started something he hadn't been able to finish and what had happened was his own fault. Whit had seen Lowendirk only once since that night, and that one day in Palomas when Lowendirk had passed him with a curt nod. Apparently the man was annoyed that Whit hadn't fallen in with his plans.

Nothing further had been heard of Bat Tiernan or Rhodes. If they had left the country for good no one could say with any certainty. Whit and Jeff Dawson had made one trip to Curtisville in the hope of learning something of the mysterious Nick Starkey, but the effort had proved of no avail. Still, Whit hadn't given up hope.

"We know John Dawson made frequent trips to Curtisville," Whit had said. "I'm going up there again soon and dig around some more."

Jeff had protested, "Whit, you and I didn't learn anything. How —"

"I don't know," Whit had interrupted, "but we might have overlooked something. I want to think things over a bit first, though."

The truth of the matter was that Whit wanted to go alone next time. When Dawson was with him they had encountered so many of Dawson's old friends that much time had been wasted in conversation. But Whit hadn't mentioned this for fear of hurting the old cowman's feelings.

Whit was even quieter than usual these days. He had a great deal of thinking to do. He had accompanied Laura Dawson on several rides, and each time their friendship had grown deeper. Now it had reached the point where Whit realized his feelings for the girl went farther than mere friendship. He was even commencing to hope that his affection was returned. On two or three occasions he had sensed that Laura was just waiting for him to speak, but Whit had always managed reluctantly to change the subject.

This was something that puzzled Laura. She couldn't

know that Whit was afraid to speak what was in his mind—afraid of himself. Whit realized that even if the girl accepted him he couldn't with any assurance promise her happiness. Of such a union children were a possibility that couldn't be ignored, and Whit didn't want to pass on to another generation that killer taint—that mark of Cain—he believed to be in his own blood. And so he continued to remain silent, gathering such happiness as was possible in Laura's company, and each day dreading the moment when he'd have to bid her good-by and pass out of her life forever, without once having spoken the words that seemed forever on his lips. And though Laura was fully aware now of Whit's history, the girl never dreamed of the reason for his silence.

The day came when Whit made the ride to Curtisville alone. He returned the following afternoon and after corralling his pony went at once in search of Jeff Dawson, whom he found mending a bit of harness in the big 2JD barn. Dawson looked up, smiling, as Whit entered. "No luck, I expect," Dawson said after they had exchanged greetings.

"I'll let you decide," Whit replied. "You know, I got to thinking that if John Dawson made a monthly trip—and you said it came about the same time each month—to Curtisville—"

"Sure, he went to see the doctor about the same time—"

"I'm not saying that isn't so. But let's say he saw somebody else. If that somebody lived in Curtisville your brother could have seen him at any time, whereas if he didn't, he might come to Curtisville at some arranged time each month—come on the train, I mean."

"That's an idea," Dawson conceded.

"So I went to the T.N.&A.S. depot," Whit continued, "and asked some questions. Finally I found a baggageman in the freight shed who had known John for some years—just by sight, that is. From him I learned that while he'd never seen John meet anyone at the train, he did see him at the depot the day before he was killed."

"What in the devil was he doing at the railroad depot?"

"What took him there I don't know, but this fellow at the freight shed told me he saw your brother having some sort of an argument with a man in cowpuncher togs. It seems there were several heavy boxes had been delivered there by a freight train—no, I don't know what the boxes contained—and one of the boxes had been dropped and a board splintered at one end. For some reason your brother was right interested, in the contents of the boxes, enough so to get him into an argument of some sort with this cowpuncher I mentioned."

Jeff Dawson shook his head in perplexity. "Damned if I can understand it. You didn't learn who the cow hand was, did you?"

Whit shook his head. "I didn't learn his name, but I did get a description of the hombre. The description fits Calgary Rhodes right close."

Dawson looked thoughtful. "It could have been him. Rhodes was away from the 2JD that day. It wasn't until the following day that I saw him in Palomas—remember, the same day I met you." His face darkened. "I certainly wish I'd knowed all this when Rhodes was still in town. I'd have a few words to say to that bustard . . . You never did learn anythin' about a Nick Starkey, I suppose?"

"I'm getting to that. Those boxes I mentioned were consigned to somebody named Nicholas Starkey. The fellow in the freight shed dug out copies of the old waybill and gave me that information. And it was the cowpuncher with Rhodes's description who took delivery of the boxes in Nicholas Starkey's name . . . So that's the story. I don't know as we have much more information to go on than we had before."

Dawson looked bewildered. "It beats me. I can't begin to understand it. And unless Calgary Rhodes returns, we won't get a chance to put him on the griddle for questionin'. I don't suppose you saw anythin' of him when you come through Palomas?"

"I didn't come through Palomas on the return trip," Whit said. "I cut straight across the range from Curtisville to here. I didn't have any reason to take me to town."

"Rhodes probably hasn't returned, anyway," Dawson said gloomily. "I'd sure like to have just five minutes *habla* with the dirty son, though. I'd get at the bottom of this mess if it was the last thing I done. I sent Red Maguire in for the mail today. If Rhodes has returned by any chance, Red will see him. He should be back any minute now, I figure."

But suppertime came and still Maguire failed to return. With the meal finished, lamps were lighted in the bunkhouse and the men busied themselves in various ways. At a rough board desk near the doorway Whitey Laidlaw and Jeff Dawson were checking over the tally book and making out a list of needed supplies. Farran, Corbett, and Cobb were seated at a round oak table engaged in a three-handed game of nickel ante. Dutch Vander was crouched on the edge of his bunk writing a letter on a pad of ruled paper and doing more chewing of the pencil stub than writing. Whit was bent over another round table, occupied in cleaning his six-shooters, a duty he never neglected for long, even though the weapons were used only occasionally. He had finished cleaning one gun and was drawing an oily rag through the barrel of the other at the moment. From the adjoining mess house and kitchen Skillet Potter could be heard banging pots and dishes as he washed up.

A staccato drumming of horse's hoofs was heard. Dawson rose and stood in the open bunkhouse door. He turned back after a minute as the hoofbeats grew louder, and again took his seat at Laidlaw's side. The other men were watching him.

"It's Red," Dawson stated. There was a certain relief in the tone. The others returned to their various labors.

A short time later Maguire, having turned his pony into the corral, entered the bunkhouse and tossed a small canvas sack on the desk in front of Dawson. "Your love letters are here, waddies." He grinned.

Skillet stuck a fat scowling face through the doorway of the mess house. "You, Red," he said with heavy sarcasm, "you're a minute or so late for supper. If you think I'm goin' to feed you now, you're mistook."

"And if you think I'm goin' to give you a chance to feed me"—Maguire grinned—"you're worse 'mistook.' Me, I et in town and I et like a king." He turned to the others, sober-faced. "Hombres, it's sure surprisin' what food tastes like when it ain't soggy or burned. I always thought food was just somethin' we had to eat to keep alive, but tonight I learned it actually tastes good—"

"Aw, you go to hell," Skillet mumbled, and retreated to his kitchen, followed by the laughter of the men in the bunkhouse.

Dawson had started to open the mail sack. "What took you so long, Red?"

"Got somethin' to tell you," Maguire stated. "Calgary Rhodes is back. I've been listenin' to him spin a windy that can't be beat—heard him tell it to a lot of folks—"

"Rhodes? Back!" Dawson put down the small sack. "What's this about a windy?"

The cardplayers put down their cards. Dutch Vander paused midway in his letter, pencil poised in air. Whit reloaded a cylinder, snapped it back in place, and ran a rag over his gun. A frown had gathered on his forehead. Somehow he couldn't get away from the notion that he was going to have to kill Calgary Rhodes someday. And he'd been hoping the man would never return to Palomas. The others were all looking intently at Maguire.

Whit said quietly, "So Rhodes is back, eh? Is he looking for trouble?"

"Me, I couldn't say," Maguire replied. He straddled a chair, arms resting on the straight back. "Rhodes says not. Says he don't hold nothin' against you, Whit. Insisted he come to Palomas strictly on business—important business."

"Business? Rhodes?" Laidlaw laughed scornfully. "What kind of business would bring him to Palomas?"

Dawson growled, "He sure did spin a windy if he claims he come on business—monkey business, maybe."

"I'm getting to that windy," Maguire said. "Look here, Jeff, I don't want to inquire into your personal affairs, but are you plannin' to sell the 2JD?"

Dawson's eyes widened. "I certainly am not. Where'd you get that fool idea?"

"Rhodes," Maguire replied promptly. "He claims he

returned to put the deal through. Says you promised to sell to him—for cash."

Dawson swore. "Of all the damn nonsense I ever heard—"

His words were interrupted by laughter from the others. Laidlaw guffawed, "Lordy, lordy! That's rich!"

"Best joke I've heard in a month of Sundays." Button-Eyes Cobb grinned. "Hell! Rhodes couldn't buy a horn off'n one of our steers if they was sellin' for two bits a head. Calgary never had any money."

"That's where you're wrong, Button-Eyes," Maguire said. "Leastwise, he's got plenty money now. I saw him flashin' a handful of gold eagles in the Shamrock, and he's buyin' drinks for anyone who'll lift one with him."

"There's somethin' damn funny afoot," Dawson snapped. "It's a wonder folks didn't hoot him outten town when he said he was goin' to buy the 2JD."

Maguire nodded. "That's what you'd expect. A few tried laughin' at him, but he convinced them and a lot of other folks that the deal was all set. He claims he met you up in Curtisville and arranged the whole business. Now he's come to tie up the deal."

"Of all the blasted liars!" Dawson snorted. "And you mean to say folks is actually believin' him?"

"That's what I'm tellin' you," Maguire insisted earnestly. "He's advertisin' himself all over Palomas as the next owner of the 2JD. Told me he was goin' to sack Laidlaw and make me foreman—"

"Cripes!" Dutch Vander jeered. "That should have proved he was lyin', Red. Nobody with good sense would promise that—"

"I doubt Rhodes has good sense if he says he's goin' to buy the 2JD," Dawson snapped. "I always figured him as a no-account, but I never did put him down for a complete idjit."

Whit asked, "Was Bat Tiernan with Rhodes, Red?"

Maguire shook his head. "Rhodes claims he parted from the two Tiernans right after the three of 'em left Palomas. He's plumb riled about Tack gettin' killed, though. Says he thought a heap of Tack."

"Make any war talk concernin' me?" Whit asked.

"Not any," Maguire replied. "He's not blamin' you. Says he understands you shot for Tack's legs. Rhodes says that's good enough for him. But he sure aims to call Lowendirk to account. Calgary is plenty sore at Lowendirk. But Lowendirk ain't in town, and nobody knows where he went to . . . There's a Mex—hombre called Torrio—with Rhodes—"

Whit said quickly, "Was he called Don Torrio, by any chance?"

Maguire frowned. "Come to think of it, I believe Rhodes did call him 'don.' "

Dawson said, "Do you know him, Whit?"

"Not personally, but I've heard things about him. Saw him once. Stockily built cuss, looks like a Mexican and talks like one, but I don't think he's purebred, if any. Got a sort of different accent, that doesn't go with a Mex. Some years back when I was in Texas he used to come raiding across the border now and then, leading a crew of bandits. The Rangers made it right hot for him, and then the Mexican Government took a hand and the fellow dropped out of sight suddenly. If Rhodes has got money, maybe Don Torrio has something to do with it. There's some bad medicine brewing or I miss my guess."

Jeff Dawson rose to his feet. "I've been wantin' to make *habla* with Calgary Rhodes for quite a spell now," he said casually. "I reckon I'll take a little ride into

Palomas." His eyes met Whit's. Whit said he guessed he'd go along too. Jeff nodded. "I'll be glad to have you sidin' me. Catch up the hawsses, Whit. I'll go get my hardware up to the house, then join you." Turning, he left the bunkhouse.

Whit strapped on his twin belts and guns, then went to his bunk for his whip. Donning his Stetson, he started out with a careless "See you later, hombres," tossed over his shoulder.

"Watch yourself, Whit," Maguire laughed after him, "or Rhodes will be trying to buy your whip along with the 2JD. I imagine he'd pay a lot for that whip—if he could have your skill along with it."

Whit's reply drifted back to the bunkhouse: "Maybe I'll get a chance to let him have it for nothing."

Ten minutes later he and Dawson were riding out of the ranch yard.

TREACHEROUS ROPES

IT WASN'T YET NINE O'CLOCK when the two men loped into Palomas. They stopped first at the Shamrock Saloon, feeling certain they'd find Rhodes there, but the man wasn't at the bar with the few other customers. Ignoring questions regarding the rumored sale of the 2JD, Dawson asked for information. Barry Flynn shook his head. "It's two hours past since Rhodes and his Mexican side-kick was in here."

One of the Shamrock's clients put in, "I saw Calgary and his greaser pal a coupla hours back down to the Chink's restaurant, but I ain't laid eyes on him since. Calgary asked me if I'd seen Lowendirk, which same I hadn't. He acted like he had a peeve against Lowendirk and was sure makin' war talk."

Dawson and Whit got back into saddles and rode to Lowendirk's house, but when they arrived there was neither a light nor any sign of recent habitation. Two horses stood in the corral back of the house. Whit said, "We can go back and make a circuit of the town's saloons." Dawson agreed, and they turned the ponies back toward the center of Palomas.

But the various drinking establishments produced no sign of Rhodes, either. Dawson sat his saddle while Whit glanced into the barrooms and asked questions. Apparently no one had seen Rhodes for some time. Several men asked questions regarding the proposed sale of the 2JD, and though Whit stated shortly there was nothing to the story, no one seemed convinced. Undoubtedly Calgary Rhodes had thoroughly persuaded a great many people that he was about to assume control of the Dawson outfit.

Finally Whit climbed back in his saddle and joined Dawson. Trotting their horses along the dusty street, Jeff growled disgustedly, "So we've come on a wild-goose chase, and Rhodes has disappeared again. I imagine he was just passin' through Palomas and, havin' a little cash to show around, did some wild takin' about buyin' my ranch. I suppose that's his idea of a joke. Well, we might as well slope back to the ranch—" He broke off suddenly, having just caught sight of Sheriff Brandon in the light thrown from the window of a poolroom. "Dan! Hey! Wait a minute!"

Brandon checked stride, wheeled, then stepped out in the road to the waiting horses. "Evening, Jeff. Howdy, Whit. What's on your minds?"

"We're looking for Calgary Rhodes. You seen him?"

"Not for an hour or so—better than an hour, I reckon.

Ain't he out to the 2JD? Don't tell me the deal's finished up already—"

Dawson snorted angrily, "Dammit! There never was no deal. Rhodes has just been runnin' a whizzer on Palomas."

Brandon frowned. "You mean you ain't sellin' to Rhodes?"

"That's exactly what I mean," Dawson stated wrathfully.

The sheriff looked narrowly at Dawson. "Cripes! Rhodes has been tellin' it all over Palomas that he was buyin'—that at the price he'd offered you, you couldn't afford to refuse. I thought it was all settled. Rhodes certainly talked like it was. He mentioned improvements he aims to make. He's goin' to import some blooded bulls and—"

"Not on the 2JD, he ain't," Dawson said grimly.

A certain coolness crept into the sheriffs tones. "Well, if you don't want to tell an old friend, you don't have to, Jeff. I can understand, I reckon. Rhodes said you'd wanted details of the sale kept quiet until things was all settled, but now that he's broke the news, I didn't think you cared—"

"Dammit!" Dawson howled. "I ain't sellin'. Come the time when you see my signature on a bill of sale, Dan, you can believe I've sold the 2JD, but not until then. Is that clear?"

"All right, all right, Jeff," Brandon said soothingly. "You don't have to get mad at me. I see I made a mistake. I ask your pardon." He turned huffily and strode back toward the sidewalk.

Dawson called after him, but Brandon kept on going, every step he took expressing hurt indignation.

Dawson looked after the sheriff a moment, then

laughed. “Now I’ve hurt his feelin’s, I suppose. He just can’t believe that Rhodes was lyin’.” He sighed. “Oh well, he’ll learn in time. We might as well slope on, Whit.”

The two men pricked their ponies with spurs and started out of town. The moon was up now but was obscured most of the time by drifting clouds. The horses moved at an easy lope along the trail. Dawson glanced at the sky. “Looks to me like it’s makin’ up to rain,” he observed.

“The range could stand it,” Whit replied. “Everything’s pretty dry. Though I’ve got to admit,” he added, “the cows look in good shape.”

The horses had been slowed to dip down across an old dry wash cluttered with broken rock. Now they were climbing out and rounding a jumble of piled boulders near the edge. One great chunk of stone the size of a small house towered above the riders’ heads.

“Yeah”—Dawson nodded—“the herd’s in right good condition. We’ll be makin’ an extra-big gatherin’ this fall. I’m figurin’ to weed out all the old bologna bulls and a lot of young culls. Next year I plan to run a smaller herd, but it will be all prime-beef stuff. Higher-grade stuff straight through. Then I can start buildin’ back—”

His words ended abruptly as there came the soft double swishing sound made by flying ropes. A pair of loops hissed through the air, dropped deftly over the heads of Dawson and Whit, then tightened viciously about their shoulders, pinning their arms tightly to sides.

The next instant the two men were jerked violently from their saddles to the rock-cluttered earth below. For a moment they were too stunned by the unexpected attack and the fall that followed to make a move. The breath had been knocked from their bodies. Then, when it was too late, they clambered to their knees and struggled to free themselves from the tightly encircling ropes. In the half-light from the moon Whit caught a glimpse of shadowy figures as they leaped down from the stacked heap of rocks above. Whit struggled to reach a gun, but his arms were held too tightly to his sides. He threshed about, endeavoring to loosen the restraining rope. Nearby Jeff Dawson was throwing himself around like a fish out of water.

"Quit fighting, you two, or I'll let you have a gun barrel across your heads!" Calgary Rhodes's voice came through the gloom, ugly, vindictive. "Quit it instanter, less'n you want your noggins blowed off!" He called to his companions: "Keep them ropes taut!"

Common sense told Dawson and Whit there was nothing to be gained from further struggle against such odds. Whit relaxed, hoping the rope about his body would be loosened, but it continued to cut tightly into his arms. He felt hands fumbling at his holsters and knew he had been disarmed. After a moment Dawson stopped fighting but broke loose with a verbal barrage of profanity when he, too, was relieved of his six-shooter. For a few minutes the air turned a deep indigo, then he fell silent when he realized his tirade produced only sneering laughter from his captors.

By turning his head about Whit had managed to make out the forms of four men in addition to Rhodes. Now a sixth shadowy figure rounded a corner of the big rock, leading behind a bunch of horses. His voice penetrated the gloom: "My congratulations, Calgar-ee. Ees the so fine ropeeng what your *compañeros* accomplish. Eet could hav' been no bettair."

This sixth man, Whit decided, was Don Torrio. Seen

in the light from the moon, Torrio was a heavy-bodied man in overalls and woolen shirt, with heavy black eyebrows, thick lips, and broad flattened nose. A steeple-crowned sombrero covered his greasy black locks. His tone carried a harsh, guttural accent not common to the softer speech of the true Mexican.

Both Whit and Dawson were in sitting positions on the rocky earth, arms still tightly pinioned. Whit said evenly, "Rhodes, you're making a bad mistake. You can't get away with this—"

"I'm doin' it, ain't I?" Rhodes growled.

"Damn you for a sneakin' son of a buzzard-eatin' rattler, Rhodes," Dawson raged. "What's the idea of grabbin' us this way?"

Rhodes gave a short, nasty laugh. "You'll learn soon enough. Just keep your traps shut and you won't be hurt—yet. We got plans. I sort of figured that if I spread a tale around Palomas that I was buyin' the 2JD you and Gallatin would come high-tailin' to town. You bit fine. We hung around just outside town until we saw you ride in, then we come out here to wait for you—"

"I got a score to settle with Gallatin too," a new voice interrupted. Whit twisted his head and saw the scowling features of Bat Tiernan above him. Tiernan went on: "Gallatin, I'm holdin' you responsible for my brother's killin'."

"I broke Tack Tiernan's legs, but I didn't kill him," Whit said evenly. "It was Drake Lowendirk killed your brother."

"Mebbe so," Tiernan rasped, "but I haven't got Lowendirk here—and I have got you."

"We can settle later who Gallatin belongs to." Rhodes chuckled. He stooped, feeling around Whit's left hand, then rose and called back to the other men: "Is

Gallatin's whip on his saddle?" The reply came back in the negative. "I want that whip, Gallatin. I aim to do some practicin' with that whip—"

"With the Señor Gallatin's bare back as the target, pairhaps?" Don Torrio suggested.

"That's a right idea, Don," Rhodes replied. He turned back to Whit. "Where's your whip?"

"It's your tough luck that I didn't happen to be carrying it tonight," Whit replied. "You've seen my whip tricks, Rhodes. I'd never be able to catch you on that stunt again."

Rhodes swore. "Damn right you couldn't." He cursed some more. Torrio said something about it being time to get away. Rhodes fell silent a moment, then, "All right, Gallatin—Dawson. You can get up now, but move awful careful if you want to stay alive. We'll be rollin' hot lead at the first false move you make."

With the guns of Torrio and Rhodes trained on them, the two captives struggled to their feet, their arms still bound tightly to their sides by the tough hempen loops. Rhodes gave further orders. Bat Tiernan and another fellow as hard-looking as Tiernan brought up the captives' horses and assisted Whit and Dawson into saddles. Then the others mounted. Once Tiernan and his companion were in saddles, the ends of the lariats were passed back to them to be fastened around their saddle horns.

"And keep them ropes pulled tight," Rhodes ordered. "Ride far enough behind Gallatin and Dawson so your hemp will stretch taut. If they try anythin' funny, yank 'em off'n their broncs. Don and me will be ridin' close, and we won't hold back our guns any, should they get to actin' up. Now let's get movin'."

The horses moved carefully along the rock-cluttered

wash. Whit glanced through the gloom at Dawson, who was swearing steadily under his breath. There seemed no way of escape from this predicament, particularly as Whit and Dawson were unarmed. As the horses got under way Whit felt the restraining rope tighten about his elbows, drawing them closely to his body. It was necessary to brace himself to prevent being jerked out of the saddle at the end of the rope controlled by Bat Tiernan. A savage exclamation from Jeff Dawson told Whit that the owner of the 2JD was in a similar situation. Whit twisted his head. Two riders rode with the pair at the other ends of the ropes. Close to the haunches of Whit's and Dawson's ponies were Torrio and Rhodes.

"What in hell is the idea in all this?" Dawson burst out abruptly, unable longer to contain himself.

"Shut your trap," Rhodes growled. "When I get ready to explain, I'll do it. Until then you won't learn a damn thing. So keep your lip buttoned."

Dawson fell silent. The horses climbed out of the wash and headed southeast, swinging wide of Palomas. Whit accommodated himself to the swing of his horse's gait and settled down to make himself as comfortable as possible. After a time the rope about his body eased slightly. Whit discovered he could move his arms from the elbows down and could even reach out from time to time and seize the saddle horn to steady himself.

But even that held little room for encouragement—not with his guns and Dawson's weapons in the hands of Torrio and Rhodes. If an escape was to be made it would be necessary to wait for some later opportunity. The moon was completely clouded over by this time.

Something large and heavy and wet splashed on Whit's hand and was instantly followed by a second drop.

"Ees raineeng, Señor Calgar-ee," Don Torrio stated.

"Let'er come." Rhodes laughed. "And the harder the better. Rain washes out tracks. Luck is with us, Don."

The rain commenced falling harder. Gradually the six riders and their two captives faded into the wet night.

A CARTRIDGE SCARCITY

FOR AN HOUR MORE THEY TRAVELED STEADILY. It was wet going for man and beast. Now and then one of the ponies slipped in the sodden adobe soil or sank hoof-deep into stretches of sandy earth. Occasionally Torrio or Rhodes directed some jeering remark at their captives, but for the most part the silence was unbroken except for the sloshing of horses' feet in the mud. Whit and Dawson were soaked to the skin; the other riders had produced slickers and were relatively dry.

Gradually, as the horses pushed steadily to the southeast through mesquite and greasewood, Whit realized that he and Dawson were being taken in the direction of the badlands section that lay below the foothills of the Encontrón Range. He wondered if they would cross the salt flats, but long before the flats were reached the horses were turned more directly to the south. Gradually the ponies got to rising ground. The way grew hilly. Now and then a cottonwood loomed up in the darkness or a clump of chaparral was passed.

The rain continued to teem down. The horses struggled and slipped around the side of a high ridge, then dropped into a long descent that finally brought them to a cottonwood grove where Whit made out dimly the blocky outlines of an adobe house. They were, he judged, in the heart of the Encontrón foothills.

The horses were brought to a halt. Rhodes and Torrio slipped from saddles. "Keep them ropes taut, hombres," Rhodes called sharpy. "I'll go in and light up."

A few minutes later rectangles of yellow light pierced the darkness. Rhodes again emerged from the house, a six-shooter in either hand. He was reinforced by Torrio, similarly armed. "All right, men, you can loosen them throw ropes now," Rhodes said, then spoke to Whit and Dawson. "You can step down now, and make it pronto. Get in the house, but move easily. I'll be pluggin' you if you make a break for it. Don has the same intentions, so move like you was treadin' on the edge of a grave."

Whit and Dawson descended cautiously from their mounts and, watched narrowly by the two armed men, entered the adobe house. There was only one room, and it was sparsely furnished with a rusty stove in one corner. There were two windows at the front and a window at the rear; rain trickled down the panes. Along the wall to the right were a pair of double-tiered bunks containing rumpled blankets. An oil lamp burned on a rickety-legged table. Empty boxes served as chairs. Shelves had been built near the stove to hold canned goods and other food.

Rhodes said, "Gallatin, you and Dawson turn your faces toward the wall. Stick your hands behind you." Rhodes gave further orders. Lariats were loosened from the captives' bodies. Strips of rawhide were produced, and Whit and Dawson found their wrists bound at their backs. Rhodes breathed easier. "All right, you hombres. I reckon you're safe enough now. You can sit on them boxes if you've a mind to."

The prisoners found seats. Whit glanced at their captors. Rhodes was telling one man to build up a fire;

another was directed to put on the coffeepot. A bottle of whisky was produced and placed on the table. Listening to the conversation, Whit learned the names of the three men he had not had a good look at before. They were called Squint, Dirty-Shirt, and Swingle. A hard-looking, unshaven trio they were, with holstered six-shooters at their hips.

Dawson's teeth were chattering with cold. Rhodes looked anxiously at him. "Don't you go to catchin' cold and croakin' on me, Dawson." He snapped an order at Dirty-Shirt to hurry and build up the fire, then drew the cork from the whisky bottle and placed it to Dawson's lips. "Got to take good care of your health, Dawson—until you've done what I want." He looked at Whit, then recorked the bottle. "T'hell with you, Gallatin. There ain't nothin' I need from you."

"You're needing plenty," Whit observed, "only you haven't realized it yet."

Rhodes swore and sent one of the men out for more firewood. The room commenced to warm up. Wet clothing steamed. The coffee boiled and was served in tin cups. This time Whit was given a drink by Swingle. The heat of the hot liquid coursed through his veins, and he began to feel better.

Dawson's teeth had stopped chattering. "Damn you Rhodes," he burst out suddenly, "what do you expect to gain by such fool stunts as this?"

Rhodes chuckled. "From you—the 2JD," he said promptly. "As for Gallatin—him and me has another score to settle. Maybe I'll let Don Torrio's firin' squad take care of him."

"Why, damn your lousy flea-bit hide!" Dawson fumed. "You ain't got enough money to buy the 2JD. wouldn't sell to you at no price!"

The other men went into paroxysms of laughter. Rhodes looked amused. "I reckon you didn't lose any time when you were in Palomas denyin' you were sellin' to me?"

"Didn't waste much time on denials," Dawson snapped. "Didn't think it was worth denyin'. Told the sheriff, but that dang idjit wouldn't believe me—" He broke off suddenly.

Rhodes laughed. "I certainly did a good job of convincin' folks, I reckon. Dawson, did you really think I meant to pay out good money for your place? You're a bigger fool than I took you for."

Dawson looked puzzled. "As I got it, you was flashin' money around Palomas and statin' you had the money to buy."

"Sure I was," Rhodes admitted. "Now when I show up with a bill of sale to the 2JD, the town will think I really bought off'n you—"

Whit interrupted, "There'd be a deed to be signed and other papers Rhodes. Aren't you overlooking a few bets?"

Rhodes shook his head. "I'm covered. By the time anybody starts askin' for a deed to be produced, it will be too late. All I need is Dawson's signature on one little piece of paper." He paused then to Dawson, "Why, damn your soul, I ain't fool enough to pay out good money for what I want when there's another way to get your spread."

Dawson's jaw dropped in bewilderment. "What in hell you windjammin' about, Rhodes? They ain't nobody can get the 2JD 'thout my say-so. Have you gone clean off'n your bean?"

"Before we're through with you, Dawson, we'll have your say-so." He grinned widely. "And you're goin' to be awful glad to give it."

Dawson shook his head in perplexity. "Damned if I know what you're talkin' about."

Whit was commencing to see what Rhodes was working toward, but he kept silent. He could see his guns—and Dawson's—on the table, but he felt it doubtful he could reach them in time to accomplish anything, even if his hands were unbound. And they weren't. Dirty-Shirt had seen to that, tying the rawhide thongs so tightly that they cut into Whit's flesh.

Dawson finally laughed with some sarcasm. "If you can't put up money for the 2JD, I don't see how you expect to get my name on any bill of sale."

Rhodes emitted a confident chuckle. "By the time we get through persuadin' you, Dawson, you'll be glad to sign that paper of your own free will. You'll be beggin' me to let you do it. Look here, Jeff"—his words took on a more genial tone—"there's no use you bein' stubborn. All you got to do is sign a paper that says I own the 2JD, and I'll release you at once to go home."

Dawson snorted, "Of all the fool idees I ever heard on, that's the damn-foolest! How in hell long do you think you'd last once I hit Palomas? Folks would soon know it was extortion and not my own free will that got you a bill of sale. Why, you couldn't—"

"That's my worry," Rhodes stated. "Once I get the 2JD, I'd hang on until Hades froze solid. Don't you fret about my interests. That Calgary hombre has been lookin' out for Rhodes's interests for a long spell now, and there won't any mistakes be made this late in the game."

Dawson frowned. There must be some way of outfoxing Rhodes. "Look here, Calgary," he said quietly, "supposin' I give you my signature on that paper, will you let Whit go the same time you release me?"

Rhodes scowled, started to speak, then hesitated. Finally, "I reckon we could arrange somethin'—"

"Don't listen to the bustard, Jeff," Whit cut in. "Once he had your name signed to that paper, your life wouldn't be worth a plugged peso. Rhodes wouldn't dare give you a chance to spoil his plans. Don't you get set to sign anything. We'll slip out of this tight yet—"

Rhodes cursed. "Gallatin, you keep your mouth outten this or I'll close it from here on out. Jeff's capable of makin' up his own mind, and—"

"You're right, Whit," Dawson broke in. "Rhodes would likely knock me off once he had my name, black on white." He glanced contemptuously at Rhodes. "You just try to get me to sign," he finished defiantly.

"I'll get your signature all right," Rhodes rasped. "There's more ways than one to skin a calf, eh, Don?"

Don Torrio smiled. "More ways than wan ees correc', Señor Calgar-ee. Pairhaps by the time we place theese so-stubborn Señor Dawson across an anthill for ten leetle minutes he weel leesten to reason."

Some of the color left Dawson's grizzled features. Whit's eyes widened, and he felt a shudder course his spine. Ten minutes on an anthill swarming with ravenous ants which crawled into eyes and nostrils and mouth in their never-ceasing search for food. It had been said that the strongest will surrendered during the first six minutes, and then the mind gave way.

A mite of spread-eaglin' across an anthill would bring you to time all right," Rhodes growled. "Once the ants have fed on you a coupla minutes, I'm bettin' you'd be glad to sign anythin' I wrote out. And by that time you'd be so plumb cuckoo folks wouldn't believe anythin' you'd say, anyhow—even if you was capable of rememberin'."

Dawson's jaw set stubbornly. "All right, try it," he challenged. "You'll learn if you can make me sign."

"There's more than one way of workin' that too," Rhodes stated confidently. "Don's got a crew of *paisanos* over in Nuevo Cesto. Him and me will be headin' over that-a-way soon. We could gather some picked men, then drop down on the 2JD after dark. Ever notice how convenient darkness is for raidin'? Once we'd wiped out your hands and brought Miss Laura here, you'd be mighty eager to sign—"

"Why, you cold-blooded—" Whit commenced, tugging frantically at his bonds. He stopped suddenly, realizing his words would have no effect and the bonds couldn't be loosened.

"Take it easy, son," Dawson advised philosophically, though he had felt a certain chilling fear constricting his heart. "No use wearin' yourself out. This coyote ain't pulled nothin' yet to worry us. You want to remember that madmen always froth at the mouth before they get caught and tied into a strait jacket. So don't you pay no mind to what Rhodes says. It's just some of his frothin' before his finish—"

"Gallatin will never live to see my finish," Rhodes sneered.

"If you're game to untie me and give me a gun, I might change your mind," Whit challenged.

"Think I'm a fool?" Rhodes snapped.

Whit smiled. "Yes, I think you are—but you're not fool enough to face me when I've a gun in my hand." There was something taunting in his tones. He was hoping that Rhodes would fly into a rage, lose his head, and consent to some sort of duel. "You know who's the best man, Rhodes. You haven't the nerve to give me a gun and face me, frank and open—"

"I got plenty nerve," Rhodes said sullenly.

"Not enough, though," Whit said derisively. "Look here, Rhodes, I'll make you a proposition. Give me a gun with just one ca'tridge in it. You have a gun fully loaded. My one shot against your five—load with all six if you like, fill up your chambers. What have you got to lose? How about it?"

"His guts," Dawson said contemptuously before Rhodes could reply. "And I figure he's already lost them."

"Aw, you two talk too much," Rhodes jowled. "For two cents I'd put a gag in your mouths. Now shut up!"

"Afraid, eh?" Whit jeered. "I'm damned if I see how Don Torrio puts up with you for a pardner. No nerve, and even with nerve I don't think you could hit the side of a barn with your gun—even if you were inside the barn—"

"Damn you, Gallatin!" Rhodes fumed, and entered into a burst of cursing. When he had run out of breath Whit continued:

"I'll give you better odds, Rhodes. Untie me and give me a gun with one ca'tridge, like I said before. But you take *two* guns fully loaded. Cripes! You can't ask for anything better. I'd have to get you with one shot, and, knowing you like I do, I'm betting you could dodge and wiggle and squirm and run until I'd fired my one shot. You claim you're going to kill me anyway. Why not give me that one chance? Even a diamondback gives an enemy a chance. He rattles first. Of course you've been doing plenty of rattling, but you haven't worked up enough nerve to strike yet. Come on, Rhodes, what do you say? One ca'tridge for me against your two guns?"

Rhodes listened, red-faced, to the proposition. He knew all the other men were listening as well. Their eyes gleamed with interest in the light from the oil lamp, and he realized his reputation was at stake. "By Gawd!" he exploded suddenly. "I'll—"

"Señor Calgar-ee," Don Torrio interrupted, "I do not theenk theese ees the time for a duel such as theese hombre propose. Hav' you forgot we hav' othair business?"

The words brought Rhodes to his senses and he cooled down rapidly. He realized now that Gallatin had almost taunted him into doing something very reckless and unwise. Even with the odds against him, Gallatin was too dangerous a man to trifle with. "That's it," Rhodes said lamely, "we got other business, Gallatin. Ain't no time to fool with you now."

The other men in the room except Torrio looked slightly disappointed.

"Awful busy, aren't you?" Whit said mockingly. "That's the only thing that prevents you from shooting it out with me. Or is it? It couldn't be that a memory of the day we shot at poker chips is holding you back, is it, Rhodes? You didn't look good a-tall that day. In fact, you looked terrible. And I'd expected to see some shooting. Two ca'tridges you wasted on one chip, wasn't it, Rhodes? Surely you can do better than that. It's a cinch you couldn't do worse—"

"Dammit!" Rhodes said furiously. "You just had luck with you that day. I admit that I didn't show up so well, but with a lame hand to slow my draw—"

"Lame hand!" Whit scoffed. "What lame hand? You're just finding excuses for yourself, Rhodes."

"T'hell I am," Rhodes insisted virtuously. "I mentioned it that day right after I'd shot. I said then my hand was stiff. Maybe you didn't hear me."

"I can't say I did." Whit laughed scornfully.

Bat Tiernan came to Rhodes's rescue: "Yeah, he did, Gallatin. I heard him. Calgary ain't makin' up an alibi. More'n once when he's missed a shot I've heard him grumble about that old scar that makes his mitt stiff. Hell! Calgary ain't lyin'. You can look for yourself. Show him, pard."

Whit looked skeptical. Angrily Rhodes crossed the floor to confront him, throwing out one hand, palm up, beneath Whit's eyes. "Knife scar," Rhodes growled. "Tangled with an Injun up in Manitoba about five years back and had to put a slug through his carcass. I figured him as dead, but he was playin' possum. When I come close he flashed his knife on me. I caught the blade in my hand, and it cut deep. Then I had to shoot him a second time. But my right hand was nigh cut in two. You can see the scar for yourself. Now and then the cut nerves get to achin' and my fingers sort of stiffen up. But look, damn you, you'll see for yourself I'm no lyin'."

Whit examined the hand thrust before his gaze. A thin red cicatrix ran straight across Rhodes's palm. No doubt about it, it had been an ugly wound at one time; and the cut, in healing, had drawn together to form a cordlike ridge slightly raised above the rest of the palm. Slowly Whit raised his eyes to meet Rhodes's.

"Is that a scar or ain't it?" Rhodes demanded boastfully, almost as though he were proud of the disfigurement. "You don't see many hands that've been cut that bad—not without a loss of the paw. I've had more'n one hombre plumb amazed when he seen that scar, and him wonderin' how I could shoot as well as I do—" He broke off. "Hey! What you lookin' at me like that for, Gallatin? There's somethin' in your eyes . . ." As though half afraid of what he had seen momentarily in Whit's face, he commenced to back away.

Whit smiled thinly. "I was just wondering."

"Wonderin' what?" Rhodes asked nervously.

"If you'd shot that Injun in the back the first time you plugged him. It sounds like something you'd do."

Two or three men in the room laughed. Rhodes crimsoned and turned away, saying to Torrio, "We'd best get started, Don."

Whit raised his voice a trifle. "Oh, by the way, Hopkins . . ."

Rhodes stiffened. Slowly he turned back, his eyes not quite meeting Whit's. Then he started toward the door again.

Whit said sharply, "Hold it, Scar Hopkins."

Again Rhodes turned. "Who in hell you talkin' to, Gallatin?"

"You, Scar Hopkins. I've been looking for you a long while."

"My name's Rhodes—Calgary Rhodes. I don't know—"

"Don't lie, Hopkins!" Whit snapped. "I never laid eyes on you before I came to Palomas, but I did hear your voice one night back near Toyah Wells. I never did forget that voice altogether, and now with you talking so much about your scar, things just sort of added up all at once. Damn you, you're one of three men responsible for my father's death. The other two are dead. I've been looking for you for a long time."

"Aw, you're crazy, Gallatin. My name's Rhodes."

"I told you not to lie, Hopkins," Whit said sharply. So completely did he dominate the situation that momentarily it was forgotten that his hands were bound behind him and he was practically helpless. The other men eyed Rhodes-Hopkins curiously. Then the man, realizing he'd have to make some sort of reply to Whit's accusation, remembered that Whit was powerless to do him any harm.

"All right," Rhodes half snarled, "I'll admit I was once known as Scar Hopkins and I was in on the plan to throw the blame for that stage holdup on your old man. Me and Hess and Talbert only wanted him for his guns in case anythin' went wrong. Old Cougar could shoot, I'll grant you that, but he was a cantankerous bustard if there ever was one. We'd made it up from the first to tip the law off to Cougar and get him outten the way—" He broke off to explain to the others: "A job me and some friends pulled one time. And then this meddlin' sneak"—indicating Whit—"had to mess into things. Killed my friends and saw to it our loot was returned. I had to leave in a hurry. I changed my name." He swung back to Whit again. "And that's another score I got to even with you. Matter of fact, Hopkins never was but one of the names I used. Scar Hopkins, they called me. But I dropped that long ago, Rhodes bein' the name I was born with—"

"Does it make any difference?" Dawson observed dryly. "A polecat by any other name would smell as sweet."

There was some laughter at the remark. Rhodes's face darkened. "T'hell with you, Dawson—and you too, Gallatin! There's not one damn thing you can do about anythin' now. I'm in the saddle and I'll do the ridin'. The time ain't far off when *you* won't even have a name. Dead men don't have names—not for long."

"I've got your name written on one ca'tridge," Whit persisted, "if you'll match it against two guns."

Rhodes swung himself angrily around, speaking to

Torrio. "Come on, Don. We'd best be startin' if we want to meet your friends by daybreak. We've wasted too much time now."

"*Sí*, Señor Calgar'ee." Torrio nodded, "I am raddy whenevair you speak the word."

Rhodes continued: "Bat, you come with us. Squint, Dirty-Shirt, and Swingle can stay here to guard the prisoners. And you hombres watch Dawson and Gallatin plumb close. They're tricky. If they get loose I'll cut out your hearts and eat 'em for breakfast. And don't hesitate to use your guns if necessary. If they escape, our hash is cooked. And, Dawson, you'd best make up your mind to sign that paper when I get back. It's your only chance for life."

Dawson and Whit remained silent. Dirty-Shirt said, "Don't worry, Calgary, these hombres won't get away. We'll be watchin' 'em."

Torrio, Rhodes, and Tiernan got into slickers. Rain was still drumming on the roof. They were about to leave when Rhodes hesitated, running his fingers along his cartridge belt. "Hell," he snapped, "I'm almost out of .45 ca'tridges. Forgot to get some when I had a chance." He glanced toward Whit. "Reckon I'll have to borrow some of your loads, Gallatin."

Whit said evenly, "I know how you could get 'em without borrowing, Rhodes. Want me to tell you?"

Rhodes swore at him and crossed to the box where Whit sat, reached down to Whit's belts, then straightened in surprise. "A hell of a killer you are," he accused contemptuously. "Your belts are empty. Don't you carry any extra ca'tridges?" Whit said no. Rhodes snapped, "You're a liar," as he ran his hand around Whit's back. "You got loads in the loops back here. What's the idea?"

Whit smiled thinly. "I leave cartridges out of my front loops, Rhodes, so the weight of the belts will balance better."

Rhodes frowned. "I don't see what difference that makes."

"Sure," Whit said smoothly. "Can't you see how a belt weighted in front would have a tendency to pull your gun forward? It might prevent a fast draw."

Rhodes pondered a moment. "Damned if I can see it. I don't understand what you're gettin' at, Gallatin."

"There's a lot of things you don't understand," Whit said coldly.

Torrio called to Rhodes to hurry. Rhodes snatched a double handful of cartridges from Whit's belts and joined Tiernan and Torrio at the open doorway. The door slammed behind them. A minute later the sounds made by departing riders carried through the downpour to those left within the house.

Dawson looked curiously at Whit. "I never noticed before, Whit, that you didn't carry loads in the front of your belts."

"I used to," Whit said briefly. "This is a fairly new idea of mine I'm trying out."

He scowled at Dirty-Shirt, Swingle, and Squint seated on boxes near the stove. They stared back without saying anything. It continued to rain, but toward dawn the downpour ceased. Swingle rose and glanced outside. When he returned he mentioned something about the clouds breaking away. "It'll be good weather for what's due to happen across the border right soon."

Dawson and Whit wondered at the words. What other deviltry was cooking? Stiffly they wiggled to more comfortable positions on their boxes and reconciled themselves to what was coming next.

THE 2JD RIDES

THE PUNCHERS IN THE 2JD BUNKHOUSE SAT AWAITING Whit's and Jeff's return from Palomas. All were in their bunks except Laidlaw, but only Bob Corbett and Button-Eyes Cobb were asleep. The others found their minds busy with the thought of Whit and Jeff and what would happen when they encountered Calgary Rhodes. A sudden gust of rain rattling the windows awakened Button-Eyes. He raised his head. "Geez! It's rainin'," he observed.

"Has been for some time now," Laidlaw replied, looking up from the paper he had been reading.

The voices awakened Corbett. "Sounds like rain," he stated drowsily.

"Probably feels like it too," snickered Shorty Farran, "if you went outside to see."

Heads commenced popping out of bunks. Button-Eyes said suddenly, "Hey, ain't Jeff and Whit back yet?"

"They should be riding in any minute now," Laidlaw replied. "Probably it's slow going in this rain."

Red Maguire consulted his watch. "Cripes! It's nigh eleven-thirty."

"Seems the two should be back by this time," Dutch Vander commented.

"Dammit," Laidlaw said testily, "they're about due, I tell you."

"What are you waitin' up for, then?" Maguire asked bluntly.

"Didn't feel sleepy," Laidlaw snapped.

A grumbling protest rose from Skillet Potter's bed: "Why don't you hombres shut up and let a man sleep?

Yap-yap-yap! All night long. If I lose my sleep you don't get your breakfast on time."

"Maybe nobody will feel sick tomorrow, then," Farran said insultingly. "The longer we put off eating, the better for our health."

"I can't see," Potter crabbed, "what you hombres can find to talk about at this time of night when all decent men are—"

"You wouldn't understand if we told you," Vander interrupted, "so you can resume your beauty sleep, Skillet."

"Beauty sleep!" Cobb snorted. "Hah! That's good. Gawd knows Skillet could use a heap of beauty sleep."

Skillet swung his legs out of his bunk. "What's wrong with my looks?" he demanded belligerently.

Laidlaw again raised his head from his paper. "Maybe I can give you an idea, Skillet," he said. He jerked one thumb toward the doorway leading to the mess shanty. "Go stand near that door with your back facing me."

Looking extremely puzzled, Skillet lifted his fat body out of the bunk and, clad only in his underwear, waddled to the doorway and turned his back. "Now, what is it?" he asked over his shoulder.

Laidlaw smiled. "You insisted on talking instead of sleeping. You're headed in the right direction. Just keep going and boil us up a pot of coffee. Nobody's sleeping anyway—"

"Aw-w-w," Skillet sputtered. "I ain't even got my clothes on."

"Just get that Java started," Laidlaw said. "If you're feeling so damn modest, one of the boys can take your pants out to you."

Without further protest Skillet proceeded on to his kitchen, where they could hear him building up the fire.

Men commenced crawling out of bunks. Pants were drawn on; cigarettes were manufactured and lighted. Corbett said, "How come the coffee this time of night, boss?"

"Nobody was asleep. I felt like a cup and figured you hombres would too."

Corbett said "You're frettin' about Jeff and Whit."

Laidlaw tried to assume a look of surprise which didn't quite come off. "Why should I be frettin'?"

"They should be back by this time," Corbett said worriedly.

"Not necessarily."

"Look, Farran cut in, "figurin' three quarters of an hour each way, and an hour in town, they should be back by this time, easy. Here it is goin' on to twelve o'clock. Where are they?"

Laidlaw furnished various reasons that might explain the delay, but the others sensed he was only side-stepping the issue. Midnight passed, and with the arrival of coffee the men endeavored to turn the conversation to other subjects, though they weren't quite successful. The talk kept drifting back to Jeff and Whit. Laidlaw said at last, "Maybe the rain decided 'em to stay at the hotel."

Farran shook his head. "This rain wouldn't stop 'em from comin' back—not when they knew we were anxious to find out what Rhodes had to offer."

Button-Eyes Cobb said, "I don't like this waiting."

"None of us do," Maguire snapped. "Boss, how about us saddlin' up and ridin' to Palomas? Then, if anythin's wrong, we'd learn—"

"We'd probably meet Jeff and Whit on the way," Laidlaw responded, "and they'd give us the laugh. Ten to one, if they aren't in the hotel, they're keeping dry in the Shamrock right now."

"If you really feel that way," Dutch Vander demanded, "why don't you go to bed?"

"I already told you I wa'n't sleepy," Laidlaw snapped.

At two-thirty there was a knock on the bunkhouse door. Laidlaw opened it to see Laura standing there, a slicker protecting her from the rain. "Perhaps I'd better not come in," she said. "I woke up and saw lights down here. Then I found Uncle Jeff wasn't in his bed. Is anything wrong?"

"Jeff and Whit went to Palomas tonight—last night, rather. They're not back yet."

"Do you think anything's wrong?" the girl persisted.

"Nothing I know of."

"Why are you all awake at this hour?"

Laidlaw scratched his head. "Oh—I dunno. We—we just sort of got to talking—well, I reckon we didn't realize it was so late. Your uncle and Whit will be along any minute now."

Laura looked searchingly at the foreman. Laidlaw dropped his eyes. The girl said finally, "I'd better get back to the house, out of this rain. Tell Uncle Jeff to let me know the instant he gets back."

"Yes, ma'am, I'll do that," Laidlaw promised. He watched the girl turn back toward the house, then closed the door and resumed his seat. He didn't speak for several minutes. Finally, "If anything has gone wrong with Jeff and Whit," he said in a troubled voice, "I think we'd best learn as soon as possible."

"Finally come around to our way of thinkin', eh, boss?" Dutch Vander said.

"Mebbe I've been thinking your way right along," Laidlaw replied. "I just sort of hated to send a man riding in this rain if it was to be a useless errand. Howsomever, mebbe I've been a fool to wait so long. Somebody's got to ride to Palomas and see if everything is all right. Get out a deck of cards and make a draw. Low man goes."

"Why can't we all go?" Maguire demanded.

"If anything is wrong," Laidlaw explained patiently, "I sort of hate to leave the ranch unprotected. Draw your cards, boys."

Cards were produced, a quick draw made, and by drawing a deuce of spades Red Maguire was elected to make the ride. He drew on his boots and other clothing. Laidlaw said, "Red, take an extra horse with you and make a fast ride. Then you can leave one horse at the Palomas livery and have a fresh animal to get you back here in a hurry—" He broke off. "I don't mind stating now that I'm worried, so make it fast, ranny. Ride the hocks off'n your ponies coming and going. You'd best take that bay mare and the little paint horse. They'll give you the best speed for short distances. One of you other hombres go help Red catch up the ponies. It'll save a minute or so."

Maguire and Shorty Farran departed in the direction of the saddlers' corral. Finally Farran returned, shaking streaming rain from his sombrero. The drumming of hoofs was already dying away. By this time all the men were on their toes with suspense. No one spoke for a time. More coffee was brewed.

"I hope nothin' ain't happened," Dutch Vander said

"What do you think we're doin'," Cobb inquired with some sarcasm, "just sittin' here thinkin' about what Santa Claus might bring us come Christmas time?"

"Aw, you go to hell," Vander growled. "You know what I mean."

The strain of waiting was commencing to tell on the men's nerves. Laidlaw commented with far more carelessness than he felt, "I really can't believe anything's happened. Not with Whit and Jeff together. Jeff's too old a hand to be drawed into anything he couldn't handle. And if there'd been any shooting fuss, somebody from Palomas would have brought word by this time—even if Jeff and Whit couldn't come. Why don't you hombres crawl into your blankets? Going to hit the hay myself in a few minutes."

"That's a right good idea," Corbett agreed. "No use of us losing sleep. Reckon I'll get me some shut-eye."

But he made no move to carry out his words, nor did anyone else. The men sat mostly in silence now, save for an occasional shuffling of feet or clearing of a throat. Laidlaw rose once, refilled an oil lamp that had commenced to burn low, and replaced it in its bracket on one wall. The others followed his movements as though he were accomplishing something of extreme importance.

Cobb, Vander, and Corbett started a game of seven-up, but the play lagged. Finally the cards were cleared from the table. The men sat, avoiding each other's eyes, as though fearful of what they might read there. Cigarettes were rolled and lighted and usually were allowed to go out, unsmoked.

"Red should be in Palomas by now," Cobb ventured once.

"Don't you think we can do our own thinkin'?" Dutch Vander snapped irritably.

Cobb didn't say anything; he understood how Vander felt. Shorty Farran went to the door, opened it, and glanced out. He came back into the room. "Looks like the rain might be lettin' up," be announced.

"Geez! You're just full of information," Corbett sneered.

Nerves were growing more taut every minute. Toward dawn the rain ceased, and only a steady dripping from the eaves of the bunkhouse was to be heard. A faint gray light began to seep faintly through the bunkhouse windows.

"Dammit!" Skillet Potter's voice rolled protestingly from his bulky form. "Red should be back by this time."

"Not necessarily," Laidlaw replied. "If Red didn't locate them right off, he'd have some inquiring around to do. That takes time. You fellers will just have to hold your horses a spell."

"I reckon." Potter nodded, unconvinced. "Anyway, I can go get breakfast started. Red will want somethin' warm when he rides in." The fat cook waddled off in the direction of his kitchen.

It grew lighter outdoors. Laidlaw glanced outside and mentioned that the clouds were breaking up. No one appeared to hear him. By the time Skillet had breakfast on the table and the men were eating, it was broad daylight. The consumption of breakfast went slowly. Food seemed to stick in the throat, but this morning there were no sarcastic comments relative to Skillet's cooking. The men sat in silence, each one's ears strained for the first sound of an approaching rider.

"By cripes!" Button-Eyes Cobb exploded. "It's been daylight over an hour now. What's happened to Red?"

"Take it easy, Button-Eyes," Laidlaw advised. "It ain't going to help any if you get all churned up about Red too—"

"But where is he? He should be back. I thought a lot of Red . . . " Words tumbled from Cobb's lips.

"Sure, we all do. Nothing's happened to him. He's

just been delayed a mite—"

Laidlaw broke off as the welcome staccato pounding of hoofs was heard across wet earth. As one man the crew rose from the table and rushed to the doorway to see Maguire's mount splashing through the mud. Red pulled the steaming bay pony to a long sliding halt before the bunkhouse and dropped from the saddle. The pony stood straddle-legged, droop-headed, as the cowboy slipped on the sodden adobe toward the doorway. He pushed inside the bunkhouse, his clothing wringing wet, his face a scowling mask of anger. Despite the torrent of questions directed at him, he couldn't seem to talk. His gestures were futile, waving tragedies. He barged past the others, his hands moving toward a box of .45 cartridges on a shelf. He was panting heavily.

"Dammit, have you lost your voice?" Laidlaw demanded.

"Do you think I'm gathering these .45 slugs to send to the heathen in China?" Red said savagely. "What in hell's the matter with you hombres? Are you glued to one spot? Buckle on your hardware! We've got to ride! They're gone. Plumb disappeared!"

This brought on a storm of queries. Someone asked Maguire why he hadn't returned sooner. Red turned violently on the speaker. "You don't make time when your hawss is slippin' sidewise one step outten every three—"

"Now calm down, Red," Laidlaw interposed. "You said something about Jeff and Whit having disappeared."

"That's exactly what I meant. Disappeared!" Maguire snapped. He told his story in short jerky sentences. He had been to Palomas. Everything was closed up except one restaurant. No one there had seen Whit and Jeff. He had awakened Barry Flynn and then Sheriff Brandon. From those two he had got some information. Yes, Whit and Jeff had been in Palomas, but they had left. Brandon said the last time he had seen them they were headed back to the 2JD. No, Calgary Rhodes hadn't been seen since the previous day. Rhodes and his Mex companion had left town sometime before Whit and Jeff had arrived.

"And you didn't meet 'em on the road anywhere?" Vander queried dumbly.

"Oh, for Gawd's sake!" Maguire stormed. "Won't you realize they're gone? Come alive! Get your irons! We've got to start—" He paused. "Didn't I meet 'em on the road? . . . That reminds me. Dammit, I left it coiled on my saddle—"

"Left what coiled on your saddle?" Laidlaw demanded.

"Whit's whip. You know that old dry wash that crosses the trail a short distance out of town?" Laidlaw nodded. Maguire continued: "Comin' back this mornin' I found the whip layin' there. Now I don't figure Whit lost it by accident—"

"Was the whip there on your way to Palomas?" Corbett asked.

"It might have been," Maguire said. "It was pitch-dark and rainin' when I rode in. I could have passed the whip in the dark. I figure somebody's grabbed Whit and Jeff, but Whit found a chance to drop his whip, knowin' we'd be searchin' for them and might find it. I looked over the earth and rock right close. There's been horses there fairly recent, but the sign wasn't too plain. Partly washed away, I reckon. Then that spot is cluttered with loose rock, and horses don't leave too much sign on rock. A scratch here and there—Oh hell, you all know that. Let's get goin'!"

"Could you tell what direction the hoofprints were headed?" Laidlaw asked.

"I'm not sure. Mebbe they followed the wash toward the south."

Men were buckling on gun belts and donning sombreros now. Everyone talked at once. It was the consensus of opinion that Calgary Rhodes had had something to do with Whit's and Jeff's disappearance.

"Just a minute, boys." Laidlaw raised his voice. "No use of us going off half cocked." His face was white, but he held his tone steady. The crew swung around to listen. Laidlaw continued: "We'd best take it easy until we know what we're doing. You're all headed to do some trailing, but you don't know for sure what direction to take. There's quite a stretch between here and that dry wash. We can make good time getting there, then we'll have to study the ground and use our heads. We can't afford to make mistakes—"

"Gawd!" Corbett burst out. "Think of trailin' anybody after this rain. All the sign will be plumb washed out. It's goin' to be a tough job."

"Do you think I have an easy job?" Laidlaw demanded testily. "I've got to go to the house and break the news to Miss Laura about what's happened. For all we know, this may be part of a raid planned by Rhodes and his Mex pardner. We just don't want to leap into something until we've considered matters with cool heads. Oh, we'll leave shortly"—as words of protest arose—"but we've got to use our heads. You fellers get ponies saddled. One of you saddle a horse for Red. No, Red, you can't do your own saddling. You're going to sit down and eat some breakfast. You might even have time to get into some dry togs. Now there's no use you fellers arguing with me. You can't leave until I do. I'm going up to the house to talk to Miss Laura right now. I'll get back soon's possible."

The men commenced to quiet down. At the doorway Laidlaw paused and glanced back. "Corbett, while I'm up talking to Miss Laura, you see that everybody has plenty of ca'tridges. Check up personal on every man. I don't want to find any of you excited waddles running short of loads, should we get into some sort of battle. And let's round up all the Winchesters around here. See that they're ready for use." With that he departed.

Ten minutes later he was back. Horses were already saddled and standing before the bunkhouse. Laidlaw's face was a mask of perturbation. "And now there is hell to pay," he growled. "Miss Laura insists on going with us. I tried to talk her out of it, but she says she can shoot and ride. Dutch"—to Vander—"go saddle up her pony. She'll be right with us. Take the pony up to the house."

Red Maguire said, "Miss Laura's as good as any of us with a gun."

Laidlaw nodded glumly. "I know, but still and all—" He paused as a new thought occurred to him. "Maybe it's just as well. I'd hate to have her here if Rhodes had any raiding ideas in mind."

The other men nodded and looked easier. Skillet Potter emerged from the kitchen carrying a double-barreled shotgun. Laidlaw demanded, "Where do you think you're going?"

"With you, if somebody'll saddle me a horse. I've been makin' up some packages of grub to take along, or I'd-a saddled my own horse."

"Thanks, Skillet, we can use that grub. But you're staying here," Laidlaw said.

"Dang your hide, boss," the cook protested in aggrieved tones, "you're just figurin' I'm too fat to stay on a horse."

At any other time this would have brought a concerted shout of agreement from the crew. Now the men remained silent while Laidlaw went on: "Your size has nothing to do with it, Skillet. We know you can ride. And that scatter-gun tells us you're ready to shoot too. I figured right along you'd be with us, but now that Miss Laura's going, somebody has to stay here at the ranch in case some word from Whit and Jeff comes. And we wouldn't feel right, either, not leaving somebody here in case there was a raid."

Skillet was somewhat mollified. "Better not no raiders come messin' around here," he stated grimly.

Laidlaw nodded. "I know you can be relied on to do what's needed, cooky. After we leave, you'd better saddle a horse and keep a sharp eye out. If you see raiders coming, you fan-tail away from here as soon as Gawd will let you. If Whit and Jeff should show up while we're gone, I reckon now we'll leave enough sign so one of 'em can catch up with us. Just remember, the 2JD is in your care. I leave it to you to make the right decisions if anything comes up."

A few minutes later Laura came riding down to the bunkhouse. Her six-shooter was strapped at one hip of her riding skirt, her Stetson pulled low on her head. She said briefly, "I'm ready when anyone else is."

The men rushed into saddles and, with Laidlaw at their head, went pounding out of the ranch yard. Skillet looked longingly after them. "Bring Jeff and Whit back," he called. "I'm counting on you-all."

Laura Dawson's voice floated back through the moist morning air: "We won't let you down, Skillet." She spurred to catch up and took a place at Corbett's side as the horses went splashing through the puddles.

Long before they had reached the dry wash the sun was breaking through the scattered clouds.

REVOLUTION

THE TWO PRISONERS STILL SAT ON THEIR BOXES. Swingle, Dirty-Shirt, and Squint lounged about the room. Torrio and Rhodes hadn't yet returned, though it was nearly eleven in the morning; sun shone through the windows. Whit's wrists were numbed and cramped by his bonds; Dawson moved uncomfortably on his box. The three guards had cooked up some bacon to eat with biscuits, and the prisoners had been fed sparingly, both Squint and Dirty-Shirt protesting that Rhodes hadn't included such feeding in his orders. However, Swingle had seen to it that they received a few bites, along with water and coffee.

Squint yawned sleepily, stretched, and gained his feet. "Me, I'm aimin' to have a shot of red-eye," he announced. "Are you with me, Dirty-Shirt—Swingle?"

Dirty-Shirt accepted with alacrity. Swingle pointed to the empty whisky bottle on the table, saying, "There's nothing to drink."

Squint grinned. "When you've been around here as long as we have, Swingle, you'll know all the tricks." He crossed the floor to the bunks, reached underneath, and pulled out a jug. "Just a little somethin' for emergencies," he said. He drew the cork and, balancing the jug against his crooked arm, drank deeply, then passed it to Dirty-Shirt. Dirty-Shirt drank and passed the jug to Swingle.

Swingle looked dubious. “I dunno. If we get to drinkin’ too much, we won’t keep our wits about us.” The other two hooted in derision, and finally Swingle took a small drink. The jug went back to Squint, who again tipped the jug to his lips. Whit looked on, a certain astonishment gathering in his mind: it appeared as though Squint would hold the jug to his mouth until it was empty. Finally he set it down on the table and smacked his lips.

“That’s the stuff to take the edge off’n that dampness I picked up last night,” he announced thickly.

Now Dirty-Shirt again applied himself to the whisky. Swingle refused a second drink. “Looka here,” Dirty-Shirt proposed, “there ain’t no use of all three of us standin’ guard. Without my sleep last night I’m feelin’ sorta tuckered. Reckon I’ll turn in for a spell, unless you two are afeared to guard these two hombres without me.”

Squint laughed scornfully. “Go ahead, grab your shut-eye. Me ’n’ Swingle is capable of doin’ all the guardin’ necessary. We’ll watch ’em.”

“Just don’t let ’em get near them guns on the table,” Dirty-Shirt warned. “I don’t care if they are tied. You can’t trust them two bustards. I’ll just grab about forty winks.” He tumbled into the nearest bunk and was almost instantly snoring.

Squint chuckled. “Dirty-Shirt never could hold his liquor too good. Coupla drinks and he’s done for. Now me, I can drink all night and never notice it.” He again reached for the jug. Liquor gurgled down his throat. He replaced the container on the table and sat down rather heavily on a box. He eyed the prisoners owlishly. “Like to offer you a drink, gents, but I don’t reckon Calgary would approve. It’s his idea to lower your resistance to the point where you'll sign that paper."

"Rhodes is figurin' all wrong, then," Dawson snapped. He shifted position somewhat stiffly. Instantly Squint was on the alert. "You sit still, Dawson. Talk all you want, but don't make no more of them sudden moves." He slid his half-drawn gun back into holster.

Dirty-Shirt continued to snore. Dawson said after a time, "I'd sure like to know what makes Rhodes so anxious to get the 2JD."

"I'll bet you would," Squint snickered. He moved his box nearer the table and again applied himself to the jug, then banged it back on the table.

Swingle put in, "Cripes, these hombres aren't goin' anyplace anyway. You might as well tell 'em, Squint."

Squint hiccuped and considered the matter. "Cansh see where it do no harm," he admitted, thick-tongued.

"Offhand," Whit put in, "with Torrio playing a part, I'd say all this had something to do with a revolution in Mexico."

"You heard something about it?" Swingle asked.

"Rumors." Whit nodded.

"Sure, theresh been rumors for months." Squint nodded heavily.

"But what's that got to do with the 2JD?" Dawson asked.

Squint yawned. "You tell him, Swingle. It won't make no difference now."

Swingle said, "It's this way: Don Torrio aims to set himself up as a new *presidente* in Mexico just as soon as he can grab off enough *soldados* for his push. Well, soldiers need guns. Guns have to come from this side of the line, and then they're run through to Mexico. Torchido Pass bein' the only route through the Encontrón Mountains for some distance either way,

Torchido is a plumb strategic point in Torrio's mind. And in Calgary's. Calgary will be a mighty important figure in the new Mex Government—"

"And in case the revolution failed," Whit put in, "Torrio and his gang would have a clear retreat through Torchido to the United States, where they'd be safe from the Mexican *federalistas.*"

"You got the idea." Swingle nodded. "To put this revolution across, a heap of guns and ammunition is needed. Regular ports of entry on the border are guarded close, so Torrio decides he needs the 2JD, Dawson, seein' Torchido Pass opens on your holdin's. Now you wouldn't allow any gun-runnin' through there, would you?" Dawson snapped out a profane negative. Swingle shrugged. "You should realize how it is, then. Torrio just has to control your property in Calgary's name. Once Calgary is runnin' the 2JD, he ain't goin' to object to Torrio runnin' guns through. In fact, Calgary will have a good investment. He'll have a nice ranch and a slice of the Mexican Treasury, once Torrio has fought his way to the capital—"

"Phaugh!" Dawson grunted disgustedly. "Revolutions ain't put over so easy as you think."

"It won't be so difficult," Swingle responded. "We've already run a lot of guns through. We got most of the men in Nuevo Cesto lined up right now. We give 'em guns. Then we move on to another town and take it over. We make prisoners of a lot of *peones,* then we give 'em their choice of facin' a firin' squad or joinin' with us. How do you think they'll decide? Especially when Torrio gives 'em one of his rabble-rousin' speeches and tells 'em they're downtrod by the present government. In that way we gather more *soldados* and move on to take another larger town and go through the same business again. Torrio's army will grow like a snowball rollin' downhill. Eventually he'll have enough men to capture Mexico City, and that's where the big lootin' comes. Rhodes and Torrio have gone to Nuevo Cesto now to plan some last-minute details before the revolution gets started—"

"You're havin' a pipedream," Dawson growled. "In the first place, I'm not turnin' my spread over to Rhodes, so there goes your revolution—nipped right at the start."

Swingle smiled confidently. Whit said, "All right, for the sake of argument, suppose Jeff did sign a bill of sale and then disappeared? How far do you suppose you'd get? Laura Dawson would know something was wrong and take the matter to court—"

"Now whosh havin' pipedream?" Squint guffawed, rousing himself from a half stupor induced by the liquor. "Once Rhodes and Torrio have worked on Dawson, he'll sign. Then to hell with your courts. Torrio and Calgary can hire law sharps. No judge is goin' to throw out a signed bill of sale. A case like that could drag through the courtsh for yearsh—anyway, long 'nough for Calgary and Torrio to do what they want." Dawson and Whit fell silent. Squint attacked the jug again. He struggled to his feet after a minute. 'Whoosh! Dawn hot in here. Reckon—I'll go get some fresh air."

"Hot is right," Dawson said, heaving a deep sigh. "I feel like I was goin' to pass out. How about lettin' Whit and me go out a minute?"

Swingle refused. "Nope. You stay right here until Calgary comes."

Dawson said hopelessly, "Suit yourself, but if anythin' goes wrong, don't blame me."

Swingle's eyes were suspicious. "What do you mean? What could go wrong?"

"Just this"—Dawson's voice sounded weak—"I've got a bad heart. Lack of fresh air might bring on an attack. If I keel over dead before Rhodes returns, he never would get that paper. Then you two would catch hell, 'cause Whit would tell him that I warned you."

"I'd tell him if I was still alive," Whit said, "but I don't feel so good neither. This sort of treatment is dangerous and right likely to kill a man—"

"What sort of treatment?" Swingle asked nervously.

"You got my hands tied so tight, my circulation is practically cut off," Whit explained glibly. "What happens when circulation is cut off? Blood commences to clot. Eventually a clot reaches the heart, and then—bang!—my heart stops."

It was, Whit figured while he talked, a pretty feeble attempt. Surely Squint and Swingle wouldn't be so dumb as to put credence in such words. But watching them from beneath lowered lids, Whit saw that he had the two men worried. His words, added to what Dawson had said, had convinced them, apparently. Swingle drew Squint up from his box, and the two men held a whispered consultation in one corner of the room. Both realized that Rhodes would raise merry hell if he returned to find his two prisoners dead.

Meanwhile Dirty-Shirt was continuing to make snoring noises in his bunk.

Finally Squint and Swingle returned to the center of the room, Squint pausing on the way to address himself to the jug. "It's this way," Swingle commenced hesitatingly. "Squint and me don't want to be too hard on you two. All that stuff about bad hearts and clots is just bosh, of course, and you ain't fooled us a minute.

On t'other hand, we're willin' to let you have a breath of fresh air. But, mind, we'll be holdin' our guns on you every minute, so don't try nothin'. We'll plug you if you try to run for it."

The two prisoners rose stiffly to their feet. Squint lurched toward the door and opened it. Sunshine poured in. As he and Dawson stepped out to the still wet, steaming earth, Whit drew a deep breath. Glancing over his shoulder, he saw that Squint and Swingle held drawn guns. One at a time the two prisoners had their hands untied and were allowed to walk about a few minutes. Then, while one guard watched, gun in hand, the other retied wrists behind a prisoner's back.

Now that neither prisoner had made an attempt to escape, the two guards breathed easier. Swingle even rolled and lighted cigarettes and placed them in the mouths of the prisoners. Dawson and Whit stood near the wall of the house, bathed in sunshine. All around were cottonwood trees, with beyond a long slope that stretched slowly toward the north. At the top of the slope nothing was to be seen but blue sky with a few drifting clouds. Whit considered: should he have tried for an escape when his hands were untied? Mentally he shook his head. The odds had been too great against him. Either Swingle or Squint—maybe both—would have shot him down before he'd run ten yards. And that would have left Dawson to their mercy. Undoubtedly the same or similar thoughts were passing through Dawson's mind.

Whit glanced again at his surroundings. "Where is this house situated, anyway?" he asked Swingle. "How far are we from Palomas?"

"None of your business," Swingle said.

"I suppose it's all right if I make a guess." Whit

smiled thinly.

"Guess until hell freezes over," Swingle said.

"I know where they brought us," Dawson put in. "We're just five or six miles from the badlands stretch of country. I've been here before. This house used to belong to an Easterner who came out here for his health. He got better and went back home. Nobody else wanted to live here—"

"That's the difference between you and the Easterner," Squint said with coarse humor. "You ain't—*hic*!—goin' to get better and go home."

Dawson fell silent. Whit studied the sky, braced his arms against the bonds. Swingle had tied them as tightly as they had been before. Whit wondered if Squint had done the same sort of job on Dawson. Probably so. Befuddled as the man was, he still had enough sense to draw the knot tightly.

Squint yawned. "Reckon you fellers had better get inside again."

Whit said suddenly, "Squint, why did Rhodes kill John Dawson?"

"John Dawson butted into somethin' that was none of his business," Squint said promptly. "He followed us—" He broke off suddenly. "Sa-a-ay, what do you know about it? Who says that Calgary killed—"

"Rhodes killed my brother!" Jeff Dawson exclaimed. "Whit, where did you get that idea? What in the devil do you know that—"

"It's true." Whit nodded. "Squint just practically admitted it. I was just guessing before, though I knew Rhodes had been there when John Dawson was killed."

"Smart hombre, ain't you?" Swingle sneered. "Just how did you learn so much?"

"I can explain that in a minute," Whit said. "When I

found John Dawson's body there was the imprint of a man's palm in the sand near the body. It was fairly faint, but I could see a sort of line running across the palm. After I'd seen the scar on Calgary Rhodes' hand I knew what had caused the line on the imprint—"

"That murderin' bustard!" Jeff Dawson exploded angrily. "All's I want is to meet Rhodes face to face, and—"

"You'll meet him, all right," Swingle said harshly, "but you won't be able to do anythin' about your brother's death. You'll be thinkin' about your own finish."

"Why was John Dawson killed?" Whit asked.

Swingle said sullenly, "None of your business."

"Aw, hell," Squint said thickly, "go ahead and relieve their curiosity. They won't be able to do anythin' about it now."

Swingle nodded. "I don't suppose it will make no difference. It was this way: We had some boxes of carbines comin' through to be delivered at Curtisville. Rhodes was to take delivery in the name of Starkey. It was just our luck that John Dawson was in Curtisville that day and saw Calgary. He bawled Calgary out for not bein' at work at the 2JD. That was a mistake. He made Calgary mad. Anyway, I suppose Dawson got curious as to what Calgary was doin' in Curtisville, so he trails him down to the depot. The boxes of guns had arrived, but one had fallen and splintered the wood at one end. John Dawson got to the depot just as Calgary was about to nail up the board on the broken box, and he got a peek at what the box contained. Calgary went ahead with his repairin' and told Dawson he was crazy—said that the box contained some windmill parts for a friend of his'n. John told Calgary he needn't come back to the 2JD and paid him off then and there—"

Squint snickered. "And the next day Jeff, here, paid him off a second time."

Jeff Dawson swore and told Swingle to go on. Swingle continued: "A bunch of us were ready at the depot, with pack horses, to load on the boxes. John Dawson left the depot and we figured we was shet of him, but I reckon we guessed wrong. He must have trailed Calgary at a distance to see where the boxes was bein' taken. Just plain snoopy, that's all. It wa'n't none of his business. Anyway, we was nigh to Torchido Pass that night, late, when John Dawson closed in on us. He ordered us off 2JD property. Calgary again gave him the story about boxes of windmill parts. Said we was takin' 'em to a friend in Mexico. With that, Dawson calls him a liar and says he guesses the boxes contain guns and ammunition for a revolution in Mexico. That made Calgary mad all over again. When Dawson turned to look for the box that had been broken, with the intention of makin' Calgary out a liar, I suppose, Calgary pulls his gun and lets him have it. Then we went on and delivered the boxes."

Dawson's face was drawn in tight, harsh lines. He shifted nervously from one foot to the other. Whit said slowly, "And so Calgary pulled his gun and let John Dawson have it—in the back."

Swingle shrugged. "Sure, why not? John Dawson had to go. He got snoopy and stuck his nose into our business. And there wa'n't no use Calgary takin' chances. Why shouldn't he shoot him in the back? You know any reason why?"

"None that you could understand," Whit said coldly.

Squint said, "Aw, cripes! It's all done and over with. Lesh go back in the house. I could stand anozzer drink.

These hombres had 'nough fresh air."

The prisoners were herded back into the house and told to take their seats on the boxes. Swingle and Squint reholstered their six-shooters. Once more Squint lifted the jug. He passed it on to Swingle, who this time drank deeply. Dirty-Shirt was still sound asleep in his bunk. Flies buzzed in and out of his open mouth.

Squint eyed Dirty-Shirt a moment. "Damned if that cuss don' look com'fable," he mumbled. "Shwingle, I'm goin' lay down a spell. Ain' goin' sleep . . . can guard jush as well layin' down. These two ain' goin . . . make no trouble . . . anyhow . . . " He half staggered across the room and tumbled into the bunk adjoining Dirty-Shirt's. His eyes closed, and in less than a minute a sound that resembled that of a power saw working its way through a knotty section of board filled the room.

Swingle swore and called, "Squint, you said you wasn't goin' to sleep." Squint continued to slumber, his snores mingling with those of Dirty-Shirt. Swingle gazed resentfully at the two, then settled back on his box, back resting against the edge of the table. "Reckon I'm man enough to guard you two," he muttered.

A half-hour passed. Swingle's eyes commenced to grow heavy. He indulged in several jaw-breaking yawns. It was close within the room. The only sounds were those of two snoring men in bunks and the myriad flies that droned through the warm air. Both Whit and Dawson were watching Swingle closely. He sat as before, back resting against the edge of the table on which were Whit's and Dawson's guns. But what good would it do, Whit mused hopelessly, if Swingle did fall asleep? True, he and Jeff would be able to reach the table, but with hands tied behind them, any thought of resistance was out of the question.

Swingle's eyes closed at last. Jeff and Whit exchanged glances. Slowly Whit commenced to slide his box back over the floor so as to place himself in a position where his bound hands could reach the knot that held Dawson's wrists together. Suddenly the box made a scraping sound. Whit froze to immovability. Swingle awakened with a jerk, eying his two prisoners suspiciously. Both men sat as he had last remembered them, it seemed. Whit and Dawson were hunched over, heads bowed.

"Did you say somethin', Gallatin?" Swingle asked.

Slowly Whit lifted his head, looking drowsily at Swingle. "No, I didn't say anything," he grumbled. "Can't you leave a feller alone? I was nigh asleep. Remember, I didn't get any shut-eye all night."

"Well, I didn't neither," Swingle growled. "That makes us even. If I can keep awake, you should be able to."

"I don't have to," Whit snapped.

"Shut up, will you?" Dawson put in.

Whit and Swingle "shut up." For a few minutes Swingle sat straighter on his box, then gradually his form began to slump down again. Slowly his eyes closed. Within five minutes he was breathing heavily. Without turning his head, Dawson whispered softly, "Whit, keep your eyes on them two in the bunk. I'll watch Swingle."

Cautiously Whit glanced over his shoulder toward the bunks. Squint was flat on his back, snoring. Dirty-Shirt was also making loud sleeping sounds, but he was lying in a huddle, face toward the back wall. Whit's gaze returned to Dawson, traveled down the old cowman's back to his bound wrists. Then Whit's heart gave a great leap. Jeff's wrists were pulling and straining at the rawhide thongs. Some of the skin had been scraped raw, but there was no doubt about it, the rawhide was looser than it had been previously.

Again Jeff whispered to Whit: "When Squint retied me outside I held my wrists edge to edge 'stead of flat together. He pulled the knot tight enough, but he was too befuddled with whisky to notice how I was holdin' my arms. It's give me some slack, and I reckon to work loose in a short spell."

Whit nodded without replying. He kept his gaze toward the two in the bunks, hearing all the time the soft sounds made by Dawson's wrists working against the leather thongs, straining, stretching, pulling, as the old cattleman worked to get free. Five more minutes passed. Something like a snore passed Swingle's lips, and he roused himself with a start and gazed bleary-eyed at the prisoners. Again Jeff and Whit slumped back to former positions. Swingle said, "Did I hear you two talkin'?"

Whit raised his head. Angrily he snapped, "Will you keep your trap closed? You went and woke me up again."

Swingle swore at him and relaxed once more. After a time his eyes closed. One minute passed. Two. Five. Something soft dropped to the floor behind Dawson and looking down, Whit saw that Dawson had freed his wrists of the rawhide, which now lay on the boards behind him. Dawson said, low-voiced, "Now if you can just wiggle yourself around to me—"

He stopped abruptly. Swingle was again awake and staring straight at him. "What in hell you two cookin' up?" he commenced.

In that moment, with a tigerish spring remarkable in a man of Dawson's age, the old cowman left his box and leaped straight toward Swingle. Even before Swingle could get his gun from holster Dawson had clutched the man's wrist, at the same moment reaching for one of the loose guns on the table.

Before Dawson could secure a gun, however, Swingle had forced him back. Swingle yelled, "Squint! Dirty-Shirt! Help!"

Whit was on his feet now. With arms bound behind him, he turned toward the bunk just as Squint was crawling to his feet. Without hesitation Whit hurled his body at Squint's knees as the man was drawing his six-shooter. The gun roared high overhead as Squint went crashing across Whit's muscular bulk and landed heavily on the floor.

Meanwhile Dawson and Swingle were struggling about the room, locked in a fighting embrace. Swingle kept wasting breath in frantic yells for Squint and Dirty-Shirt. The old cowman grappled in silence, his left hand clinched about Swingle's right wrist, preventing the drawing of Swingle's weapon, while at the same time he fought to reach the guns on the table.

Dirty-Shirt was just emerging from his bunk, mouth open, eyes clouded with sleep and alcohol, not yet quite realizing what was taking place. Whit, wiggling loose from under Squint's form, threw out his legs as Dirty-Shirt stepped from his bunk. Dirty-Shirt tripped and went sprawling on his face.

Whit struggled to his feet and whirled toward Squint, who was on hands and knees, reaching for the gun which had gone flying from his grasp as he went down. Raising his right foot, Whit kicked with all his force, his booted toe landing squarely on Squint's jaw. Squint groaned and slumped back to the boards, face down.

Whit laughed with savage exultation, turned toward

Dirty-Shirt, who was just rising, one hand clawing at his gun butt. Again Whit drove his right foot in a vicious kick. Dirty-Shirt whimpered as his head was knocked violently to one side, then crashed down again, jaw slack and eyes glassy.

Now Whit whirled back toward the struggling figures of Dawson and Swingle. With hands bound behind him as they were, there was little Whit could do except dart to Swingle's rear and drop to hands and knees. Dawson increased the ferocity of his attack, wrestling Swingle back and back. At the same instant Whit flung his muscular form at Swingle's knees. A startled yell was torn from Swingle's lips as he tumbled back, heels over head, to land on the back of his neck as Dawson released his grip. He lay there, half stunned, as Dawson leaped to the table and secured a six-shooter.

A wide grin parted the old cowman's lips as his gaze fell on the prone figures of Dirty-Shirt and Squint. He swung back toward Swingle who was thrashing futilely on the floor. "By Gawd!" Dawson panted. "We'll show you stinkin' bustards what a revolution really means! Whit, you done elegant! Crawl into the clear until I get a shot at this scut!"

LUCK RUNS OUT

WHIT WAS JUST STRUGGLING TO HIS FEET when the door banged open and a voice snarled furiously, "Drop that gun, Dawson!"

Whit glanced toward the open doorway and saw Calgary Rhodes standing there, six-shooter clutched in his fist. Behind him was the tall figure of Drake Lowendirk, and beyond some fifteen riders just pulling mounts to a halt. So intense had been the struggle in the house, neither Whit nor Dawson had heard the approach of Rhodes and the others.

Dawson slowly lowered his gun as he turned to the door, then allowed it to drop to the floor. His arms lifted into the air as he said grimly, "Whit, it looks like our luck's run out. But we sure made one hell of a try." He glanced around the room and laughed harshly.

"Anyway," Whit replied quietly, "it was good fun while it lasted."

Squint and Dirty-Shirt still lay as before. Swingle climbed stiffly from the floor. Calgary Rhodes barged angrily into the room. "Your fun's all over, you buzzards," he fumed. "You'll pay for this, by Gawd!"

"You murderin scut!" Dawson charged. "If anybody's due to pay, there's an account against you for murderin' my brother."

Rhodes stopped short. "Where'd you get that idea?" he commenced, then stopped and shrugged his shoulders. "All right, I killed him. I suppose somebody's been talkin' out of turn. T'hell with it . . . Drake, keep Dawson covered until I can tie him up."

The old cowman had taken a sudden angry step toward Rhodes, but at a sharp warning from Lowendirk he stopped. The section of rawhide was found, and a few minutes later Dawson's hands were bound tightly, and he and Whit were again seated on their boxes. Bat Tiernan and other men now crowded into the room. Whit looked them over. A dirtier more murderous-looking group he had never seen. Just border scum, he concluded.

Rhodes stormed furiously about the room. He turned savagely on Swingle. "Fine guards you three turned out to be, letting two bound men put it over on you. Only that we got here in time—"

"It ain't my fault no more than Squint's and Dirty-Shirt's," Swingle whined. "Them two went to sleep in their bunks. I figure that Squint done a poor job when he tied Dawson up again. That's how come—"

"Tied him up *again*!" Rhodes' jaw dropped. "Do you mean to stand there and say that after all my warning you had these hombres untied once?"

Swingle sheepishly mumbled something about bad hearts and the prisoners needing air so they wouldn't die. That sent Rhodes into another explosion of anger. "You fools, you utter goddamn fools," he snarled.

He jerked furiously away from Swingle and crossed the floor to the recumbent forms of Dirty-Shirt and Squint. Here some savage kicks in the ribs got that pair stirring and moaning with pain. After a few minutes they stumbled to their feet. By the time they were in condition to listen they, too, came in for their share of the tirade while they mumbled excuses and each tried to lay the blame on the other two.

Lowendirk cut in finally: "All right, Calgary, what's done is done. There's nothing happened in this place that's beyond repair. But you'd best get your men out and watch for that Mexican cavalry. It might come clear through the pass."

Whit pricked up his ears. "What about Mexican cavalry?" he asked.

"None of your damn business," Rhodes spat. He turned to the other men in the room. "You hombres get outside. Keep a sharp watch. Fire on any riders you see. Bat"—to Tiernan—"you know what's necessary. You go along as boss. And hurry up about it."

Men commenced to shuffle out of the room, and Whit

could hear them remounting outside. Hoofs moved away from the house. Rhodes slammed the door with a muttered oath. Lowendirk was seated on a box near the table. Squint, Dirty-Shirt, and Swingle stood about, looking still dazed. The former two had bloody, swollen jaws showing where Whit's boot had landed.

"I'm still wondering," Whit said quietly, "if the Mexican Government put a stop to the revolution."

Lowendirk frowned. "What do you know about it?"

Whit laughed. "I was up in Curtisville a couple of weeks back and I sent a telegram to Mexico City tipping the authorities off to the fact that a revolution, centering in Nuevo Cesto, was brewing—"

"Why, you goddamn—" Rhodes leaped across the room and swung his fists on Whit's head. Whit let his head roll with the blows. Rhodes finally stepped back to land a finishing punch when a sharp word from Lowendirk stopped him.

"Take it easy, Calgary," Lowendirk said. "Let's see what Gallatin can tell us."

Rhodes stepped back, glowering. Blood ran from a cut on Whit's cheek. One of his eyes had commenced to swell. "There's nothing more that I can tell you." He laughed contemptuously. "Jeff and I were in Curtisville one day, and while Jeff was talking to some friends I dropped down to the depot and sent the telegram."

Dawson chuckled with grim humor. "That's somethin' I should have thought of doin' myself a long spell back. So the revolution's busted up, Lowendirk?"

"I guess it is," Lowendirk admitted calmly. "A few companies of Mexican cavalry dropped down on Nuevo Cesto and captured Torrio's *soldados* before they even got started. Torrio was grabbed too. If he hasn't already faced a firing squad, I'm surprised. The revolution is done for. Calgary and I and some of our men just managed to get away in time."

"That's too bad," Dawson growled.

"Things aren't bad at all." Lowendirk smiled. "I never did have too much faith in Don Torrio's revolution, but when he came to me with gold for guns—"

"Why should he come to you?" Whit asked.

"I own a factory up in Denver. The machinery I had wasn't intended for gun manufacture, but I was able to convert it to making cheap imitations of guns turned out in this country. Then when Torrio commenced to run low on money he offered me a share in his revolution if I'd continue to furnish guns. It looked like a fair gamble, and I took it. I'm still money ahead." He chuckled nastily. "So you see, I'm not a detective after all, Gallatin. I don't mind admitting when I first saw you I suspected you were a government agent snooping into revolutionary activities—"

"And so," Whit interrupted, "you let it be known around that you were a detective, hoping to throw me off the track. And acting friendly to me was part of the same idea. I'll admit to being thrown off the track, sort of, but you never did have me entirely convinced. I suspected something was wrong from the first. You were supposed to be down here for your health and to do some riding. One horse would have been enough for that. You kept three. So I knew you were covering a lot of territory and weren't just pleasure-loping around. You claimed you weren't familiar with guns, but the day you handed me your six-shooter 'to examine'—another *friendly* gesture—I noted it was loaded with only five ca'tridges. A greenhorn with guns would have loaded all six chambers."

Lowendirk's eyes narrowed. "You're smarter than I thought you were, Gallatin. You should have joined me when you had a chance. You and I could have made some very profitable deals—"

Whit cut in: "The night before I came here I saw you in Nuevo Cesto. Just happened to look through a window of the posada where I was staying and saw you talking to some Mexes. When I heard the talk about you coming here for your health I thought something was queer."

"You never told me all this, Whit," Dawson said.

"I wanted to be sure of my facts, Jeff, before I shot off my mouth," Whit explained. He turned back to Lowendirk. "It was fixed for me to be killed the night I visited your house, if I didn't fair in with your plans. When Tack Tiernan didn't succeed in shooting me, you killed Tiernan to keep him from talking. Isn't that correct?"

"I'll grant you're on the right track." Lowendirk admitted coolly. "But how did you arrive at that? I'm curious."

"You failed to warn me not to tell people that John Dawson had brought you here until *after* Tack missed his shot. As you had it arranged, I was never going to get a chance to talk to other people. Right?" Lowendirk answered in the affirmative. Whit went on: "And that business of trying to get me to go to San Diego—if I'd fallen in with your plans—was just to get me out of the way—send me off on a wild-goose chase. And Nick Starkey was just a name you made up in your mind."

"You're wrong there," Lowendirk said. "Nicholas Starkey is the silent pardner in my factory. He put up the money to finance the business. And he really has gone to San Diego. Of course he doesn't know the factory is furnishing guns to revolutionists. His honest soul would rebel at doing anything like that. But he has a name for integrity. It's a very good name under which to ship contraband weapons. I'll concede I might have employed a little more originality when I gave you his name as that of the man John Dawson feared—nice little bit of fiction, that was—but I had to give you some sort of story, and Starkey's name just popped into my mind. Of course if you had believed me and gone hunting for him in San Diego, he would have denied knowing John Dawson."

"And if he put up too much of an argument, you figured I'd either shoot him or at least arrest him and bring him here," Whit said grimly.

Lowendirk nodded. "Starkey would listen to reason if I had him here."

In other words, you'd have had him murdered," Whit snapped, "so you wouldn't have to return the money he invested in your factory."

Lowendirk said boredly, "You make it sound rather crude, but I must say you're correct in your surmise—"

"Hell!" Rhodes broke in irritably. "What's the use of all this talk? Let's get down to business, Drake."

"I quite agree, Calgary." Lowendirk nodded. "You see, the end of the revolution doesn't entirely destroy my plans. After a time things will settle down along the border. I can see a vast profit in promoting revolutions. Meanwhile Torchido Pass is very convenient for smuggling purposes. Both the United States and Mexico require certain articles that are contraband, and I see profit in that direction too. That means we need Torchido Pass, and to control the pass we have to own the 2JD Ranch. I hope you're ready to listen to reason, Dawson. Calgary and I have talked things over, and the deal might convince even more people if you put my name on that bill of sale. I'm supposed to be a wealthy businessman. What is more natural than that I should take over your property?"

"You can go plumb to hell!" Dawson snorted.

Rhodes flung himsef across the room to confront Dawson. "I'm sick of arguin' with you, Dawson. We want your name on that bill of sale, or I aim to start slicin' you up in little pieces. Don Torrio ain't here, but I know all the tricks he had for persuadin' stubborn hombres. Now you'd best listen to reason—"

"Aw go off and die in some rattlers' nest," Dawson growled contemptuously. "That's where you belong. I'm sick of your threats. But get one thing straight: I ain't signin' that paper!"

A baffled howl of rage was torn from Rhodes's lips. He swung his clenched fist, catching the old cattleman full in the face. Dawson went topping from the box and went down like a poled ox. He struggled slowly to his feet, a thin trickle of scarlet coursing down from his mouth. "I could expect somethin' like that from a sidewindin' bustard," he said quietly.

"That's only a small sample of what you're due to get unless you see things our way," Rhodes commenced. "Now I'm goin' to give you one more chance to be reasonable. Ever hear of that Chinese torture—the Death of a Thousand Cuts? We can slice your carcass a mite at a time, Dawson, until you've had enough. Or maybe you'd sooner be staked on an anthill. A lighted candle held to the soles of your feet can be plenty persuasive, or we can drive some slivers under your fingernails—"

"I'll take more'n your talk to make me sign, Rhodes," Dawson interrupted. His face had gone pale beneath its tan, but his voice was firm.

"You're wasting breath, Calgary," Lowendirk put in. "If Dawson thinks your ideas are too crude to make him cooperate, I'd like to point out that he'll change his mind when we bring his niece here and—"

What more he intended to say was never learned. A shot sounded some distance from the house. It was immediately followed by a ragged volley coming from various points. Then an abrupt yelling burst in the air. There came the drumming of horses' hoofs.

Rhodes and Lowendirk stiffened. "What in hell's that?" Rhodes demanded.

Lowendirk said, "Some of that Mex cavalry has probably followed us through Torchido Pass—"

"I'm betting you're wrong," Whit laughed. "That's the 2JD hands on your trail. They've probably got an army of riders—"

"You're a liar!" Rhodes swore. The firing increased.

Rhodes and Lowendirk rushed to the door, flung it open. Squint, Dirty-Shirt, and Swingle were close behind. Rhodes spun back, speaking to his three henchmen. "You hombres stay here and keep the door closed. Watch them prisoners . . ."

The door was slammed shut behind him as he hurried after Lowendirk. Squint, Dirty-Shirt, and Swingle came back into the room: " 'Sall right with me," Swingle said, shrugging his shoulders. "I don't crave to go out and expose myself to no bullets if Calgary wants I should stay here." Dirty-Shirt and Squint voiced similar comments. All three guards were crowded at the front windows now. Outside guns were cracking wildly. Horses thudded past the house, and the hoofbeats receded as they moved away.

"You three might tell us what's doin'," Dawson

growled impatiently.

"I tell you it's the 2JD—" Whit commenced.

Swingle moved back toward the prisoners. "Can't see much of anythin'," he grunted. "Mostly what's goin' on is takin' place beyond the trees. I saw Bat Tiernan lope past a minute ago—" He stopped and said to Whit, "What makes you so sure that's the 2JD? They wouldn't know where to find you."

"I gave 'em a good start, I'll bet." Whit grinned. "I knew they'd be looking for us when we didn't return to the ranch. Last night, the instant that lariat dropped over my head, I realized what was happening, so I let go of my whip—dropped it on the ground. You fellers overlooked it in the dark. The 2JD boys could take up the trail from where they found it."

Swingle commenced to look worried. "Sure," he said uncertainly at last, "but how could they trail us from where they found the whip? The rain would wash out our tracks."

Another burst of fire interrupted. It was nearer now.

Whit continued: "Sure the rain would wash out a lot of the tracks, but if the 2JD hands was to run across a ca'tridge layin' on the ground every so often, they'd know what direction we were traveling."

"Ca'tridge?" Swingle asked dumbly.

"By Gawd!" Dawson exploded. "That's why you didn't have no ca'tridges in the front of your belts last night when Calgary wanted some loads." He looked admiringly at Whit.

Whit nodded. "I knew they wouldn't find all the ca'tridges I'd plucked out of my belt and dropped while we were riding—but if they could just find enough to show 'em the general direction, I figured they'd arrive here—"

The words were interrupted by alarmed exclamations from Squint and Dirty-Shirt as they turned back from the window. "Swingle," Squint cried, his face pale beneath his whiskers, "there's a rider herdin' Tiernan and Jackson up this way. They both got their hands in the air and they're afoot. Do you reckon—"

"You hombres are licked!" Whit yelled triumphantly. "Better use your heads. Surrender to Jeff and me and untie us. It's your only chance to save your necks."

"That," Swingle stated nervously, "sounds like good sense to me." He started around behind Whit.

Squint and Dirty-Shirt had drawn pocketknives, "Don't take time to untie them rawhides," Squint exclaimed. "Cuttin' is quicker!"

CONCLUSION

WHIT CAME RUNNING FROM THE DOORWAY of the house, stuffing six-shooters into his holsters. Through the trees he could see men and horses on the slope that descended to the house. Several men were afoot, arms raised in the air. Nearer at hand he saw Red Maguire approaching, driving before him two individuals whose arms appeared to be trying to reach the sky. One of the captives was Bat Tiernan; the other, one of the "border scum" who had arrived with Lowendirk and Rhodes. Whit let off a wild yell of greeting: "Red! How's it going?"

Maguire's head jerked up from his prisoners. A wide grin split' his features. "Whit! You ornery ol' bastard," he cried fondly. "You're safe!" He pulled his pony to a halt and spoke to his prisoners: "Tiernan, you and your sidewinder pal hold up a moment." Then to Whit,

"Where's Jeff?"

Whit jerked his thumb over one shoulder. "Back in the house there, guarding three more prisoners. You must have found my whip—"

"Got it right with me." Maguire pointed to the whip coiled about his saddle horn. "Found your ca'tridges too."

"Talk fast," Whit suggested. "I want to get into this fight."

"Fight's over. You don't hear any shootin' now. The others are just sort of moppin' up the remains. Like I say, we found your whip and then followed along the dry wash. When we got to higher ground, any tracks that might have been made was washed out by the rain. We were stumped for a minute, until Dutch Vander spotted a ca'tridge layin' on the ground. We figured you might have dropped it—it looked bright and not like it had been there a long time. It was you dropped them ca'tridges, wa'n't it?" Maguire scarcely waited for Whit's nod of confirmation before continuing: "Later we found another ca'tridge. We kept goin'. Then we hit some more tracks that hadn't been clean washed out. We figured at first you and Jeff were bein' taken through Torchido Pass, but a ca'tridge dropped at the right place told us where to swing to the southeast—"

"I'll bet a lot of my loads got washed over with mud."

"Probably. We found enough to keep us goin', though it was some slow at times when we couldn't find neither ca'tridges or tracks. This mornin' we run across Sheriff Brandon. Your disappearance had got him worried, and he was out to see what he could find. He joined us. Seein' the direction we were headed, he happened to remember this house here. Well, more ca'tridges pointed the way. When we got near here we sort of fanned out along the top of the slope to look things over. We saw some riders arrivin' from the direction of Torchido Pass. They disappeared in the trees around the house. Later a bunch of 'em come into view again. They kept lookin' off toward Torchido, as if expectin' somebody from that direction. That give us a chance to sneak a mite nearer. Finally one of 'em turns and spies Laidlaw before he could duck out of sight. With that, the hombre shakes a load outten his barrel. That started it. Laidlaw and the rest of us cut loose from behind rocks and brush."

"You made plenty noise." Whit chuckled. "It sounded like an army attacking."

"That was the impression we tried to give. We let loose plenty lead from various points in damn little time. First thing we knowed, one of them scuts goes yellow and yells that he craves to surrender the instant he sees us come racin' down the slope. I guess his disease was contagious, 'cause some more starts belly-achin' the same song. There just wa'n't no fight in them bustards"—disgustedly—"so we commenced roundin' em up. We'd only plugged three or four when the rest quit and threw down their guns. Then Laidlaw sends me up this way to see if I can find you—"

"Did you get Rhodes and Lowendirk?" Whit cut in.

"Lowendirk?"

"He's in it too."

"I'll be damned! I saw Rhodes ride past once, but I was busy at the moment shootin' the rattles off'n a sidewinder. But Lowendirk—"

Bat Tiernan interrupted in a sullen voice: "I can tell you right now, Maguire, your crowd didn't get either of 'em. They've lit out to save their skins. Calgary yelled at me as he rode past to stand you hombres off as long as possible and that he'd meet me in Curtisville if I could get away. Them skunks quit us cold. That's why we didn't have no heart to fight. Gallatin, I'd like to see you get Lowendirk. That smooth-talkin' son of a leech killed my brother Tack—"

"Too bad you didn't do something about that long ago," Whit said coldly. He turned back to Maguire. "Red, get down off that horse. Go on to the house. Jeff will fill in the story for you. I need your pony—"

"Where you goin'?" Maguire asked as he climbed down from the saddle.

"After Rhodes and Lowendirk."

"You don't know which direction they took out for."

"I can make a guess. Rhodes will realize they wouldn't have much chance in open country. I figure he'll lead Lowendirk down into the badlands, hoping they'll be able to hide out down there."

"You'd best let me go along with you."

"You stay with your prisoners." Whit stepped up on the pony's back. The familiar sight of his whip on the saddle horn gave him an added confidence.

"But Laura will want to see you before you leave," Maguire said.

Whit hesitated in some surprise. "Laura?"

"She insisted on comin' with us. She was rollin' lead outten her barrel as fast as any of us."

Whit paused. Then determinedly he whirled the pony around and plunged spurs into its flanks. "Tell Laura I'll see her later," he called over his shoulder.

He glanced back once and saw Maguire urging his plodding captives on toward the house. Jeff Dawson had appeared in the doorway and was waving to Red with the six-shooter held in one hand. Then Whit was through the cottonwoods and flashing into the open, the pony gathering speed at every jump. Whit drove up the slope, eyes alert for a sign of Laura. Finally he spied her riding far to one side. Somewhat nearer he spotted Dutch Vander and Laidlaw, each herding a captive toward the house. Other riders were scattered about, a couple of whom hailed Whit as he dashed by. A dead horse lay on the ground, and caught beneath it was a motionless figure whom Whit recognized as another of the "border scum" contingent.

As he reached the top of the slope Whit took one last look back toward the wide saucer of land with its clump of cottonwoods and house at the bottom, then he drove on, again using his spurs to urge the pony on its way. "This horse is none too fresh," Whit muttered "but Lowendirk's and Rhodes's ponies can't be much better off." At the thought of Rhodes the old burning hate commenced to rise in Whit, and the incitement to kill and kill and kill surged through his being. He glanced down at the guns slung at either thigh. His face was a bleak mask of vengeance now, his lips a hard straight line; his gray eyes seemed to glow with cold blue flame.

He drove furiously on, crouched low behind his pony's head so as to offer less resistance to the wind whipping past. A moving panorama of greasewood, mesquite, and prickly pear slid smoothly by. After a time the growth thinned out; the earth over which the pony's hoofs thundered took on a lighter grayish tinge. Finally Whit saw what he'd been seeking: hoofprints. The marks were widely spaced, showing that the horses which had made the prints were moving fast. The prints were fresh, easy to follow.

After a time Whit raised his head. Two miles farther on a blinding stretch of white glare met his eyes: the salt flats lying just north of the badlands area. The salt flats shimmered and undulated brilliantly under the light of the bright afternoon sun. Whit narrowed his eyes, straining his gaze for a first sight of the two men he was pursuing. At last he was rewarded. There, cutting across one corner of the salt flats, a pair of black figures, traveling fast, were silhouetted against the expanse of glaring white.

"It's them," Whit muttered harshly. "Just as I thought, they're cutting toward the badlands. Moving fast too. But I'll catch up, once they've hit the badlands country. Or will I? No horse makes very good time through that jumble of broken land. I'll have to risk a short cut, I reckon."

Now that he knew where his prey was headed, he swerved at a tangent to save time. After a while the way became cluttered with broken chunks of sandstone, and wide cracks appeared in the crusted alkali earth, where the slightest misstep could result in the pony's crashing down. Recklessly Whit urged his mount on, leaving it to the pony's good sense to avoid all pitfalls. He dipped suddenly into a rough-bottomed gully flanked on either side by sandstone walls. Deeper and deeper he descended, until the sky overhead was only a narrow winding ribbon of blue.

Abruptly the way ended in a steep incline. Whit tried to slow the thundering horse, but he was too late. With all the strength of his muscular arms he jerked the pony back to haunches, and it went sliding down and down the precipitous grade, loosened rock tumbling about on both side of its rider. The bottom was reached, with both man and horse right side up, stopping in a billowing cloud of thick yellow-gray dust that entirely blotted out the surrounding scene.

"That was mighty close." Whit coughed as the dust

once more settled about him. He glanced about. Ahead stretched a wider canyon with rising on either side, eroded bluffs of sandy earth and rock. The badlands were a tortuous maze of broken and blind canyons, gashed by centuries of erosion. Wind and water since time unknown had cut the earth into fantastic formations, leaving queerly shaped turrets and spires lining the walls on either side. There seemed to be one main canyon running through this area, with hundreds of smaller canyons opening into this twisting main chasm.

Whit reined the pony to a slower gait. There were very few level stretches through this winding abyss, and the way was cluttered with chunks of sandstone. Ravines opened on either side, most of which were large enough to conceal a horse and rider. And there was no telling where such ravines led. Occasionally, instead of deep rifts and gashes, a section of wall would present a flat, fluted appearance with a great mound of loose rock fanning out below it. There seemed no sign here, deep in the earth, of the previous night's rain.

"Probably," Whit mused, "the storm didn't reach this far. If Rhodes is hoping to find some pools of rain water down here, he's due to be fooled."

He wished that he could have moved with more silence, but that was impossible: each hoofbeat resounded eerily from the walls on either side. Any sound made by the slightest shifting of rock seemed to be magnified and threw out echoes which rolled loudly through the canyon.

"Rhodes and Lowendirk," Whit told himself, "will be coming down here someplace ahead, or I miss my guess. They'll look for an easier descent than I took. I might run onto them any minute now. I just hope I see them first." His features became even more grim. "There's so damn many hide-outs through here that could be used for ambushing me. If either of those scuts saw me first—"

He broke off, eyes narrowing, as a movement ahead caught his attention. Two riders, fifty yards farther on, were just emerging from a side canyon that gave on to this main defile. Rhodes and Lowendirk! The two men weren't hurrying now. Undoubtedly the noise of their own mounts had drowned out any sounds made by Whit's pony. Reaching the floor of the canyon, the two men turned their ponies, backs to Whit, and proceeded at a walk.

Some inner sense must have warned the two, because even before Whit drove spurs to his pony's ribs they suddenly turned and looked back. A wild yell from Rhodes rang through the canyon. Both men pulled to a halt, as though about to turn back from the direction they had come. Then with one accord they urged their ponies to flight, Rhodes turning in the saddle to send a wild shot whining in Whit's direction.

Whit was closing in fast now, disregarding the danger of the unsure footing for his mount. Rhodes and Lowendirk were losing time in their more cautious riding. Now Lowendirk turned and fired, but the speed of his horse and Whit's over the uneven, rock-cluttered canyon floor caused him to miss.

Whit hadn't yet drawn a gun as he drove on, riding low behind his pony's neck, though he was already coiling his whip in his left hand. Now only twenty-five yards separated pursuer and pursued. Rhodes forged ahead of Lowendirk where the canyon narrowed, his horse sideswiping Lowendirk's mount and nearly knocking it from its feet.

Lowendirk howled a curse at his companion and, turning in the saddle, sent another shot in Whit's direction, but his horse hadn't yet righted itself, and its sudden lurch to one side made accurate shooting impossible. Even while Lowendirk was setting himself for another shot, Whit's hand flashed to his right holster, came out and up, to end in a sudden mushrooming of smoke and flame. The detonations of the six-shooters rolled through the canyon and hadn't yet died away when Lowendirk toppled sidewise from the saddle.

Even before he had struck the earth Whit had flashed by in swift pursuit of Rhodes, who had just disappeared around a bend. A few seconds later Whit caught sight of the man again, just a short distance ahead. Rhodes flung one wild shot from beneath his arm, and Whit felt the breeze of a leaden slug fan his cheek.

With his whip clutched in left hand and six-shooter in right, Whit knee-guided his pony, urging the horse to the utmost in an endeavor to overtake Rhodes. Rhodes leaned suddenly from the saddle, swinging his pony far to the left in the hope of darting into a side canyon which had suddenly opened to view, leaving Whit, if unable to turn his pony in the same space, to drive straight on past and thus lose more time.

The maneuver was almost successful, but just as Rhodes changed direction Whit's left arm snapped out to send his long lash hissing through the air and winding about the flying hind hoofs of Rhodes's pony. This time Whit released his grip on the whip butt. Rhodes's mount faltered, then tripped, and suddenly crashed on its side, a wild scream of terror leaving its throat as it went down.

Even before the horse struck the earth, however,

Rhodes had felt it falling and, releasing his feet from stirrups, had leaped wide to land on his feet, facing Whit, upraised six-shooter in hand.

"Damn you, Gallatin!" Rhodes yelled furiously. "This is your finish!"

Whit had turned his mount and checked it. Now he dismounted and started toward Rhodes, all the hate of years concentrated in the gun he carried in his right hand. "You should know whose finish it is, Rhodes," he said sternly, his long legs carrying him relentlessly toward his foe.

Deliberately he lifted his gun to bear on a spot just below Rhodes's left ribs. His finger commenced to tighten on the trigger. His six-shooter and Rhodes's thundered at the same moment, but a split instant before he fired Whit had shifted aim a trifle.

He felt the bullet from Rhodes's weapon cut through the bandanna at the side of his throat. Whit saw Rhodes swerve suddenly to one side, then right himself and scoop from the earth the gun that had fallen from his right hand. Again Rhodes lifted his weapon and again Whit fired.

Through the drifting black powder smoke Whit saw Rhodes slump back against the side of a boulder, all blood drained from his face, both arms hanging disabled at his sides. A dark, seeping stain had appeared on each shirt sleeve. Whit's even strides carried him to the wounded man. Rhodes cringed back, terror-stricken. "My Gawd," he whimpered, "you wouldn't kill me now, Gallatin? You've busted my arms. I'm helpless. For Gawd's sake, show a mite of pity—for the sake of your father. I was a pard of his once . . . "

Rhodes's voice died away before the look in Whit's eyes. "Pity?" Whit said in a weary tone. "*You* are asking pity? You ran away from Toyah Wells, after you'd planned your deviltry, and now you're trying to escape again . . . Well, you're free of any further harm from me. I've just realized, Rhodes, that pity is all I have for your kind. It's not my place to be your executioner. We'll let the law decide what's to be done with you."

Contemptuously he strode past Rhodes to retrieve his whip. Rhodes's horse had finally managed to disentangle itself and was now on its feet, shivering slightly, but unharmed beyond a few scratches. It required some time to tear up bandannas and bandage Rhodes's wounds. Then Whit helped him into the saddle and mounted his own horse. They got started and traveled at a walk around the bend in the canyon, where Whit spied Lowendirk's horse waiting patiently, while its owner sat disconsolately on a rock, face twisted with pain. There was no fight left in Lowendirk, and the man submitted quietly while Whit dismounted and examined his smashed shoulder. There was more brief bandaging done, then Lowendirk, too, was helped into his saddle. Whit used lariats to lash each man securely on his mount's back, then the horses were started again . . .

The sun had set by the time Whit, with his two bandaged prisoners riding before him, had emerged from the canyon and climbed back to level land. Darkness was creeping across the greasewood wastes, and along the eastern horizon the first faint stars were winking into being. Both Rhodes and Lowendirk were weak from loss of blood, but beyond an occasional groan, neither made a sound. They were, Whit suspected, extremely thankful at being still alive; and their future fate at the hands of a judge and jury was something they were satisfied, at present, to leave to the future.

The night deepened. The horses traveled slowly, their hoofs making soft thudding sounds across the sandy earth. Suddenly, from some distance ahead, Whit caught the drumming of horses' hoofs above the soughing of the evening wind. He raised his voice to hail the riders. Almost instantly an answering yell came back to him. A couple of minutes later four shadowy figures took form against the night sky. Then Jeff Dawson's voice, querulous with anxiety: "Is that you, Whit?"

"It's me," Whit called back. The hoofbeats were nearer now, and Whit caught words in a feminine voice: "Thank God . . . "

The riders closed in and halted about Whit and his prisoners as he brought them to a stop. Whit found himself speaking to Laura, Jeff, Sheriff Brandon, and Laidlaw. Brandon said, "Looks like you got Lowendirk and Rhodes here."

"Lowendirk and Rhodes," Whit repeated. "A broken shoulder and a pair of busted arms."

Laidlaw said, "You should have killed 'em, Whit."

Whit said quietly, "It came to me that it wasn't my job. This way is best."

They talked a minute or so more. Finally Laidlaw said, "Sheriff, why don't you take these prisoners off Whit's hands? Jeff and I can ride with you to make sure they don't escape. We can pick up the others and their prisoners at that adobe house and head on in to Palomas. Whit's had enough hard riding for a spell. He and Laura can take their time coming on." Brandon and Dawson were quick to agree.

Laura and Whit sat their saddles, watching the others fade away in the night. Then, as though by some unspoken agreement, both slipped down from saddles and stood facing each other, their features just visible under the night sky. Laura was saying, ". . . and as soon as we could get going we followed you. It was more or less aimless riding after we got over this way. You see, we couldn't know at what point you'd climb up from the badlands, or"—her voice caught a little—"or even if you'd ever climb out.

Almost as though he hadn't heard her words, Whit was telling the girl of his meeting with Rhodes. "I could have killed him easy as not," he said earnestly. "I'd intended to kill him right along—it seemed that was the only way I could rid myself of all the hate and anger that was building up inside me, and then—and then"—he laughed a trifle sheepishly—"the queerest feeling came over me. Right up to the time I pressed the trigger I meant to kill him. I don't quite understand it myself, only somehow I suddenly hated the thought of killing. I couldn't do it. And so I shifted my aim. Maybe—maybe I've licked that killer strain. Perhaps I'm not a killer after all. I think I've beaten that thing that's in my blood." Whit's voice wasn't quite steady.

"Of course you've beaten it, Whit." The girl's words brought him a new strength. "Uncle Jeff and I realized you had beaten it the first day you met Calgary Rhodes in Palomas. You had a firm grip on yourself that day. No real killer would have acted as you did. Oh, Uncle Jeff and I have talked about it a lot. We could have told you, but you'd let your imagination run away with you. It was something you had to learn for yourself. I tried to convince you that first day we rode to Palomas, but I could see I wasn't making much headway—"

A laugh of sheer joy suddenly burst from Whit, as though he had made some marvelous discovery. "I have beaten it, Laura! I know I have. I'm not a killer! I'm normal, like any other decent man. Is that clear to you?"

"It's been clear to me for a long time, Whit." Laura smiled in the darkness. "Only—only"—her words were soft through the gloom—"I wish you'd act normal." Her arms lifted to his shoulders, and now her face was very close to his own. "I'm waiting to be convinced that you're normal—" And then further words were smothered completely by his lips. A long minute passed, then Laura's voice came again, somewhat breathless: "By golly, Whit, you *are* normal. I'm—I'm thoroughly convinced . . . "

We hope that you enjoyed reading this Sagebrush Large Print Western.
If you would like to read more Sagebrush titles, ask your librarian or contact the Publishers:

United States and Canada

Thomas T. Beeler, *Publisher*
Post Office Box 659
Hampton Falls, New Hampshire 03844-0659
(800) 818-7574

United Kingdom, Eire, and the Republic of South Africa

Isis Publishing Ltd
7 Centremead
Osney Mead
Oxford OX2 0ES England
(01865) 250333

Australia and New Zealand

Bolinda Publishing Pty. Ltd.
17 Mohr Street
Tullamarine, 3043, Victoria, Australia
(016103) 9338 0666